STE
O_ER
BODIES

CW00860312

Ye Olde
Cheshire
Cheese

MARK
MOORE

STEPPING OVER BODIES

MARK MOORE

Copyright © 2016 Mark Moore
All Rights Reserved

Maps by Rosie Collins
Image by Ruth Hydes

For CRM & DMC

CONTENTS

CHARACTERS

Front Page's masthead…

Scipio Africanus Moriarty ("SA", "Essay") *editor*
Colin Cuddleigh-Cook ("Cuddles") *deputy editor*
Bill Roadhouse *business editor*
Jerry Carter *news editor*
Judy Bodkin *features editor*
Eddie Osmoe *chief sub-editor*
Rex Spurgeon ("Splurge") *opinion editor & reviews*
Cyril (Cill) Weaver *senior reporter*
Liz Tintwistle ("Tintin") *reporter*
Simon Ridge *reporter*
Mike Philbert ("Three Fellas") *deputy features editor*
Margaret Hardman *deputy chief sub-editor*
Peter Bowling *sub-editor*
Kate Clore *sub-editor*
Robert (Rob) Blynde *art editor*
John Hodger ("Enver") *assistant art editor*
Caroline Clipper *layout artist*
Kim Sook *layout artist*
Bill Aykroyd ("Billy Ayk", "The Ache") *production editor*
John Smigley ("Smegs", "Smigs") *chief photographer*
Cathy Wight *assistant photographer*
Alison Wong *librarian & archivist*
Janet McLing *editor's assistant*
Carmen Siguenza *editorial secretary*
Lydia Scant *receptionist*
Roderick (Rod) Crowcroft *publisher*
Alex (Sandy) Growler *managing director*
Don Phurse *advertisement manager*
Arthur Hinchcliffe ("Arf-Inch") *head of classified advertising*
Yan Yoonick ("The One", "Yooneek") *head of the post-room*
Bartholomew Gonner ("Gonner Rear") *barrister, legal correspondent*
Derek Goodbread *MP, political correspondent*
Darien Macdaniel *proprietor of "Medallion Trype"*

Thompson family...
Tom Telford Thompson, Lord Ironbridge *founding editor*
William Thompson *Tom's brother*
Rebecca (Bex) Thompson *Tom's daughter, married to Sidney Dudley*
Major Sidney Dudley ("Silent Sid") *Bex's husband*
Dryden Thompson *William's son*
Anna Aphra Thompson *Dryden's daughter*
Samuel Taylor Thompson *Dryden's son*
Stella Thompson *Dryden's wife, deceased*

friends, others...
Sarah Deeds *works at BBC, Cill's girlfriend*
Christian (Christy) Beeby *works at BBC*
Molly Stelfox *lives in Sarah's house*
Eva (Leeva) Malone *lives in Sarah's house*
Philip Flagstone *Eva's boyfriend*
Esra Oz *banker, Bill Roadhouse's girlfriend*

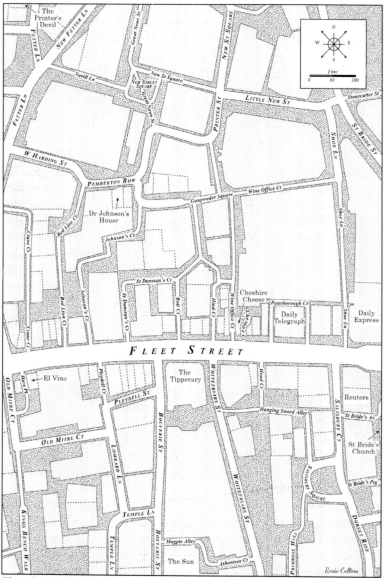

Fleet Street London EC4 in 1982

1. TUBE

The best pub in Fleet Street was the Tipperary, Weaver was thinking as he walked down the street to the tube. He had to keep his eyes scanning the concrete flags in front of his feet. It wasn't only what the dogs had left, there were gobs of phlegm and spit and snot to be avoided, there were spat out chunks of darkling gum, there was litter, and there were unidentifiable sticky black stains of god knows what streaking part way across the pavement.

The thought of the Tipperary momentarily unfocused his eyes from where to place his next step. The underside of his heel caught the raised edge of a cockeyed wonky paving flag and he stumbled forward awkwardly, spreading his arms wide instinctively to lower his centre of gravity to keep his balance and prevent a fall. He succeeded, but the thought of lunchtime and a visit to the pub only four hours ahead was driven from his mind until he was standing inside the tube train, his hand locked rigidly to the steel bar running along the roof, trying to match the rolls and lurches of the train with counter lurches and rolls of his own, and failing mostly, and trying even more to keep out of the firing line of the foul breath of the man crushed up against him by the squash of a standard Monday morning rush-hour on a tube train in London.

<<REPORTER IN SUBTERRANEAN CATTLE TRUCK POISON-GAS HORROR. OUR MAN FOUND STILL AT HIS POST. SANCTIONS CALL BY LEAGUE OF NATIONS. GERMANS DENY COMMUTER EXPERIMENTS>>

As always Weaver found his mind wandering away from his imaginary headlines to things even less concrete: The last syllable of recorded time is always now, he thought. What's a time syllable? How long is it?

He looked up momentarily as another hand brushed his, and he tightened his grip on the bar and tried to angle his elbow and arm outwards to take up more space. This bar's nice. Is it solid? How easy is it to take off? Does it unscrew? Yes, but what would you use it for? Nothing, but it's nice though, all shiny and machined; engineered almost.

Is time multisyllabic? Or do you take it, pronounce it he supposed, one syllable at a time. He had a lot to answer for that Shakespeare with his sodding time syllables and all like that. I need a pint, I need a drink: the last pint of recorded time. Still, only four hours to go now before I can lead a raid on the pub.

<<DARING RAID ON ENTEBBE ARMS. SPECIAL FORCES UNIT LED BY CRACK COMMANDO VETER- AN CYRIL "OTTO SKORZENY" WEAVER LEADS DARE- DEVIL MISSION BEHIND ENEMY LINES TO LIBERATE VAST QUANTITIES OF LAGER FROM CRUEL INCAR- CERATION IN PUB BARRELS. "MAGNIFICENT FEAT" PRAISED BY CIGS. KING SENDS NOTE>>

Yes, the Tipperary today, Weaver thought. We did the Printer's Devil yesterday. The Cheshire Cheese is no good, too many tourists. Upstairs at the Tipp, clustered on stools round the coal-effect gas fire.

We're inside a giant hollow steel mole. Lined up like air- borne troops on a mission, ready to drop onto enemy strong- points: Arnos Grove, Turnpike Lane, Seven Sisters, Eben Emael: armed with our twice-folded newspapers to avoid invading the defensible space of the next seat, our collapsible umbrellas, our headscarves, our assorted and often oddly shaped briefcases, our Barbour jackets, our camel hair overcoats, our tights, and our freshly washed cotton underwear. Come back nylon socks, all is forgiven.

<<TIME SYLLABLE DISCOVERED BY SCIENTISTS. COAL-EFFECT GAS FIRE GIVES BOFFINS CLUE TO BREAKTHROUGH>>

Yes, "boffins", he thought, that's it. Must be the last surviv- ing wartime slang word, stuck in the time-warp of newspaper headlines. His mind wandered again. We've been devoured by a giant steel mole like a tribe of Jonahs inside the whale; avoid- ing each other's eye, staring at the ads above the heads opposite, reading, doing the crossword - or as like as not sucking our pens while staring at the crossword, watching the black walls slither by. What are all those pipes for? Where are they going? What do they do?

Well it's not the Marrakesh Express. All aboard be buggered. Commute. Commute. A death sentence commuted to life imprisonment. Doomed like some Tantalus... Forget that analogy, it would have been a stupid Classical one anyway. Who needs the idiotic Classics. Why was I lumbered with an education that enables me to go to Rome and translate what it says on the statues, but left me knowing sod-all about electricity?

Weaver blamed that Arnold bugger. The one that was the brother of the poet. Dover Beach's brother. Was that right? Or was it Dover Beach himself? Weaver couldn't remember if he'd ever known which Arnold was which, or one from the other. "Where ignorant armies clash by night" - about the most apt description of private boarding school education Weaver had ever heard - so maybe it was Dover Beach and not his brother, if he had a brother. He felt his mind slipping out of focus and he dozed off into an almost comfortable lurching standing semi-trance.

The tube train slowed and stopped (Weaver opened his eyes), but not at a station. The standing passengers noted this fact before the seated ones, who looked up and tried to see through the windows, peering round standing bodies expecting to read the name of a station, craning to see through the open doors - when they opened - because the designers of the aluminium tube train, or the interior decorators of the tube stations - take your pick - had ensured that you could never read the name of the station from a seat through the windows for some reason, the angles were all wrong, then disappointed at seeing only tunnel wall, perhaps with a grimace or groan, a tut or pursed lip or breath sucked in through front teeth, looked down again at their newspapers or books, or resumed their repeated and random reading of the publicity material filling all the available space above the window line; or some perhaps cast appraising and sidelong glances at members of the same or opposite sex, ready to glance away immediately if the subject's eyes intercepted theirs.

Weaver peered out through the glass of the sliding doors at the sooty wall. what were all those pipes for? Where did the soot come from?

<<SECRET LAGER PIPELINE DISCOVERED UNDER LONDON>>

The train began to move again. The commuters pretended not to notice. It shuffled with a slow clatter into the next station. Some, not many, of the seated passengers rose and made their way with a muttered pardon or excuse me through the crush towards the sliding doors. Their empty seats were seized readily by standing passengers who though exchanging a sham of polite after-yous and no-thank-you-it's-all-right-I'm-getting-off-at-the-next-stops, had in fact at some point moved tactically along into the space between the banks of seats, and while pretending to read or stare about had been keeping a sharp eye on the seated ones most likely to be getting off at the next stop. Mmm, suit and umbrella, FT; he'll be going all the way to the City, perhaps changing at Holborn. No luck there. Ah, now, jeans and some sort of combat jacket. Is that shoulder flash the German flag? He could be getting off anywhere, could be the next stop. See if I can move in front of him and keep an eye on him in case he moves.

The doors wheezed shut again. The train picked up speed and then slowed to a halt as soon as it cleared the platform and entered the dark oval of the tunnel. Pipes all over the bloody place, Weaver thought. There's a green one, plastic covered, looks new. They all seem insulated. What's inside them? How many hands have gripped this bar before me? Let's see. He attempted to start a calculation then thought sod it, can't be bothered. The train moved again, but slowly and in fits and starts. Now there was an audible and widespread sound of tutting. Some people glanced round and made rapid eye contact for a moment with each other.

Weaver took his eyes away from the tunnel wall and read what he could see of a newspaper over the shoulder of a woman standing to his left. Something about the Task Force. Wouldn't mind task-forcing her he thought loosely and without any real desire, more interested in the pun and innuendo than gauging the extent of his attraction to the woman or in the act he was imagining he was expressing. But how can you actually meet people on the tube? There's no way you can casually strike up a conversation, he thought, the Underground is the most silent form of transport, absolutely no conversation at all; no point at all in saying "Do you lurch and sway and get squashed here often?" There's no visible weather to talk about, and if you said something everyone else in the carriage is going to hear and think: hello here's a chat-up in operation, you've got no chance mate. So he wasn't going to start anything for that reason alone. Sometimes afterwards though he wished he had.

The train gushed into Holborn station, doing the last 100 yards or so at full speed, as though done deliberately as a malicious act to fool the waiting passengers. That'll fool them, Weaver smiled inwardly at the thought, those about to get on here will think they've got a real fast train all right; little do they know they'd've been better off on beach donkeys.

He stepped off onto a platform pulsating with people and bobbed and weaved his way along the exit passage. He joined a human snake, a sullen silent wormlike human conga shuffling along making instinctively, automatically, for the light.

A bald man in tatty jeans and a brown suede jacket with tears and holes on the upper arms and on the back (Weaver thought: how did he do that? Leaning against a barbed-wire fence? Caught in a razor-blade hailstorm?) was tuning up an electric guitar on a bend in the yellow tiled passageway. The long guitar box lay open on the floor forming a well to catch any coins that might be lobbed in that general direction as a consequence of his playing and singing.

Weaver dug out a ten pence piece and threw it into the case as he passed. It bounced on the bottom of the box and out over the far lip and then, demonstrating the inexplicable property of the conservation of angular momentum that has so baffled scientists down the ages, rolled down the slope and disappeared

<<REPORTER SOUGHT IN RUBBER MONEY

FRAUD>>

under the waving weaving thrashing impenetrable nettlebed of legs. The man looked up, surprised since he hadn't yet played a note. Weaver delved for, located, and assumed a look of complete innocence and non-involvement, a little embarrassed, aware of bored eyes watching. He knew the busking musician knew he'd thrown something into his box, but did he know it had rolled off down the passage? Weaver wasn't going to crawl and grope around after it. He tried to pretend it was all nothing to do with him and tried to shuffle on as quickly as possible, stepping in the quick little strides that were all this conga would allow. It was a pity really because he liked electric guitars and wanted to encourage the player. Buskers with electric guitars were rare in the tube. Mostly they were saxophonists, and sometimes a bloke with an accordion. Maybe the musician would find the coin when the crush had passed. Weaver never gave saxophonists anything. He hated wind.

A bottleneck was forming round the access point to the launchpad to the escalator. All aboard for the Stairway to Heaven. Weaver's turn came to step on.

<<REPORTER IN ESCALATOR NIGHTMARE. YARD SWOOPS ON SWEENEY TODD ESCALATOR CO. SAUSAGE FACTORY DENIES CHARGES>>

Sometimes he went in the fast lane on the left and walked up: sometimes he went in the slow lane and stayed put on one going. This time he stood still, his energy banks feeling not up to the walk. He looked up to the far top of the giant escalator, clattering away like the underground workings of the Morlocks. Perhaps it was the underground workings of the Morlocks.

Was that..? Surely it wasn't..? Yes it is..! Oh yes… Weaver convinced himself a woman just about to step off the escalator way up at the top was an old girlfriend, lost and gone forever but warmly remembered. He girded his energy banks about him and set off in pursuit, a course of action very difficult to perform on a cramped escalator in the morning rush hour. He went up the moving stair like Jack up the beanstalk, like slag on a conveyor belt, like Ulysses 'twixt Scylla and Charybdis, like a ladder in a pair of tights, ducking and dodging, sliding and skipping and sidestepping, clutching his long white mac about him and hanging on tight to the small WW2 rucksack on his shoulder, muttering apologies all the while, hoping he didn't knock into anyone bigger and surlier and more aggressive than himself. Briefly he worried about the Domino Effect

<<VIETNAM..LAOS..CAMBODIA....HOLBORN NEXT TO FALL?>>

then thought he might do better if he pulled out a handkerchief and waved it about like a white flag and pushed forward urgently, shouting "Emergency. I'm a doctor. Emergency. Let me through." But he didn't have a hanky. And besides it was Monday morning and he knew his heart wasn't really in it.

By the time he arrived at the top the woman was nowhere in sight. She could have gone up the next escalator to the surface, or turned down a side passage to the Central Line and points east to the City or west to the West End. There was no way of telling where she was. Damn, piss, shit, he thought and made his way up the next escalator to the surface.

It was raining again on the street.

A fine drizzling rain gusting and swirling off the buildings and seeming to come from all directions at once; lifting under umbrellas, creeping down collars, depositing a fine mist on glasses, endangering make-up stability, and setting the tone for the day till lunchtime.

Weaver turned up his mac collar and walked through the shallow pavement puddles, making his way across Lincoln's Inn Fields towards Lincoln's Inn and its back door and the alleyway down the side of the Three Tuns pub with its marvellous handy little lean-to urinal against the brick wall of Lincoln's Inn, in the cut-through to Chancery Lane. He always walked through puddles, it allowed him to walk in a straighter line, and he could show the other daintier walkers he wasn't afraid of a little water. It also made him feel he was out in the venturesome wild, in the Wild Woods like the Cat that Walked by Himself, on some expedition or adventure or some heroic military march through impassable terrain instead of walking drudgingly to work from the tube.

<<MERCENARY COLUMN BREAKS REBEL SIEGE TO RESCUE CONVENT NUNS. REBEL FORCES SCATTERED>>

He walked across the central area of Lincoln's Inn, home of lawyers, barristers, and judges in their chambers. A large lawn gleamed greenly in the middle through the drizzle. Keep off. Residents and members only; a sign said. Another sign said: The police have instructions to eject anyone making a noise in this Inn. Wankers, Weaver thought, dickheads, how can you give the police instructions like that? But then, saddened, he thought that if anybody could these were the boys that could. Bastards. He wanted to throw something on the grass. Acid, Greek Fire, a flamethrower, tons of litter, raw sewage, fresh concrete, anything to break the complacency, upset the certainty of social superiority, the surety of immunity from revolution and change.

<<CAT THAT WALKS BY HIMSELF CRAPS IN JUDGE'S CHAMBERS>>

Fuckers, he thought finally as he passed through the doorway in the perimeter wall and entered the alley behind the pub.

He glanced over superstitiously to make sure the curious little georgian-wired glass-roofed iron-sided four-stall urinal was still there. An essential armament of any hardline serious urban drinker is to carry a mental map of the available public pisshouses. Sometimes at work Weaver would lean back in his chair at the newsdesk and mentally try and plot certain routes across town by landmarking in his mind where the urinals were, like stepping stones across the city stream. That's an idea, he thought, produce a map locating all the public lavatories, then sell it to all the pubs, wine-bars, restaurants, cafes, and breweries. It'd make a bomb.

The offices of *Front Page* magazine where he worked as a news reporter were in a building in one of the tight little alleyways cascading down the slope on the north side of Fleet Street. You could walk down the street on that side making your way east towards Ludgate Circus, to the King Lud say or round the corner to the Blackfriar with the exotic starry ceiling, and cross entry after entry of alleys disgorging into the street. Crane Court; Red Lion Court; Johnson's Court; St Dunstan's Court; Bolt Court; Hind Court; Wine Office Court; Peterborough Court; Racquet Court; and Poppins Court; and the only street on that side between Fetter Lane and Ludgate Circus was Shoe Lane which was hardly more than an alley anyway. And where, Weaver wondered as he approached his workplace, were Red-Handed Court and With Your Trousers Down Court?

It was 9-40 when he pushed through the glass front doors of the office building housing the weekly news magazine he worked for as a news reporter.

He smiled and said "morning" more brightly than he felt to the receptionist behind the desk handling the phone like an inky slime-covered one-legged octopus with a look of utmost distaste welded to her face.

He noticed she was wearing bandages wrapped round both her wrists.

Oh no, he thought, Lydia's slashed her wrists again.

2. CAR

Moriarty thought of himself as a director. Moriarty the Director manoeuvred his motor, a BMW, sufficiently far towards the centre of the road so he could see round the van in front but not far enough to let any clown behind slip through on the inside. The traffic queue was backing up from the lights about forty yards. For God's sake, he thought, would you look at that, it's not green long enough. It's quite clear this is going to be the busier road at this junction, yet the lights were green an equal amount of time in both directions. This road should be green twice as long as the other road. Clowns. Raving clowns. Sack the lot.

Moriarty was an editor, but he didn't think of himself nowadays as editor. He thought of himself more as a director. In the early days, six years before when he first made it to editor, he used to play the phrase SA Moriarty, editor, round in his mind. It had a good feel - solid, established, worthy of respect, essentially powerful. As editor he felt he had arrived. He used to like the sound of it. But now he was bored with editor. People didn't seem to look up to the title quite as much as he imagined they would. The sound and feel of it weren't quite so solid, not quite so established or worthy of respect, less essentially powerful than he would have liked. As editor he felt he still had yet to arrive. He was no longer content with the sound of it. But director, now you're talking. As director he could imagine himself soon a main board director. And why not go further, he often wondered to himself, and become managing director?

There was one small problem with Moriarty's intention of becoming managing director. Someone told him once that as editor of *Front Page*, a leading national - and international - weekly news and current affairs magazine he would be included in the roll call in *Who's Who*, and it was true, he was. In it his interests were listed as: golf, sailing, and collecting first editions. All of which were completely untrue; he didn't play golf, was bored by boats, in fact had never knowingly stepped on a boat smaller than a Channel ferry, and even if his next year's pay rise depended on it couldn't tell a first edition from a toffee apple. He thought they were the sort of interests people listed in *Who's Who* ought to have. He didn't list his real interests which were going to the races and betting on horses and screwing the latest female recruits on the editorial staff of his magazine.

But he now believed that as manager of the publishing company, or a director, or even one day as its managing director, and why not chairman, the pages of *Who's Who* would be barred to him, so though he thought of himself as a manager, he still ensured that he spoke of himself as editor. Still, Moriarty thought as he inched forward towards the traffic lights, I'll roger that roll call when I get to it. Harder surely, he thought, to get into the book in the first place than to get taken out once you're in. Moriarty lived with the constant expectation that the rules could and would be changed to accommodate him. The amazing thing was they often were.

He pressed his foot on the accelerator slightly, just enough to hear the throaty catarrhal build-up of power lurking under the bonnet like a bad-tempered but powerful genie in a bottle. He wasn't moving forward at all, but he liked to hear that sound. He liked to imagine other people around could hear the sound too. Look, they'd say, look at that, that's a motor; that's a real car. And look at the driver, that's a real man. Someone who drives a car making that growly big cat sound must be someone special. One day, Moriarty dreamed to himself, they'd recognise him and say look there goes SA Moriarty.

Moriarty looked in the mirror. The clown behind was getting too bloody close. He always seemed to brake too late and almost ram his back end every time the queue halted. Moriarty had a feeling someone had once told him that it might be an optical effect of the mirror, but he wasn't a hundred percent sure about that. He couldn't see the sense in it. Now if that clown gets right up my arse one more time, he's going to get - Moriarty's train of thought was interrupted as he realised he hadn't been concentrating on the van in front, which had moved off a small distance and had left a gap. Moriarty floored the accelerator all the way to the rubber mat and his BMW lurched forward and stalled. He could see the lights on green and the other cars in front darting through while they could. The gap widened as the van approached the lights. Moriarty managed to get his car restarted. He set off in pursuit of the van. The van sped across the junction. The lights changed to amber and red. Moriarty thought for a fraction of a second whether to carry on and cross over while the lights were on red, but his legendary luck was still with him because just as he had committed himself to cross over he saw a police car waiting at the junction on the other side watching the action. Moriarty braked and waited at the lights. He'd missed the lights, but at least he was now first in the queue. Confucius Moriarty he say better be first in second queue at lights than last in first queue at lights. Now then, he thought as he watched the traffic crossing in front at ninety degrees to him, there'd better not be any clowns turning my way in front of me from the other road.

The lights changed and Moriarty surged the car forward, gauging the gear changes by the high pitched scream of the engine, and taking the revs right up to the start of the red section on the rev counter, and sometimes well into it before changing gear. If queried whether this was a way of driving that tended to shorten the life of the motor, Moriarty would respond with a look of incredulity, suggesting what the hell, it's only a company car, it only has to last three years or 40,000 miles, whichever is the sooner. And initially when he had chosen this car from the shortlist of those available through the company's car buying policy, Moriarty had immediately and instinctively rejected the option of an automatic gearbox as unsuited to his vision of himself as a good, and fast, driver. One of Moriarty's ambitions was to leave a trail of rubber at every set of traffic lights on his route from Blackheath to Fleet Street.

The next junction approached and now Moriarty had to make a judgement. Though not a dual carriageway, the road at the lights was marked into two lanes. Moriarty had to decide which lane to line up in. If he went in the outside lane there was the danger of cars turning right and holding him up as they waited for the chance to turn against the oncoming traffic; and while Moriarty waited behind them all those clowns he had left for dead at the previous traffic lights would swarm through on his inside, and laugh at him, he was sure, as they passed. But if he went in the inside lane, which tended to have more vehicles in it anyway, there was a twofold risk, one that a parked vehicle on the other side of the lights would rapidly restrict the two lanes back to one again, and those in the inside lane would be held up longer than those speeding through on the unblocked outside, and two that the outside lane would this time not have any cars wanting to turn right in it, and the cars would all get away faster than he would, and leave him for dead in his turn.

Moriarty craned his neck as he came up to the lights to see if any cars were indicating to go right. It didn't look like there were, but that didn't mean no one was going to turn right. It was quite normal, Moriarty knew, for clowns like this to indicate and signal their intentions only after the lights had changed, when it was too late for drivers behind to move into the inside lane. Moriarty decided to take the risk and moved into the outside lane. He passed the van that had been in front of him at the previous lights, now queuing in the inside lane. Damn, he thought, has he seen someone indicating to go right? Damn again. Too late now, I'm committed. Moriarty stopped behind a grey Cortina. There was a sticker in its back window saying *Caution, baby on board.* What the hell difference did that make? Moriarty wondered. He'd be better off with a sticker that said *Caution, clown behind wheel.* There were four more cars in front of the Cortina in the queue to the lights.

The lights changed to green. The five cars in the queue in front of Moriarty started to speed forward. The first four gathered speed and hurtled off, but the fifth one, the Cortina, suddenly switched on its right indicator. Moriarty banged the steering wheel with his fist in frustration and cursed aloud. He started revving up violently. The Cortina edged painstakingly towards the centre of the road, its exhaust throwing out a constant cloud of black smoke. That'll do the baby's lungs a lot of good, Moriarty thought; pretty soon they're going to have to put a sticker on the back window saying *Caution, sick baby on board.* In his left hand wing mirror Moriarty could see the van coming up to overtake him on the inside, and behind it the clown who had been behind him only a few moments before at the other lights. He inched forward behind the Cortina, willing it to go further out into the middle of the road. There were no breaks appearing in the oncoming stream of traffic, so no chance looming for the Cortina to turn. Moriarty saw that a slight gap had opened up in the inside lane between the van and the car in front of it. Grasping the steering wheel tightly in both hands, Moriarty turned it rapidly to the left, missed the back of the Cortina by a fraction of an inch, made the van on his left brake violently as Moriarty's black BMW leapt into the space in front of it, and accelerated with a scream of valves across the junction, swerving again back into the outside lane as he left the Cortina behind still waiting to turn at the lights. In his mirror Moriarty could see the van driver vigorously waving the first two fingers of his right hand out of his window in the rain and flashing his headlights in the direction of Moriarty's fleeing car. Moriarty made no response, he pressed his accelerator further and left him for dead.

He turned right off the A2 into Deptford Church Street, the dual carriageway allowing him to put his foot down and pass a line of slower vehicles on his left, proceeding sedately behind a Luton van. At the lights at the end of that section he turned left into Evelyn Street which became Lower Road shortly before the large roundabout at the southern mouth of the Rotherhithe Tunnel. A solid steel-link chain of traffic was disappearing down into the subterranean world. A steel chain with links more spread out was emerging from it. Moriarty swerved left onto the inside track and hurtled round the roundabout, ignoring the sound of a car horn behind him, and turned left on the first exit off the roundabout into Jamaica Road.

He built up speed on the dual carriageway of Jamaica Road. Only yards in front of him the lights of a pelican crossing turned from green to red. Moriarty ignored them and sped through the crossing, making a young black man with long dreadlocks hanging down round the back and sides of his head to his shoulders jerk his foot and his head back onto the pavement from where he had a split-second before stepped. The sudden movement disturbed the carefully arranged layers of the dreadlocks and the long plaited strands of hair fell across his eyes like the overbred pelt of a black old-English sheepdog. In stepping back he banged into a rust-speckled pram pushed by a woman in tight blue jeans, tighter fitting than the swaddling clothes of the infant Jesus, and a low-cut nearly-white tee-shirt that exposed the top two-thirds of heavily freckled breasts like a matching pair of seeded bloomer loaves. The baby in the pram, no infant Jesus this, started screaming viciously and violently and inexorably and incessantly. Moriarty was a black speck in the distance. Moriarty drove on. He drove furiously.

Moriarty's stream of traffic curved left off Jamaica Road into Druid Street and swept past a marching column of railway arches carrying the line in its final elevated approach to London Bridge Station. Each arch was doored off and each one, there were perhaps forty in all paralleling Druid Street, housed an auto repair yard. Steering problems? Servicing. MOTs. Exhaust repair and fitting. Undersealing. Body repairs. Duckhams. Castrol. STP. Clutch and brakes. Michelin Tyres. The names and services offered flashed into and through Moriarty's mind without stopping as he took his BMW up to a few inches from the bumper bar of the car in front, then pressed heavily on the brake. Move over you clown: one side of the road or the other - Moriarty didn't mind which as long as there was enough space either on the inside or the outside for him to force his car through - with this clown stuck in the middle of the road there was no room on either side to overtake. He blew his horn. The car in front didn't move. The lanes marked in the road at the next lights forced the driver to decide which lane to run in. Moriarty went in the other. When the lights changed he left him for dead.

He steered through the double-light chicane where St Thomas Street intersected with the A3, Borough High Street, and crossed over into Southwark Street. Moriarty was heading for Blackfriars Bridge.

On his right as Moriarty weaved down Southwark Street changing lanes at will, passing on the inside and the outside, flooring the accelerator, pumping the brake like there was water in the hold, and ramming through the lower gears, between London Bridge, Cannon Street railway bridge, Southwark Bridge, and Blackfriars Bridge were the sites of The Clink debtors' prison and also here, somewhere under the mass of Victorian shambles and power station yards and soon to be demolished 1960s office blocks, were the yet to be discovered remains of three of the most famous theatres of Shakespeare's day, the Globe, the Rose, and the Fortune. Moriarty neither knew nor cared. He had no time for history. If he had been aware that Henry Ford had said that "History is bunk", Moriarty would have definitely agreed with him. As far as Moriarty was concerned history was now, and here: history was him.

Moriarty turned right into the approach to Blackfriars Bridge. The blue-turquoise painted parapet obscured much of any view of the river drivers might wished to have had. Ahead on the other side and slightly to the right the dome and frontal edifice of St Paul's Cathedral rose up on its hill like the Crab That Played With The Sea to dominate the skyline despite being surrounded by drab square truncated glass towers and rain-streaked concrete office boxes. Moriarty didn't glance at it. He'd seen it before. It wasn't relevant to the morning ritual of the race to the office.

Across the bridge the road became New Bridge Street. Moriarty darted in front of a car to place himself in pole position on the inside lane at the traffic lights at Ludgate Circus. He didn't look over half-right to the blue cast-iron railway bridge over Ludgate Hill carrying the railway commuter line from Blackfriars Station up to Holborn Viaduct Station. The blue cast-iron railway bridge was famous for blocking what should have been one of the finest sights in London, the view of St Paul's from Fleet Street up Ludgate Hill.

The lights turned to yellow and before they had reached green Moriarty was already in second gear and round the corner left into Fleet Street.

The street was littered with newspaper offices, pubs, and sandwich shops. There had been printing houses in Fleet Street ever since the very early 16th century when Caxton's assistant Wynkyn de Worde moved the press there after the master's death, from Westminster Yard where Caxton had first set up his printing business.

On his right as Moriarty accelerated up the long incline of the street behind a doubledecker bus he passed the black glass Modernist peoples' palace of the *Daily Express*, known as "the black Lubyanka". Here not only the *Express* but London's sole evening paper, the *Evening Standard*, were produced and printed and published. Shortly after it on the same side came the 1930s stone-faced edifice of a completely different style of building, yet erected within two years of the *Express*'s home: the *Daily Telegraph* building. Then on his left Moriarty passed Bouverie Street, home of the stablemates the *Sun* and the *News of the World*. And in between on both sides up and down the street there were offices of regional papers and magazines. Between the newspaper offices there were pubs. And between the newspaper offices and pubs there were sandwich shops. And between the newspaper offices and pubs and sandwich shops there were newsagents. And between the newspaper offices and pubs and sandwich shops and newsagents there were newsvendor stalls. And between the newspaper offices and pubs and sandwich shops and newsagents and newsvendor stalls there were the occasional retail outlets such as a tailor or gents outfitter, a bookshop, a restaurant, and a jeweller. And that was all.

Moriarty turned right into an entry to an underground car park on the north side of the street under one of the newer buildings. He parked his car in the space allocated to his company, and noticed momentarily, but immediately ignored, the loud tinkling sound the car's bonnet made as the engine cooled after the hard and hectic drive. He came up in the car park lift that opened out in an alleyway behind Fleet Street. He walked along the alley to his office.

It was 9-50 when he pushed through the glass office doors. On the door the words *News World Publishers* and *Front Page Magazine* were written. Below them were the words *Founded by Lord Ironbridge in 1932*. I edit that, Moriarty thought as he entered the red carpeted reception area.

He didn't say anything at all to the receptionist behind the desk wrestling with the phone like a slim wiry giant anaconda with a look of utmost distaste welded to her face, even though she said "good morning" brightly to him, more brightly than she felt, as he passed. He had no wish to encourage her into thinking that a recent leg-over entanglement between them would lead to further things. But he did notice that she had bandages wrapped tightly round each wrist.

For Christ's sake, he thought as he carried on to the lifts, the dozy histrionic bint's not gone and slashed her wrists again?

3. BUS

Elizabeth Tintwistle was worried. She sat on the number 11 bus and worried. She worried about many things. She worried whether she'd left the iron on after she ironed her blouse that morning. She couldn't remember turning it off. She worried whether she'd left the bathroom light on. She worried whether she had turned the dripping tap off tight enough to slow the trickle to an occasional drip - which was all you could do at best - but she couldn't remember. Had she locked the front door? She had no mental image of doing so.

She worried too about muggers, burglars, rapists, but not primarily for her own safety but for other people's. She cared about the victims of the world. She cared deeply about other people. She worried about famine in Africa. She worried about the Boat People. She worried about Apartheid. She worried about the Front Line States. She worried about the war in Angola and the war in Mozambique. She worried about Ulster and believed the British should leave and it would be nice to have a united Ireland. She worried about the West Bank. She worried about Mrs Thatcher.

And now suddenly there was Argentina to worry about. Or rather the Falkland Islands. Liz deep in her heart, as she was fond of putting it, couldn't really blame the junta - she took care to pronounce it "hoonter" - for invading. After all, they had a better claim to them. And while she worried about the disappeared ones in Argentina, she felt also that they really did have a better claim to the Malvinas than the British, and the British government ought to respect that. We had no business being there and ought to leave. The people could go to St Helena or Tristan da Cunha. After all they were islands in the Atlantic just like the Falklands, and there was plenty of room. It wouldn't be much different, surely? They would just have to leave and let the Argentineans have what was rightfully theirs.

She worried about war and poverty and injustice and racism and colonialism and imperialism, especially American imperialism. She worried about the Right and military dictators. She worried about the CIA and interventionism. She worried about defoliation and destabilisation. She worried about nuclear weapons and nuclear fallout and nuclear radiation. She worried about the Third World. She worried about famine and encroaching desert. She worried about DDT and rare earths. She worried about the rain-forest. She had a deep and wide-ranging worrisome compassion for all those less well-off than herself. In fact she often described herself as a "passionate compassionate", or as being "passionately compassionate", and was pleased with the phrases, with the identity she imagined the phrases lent her.

She used to worry about the war in Vietnam and the bombing of Cambodia. Above all things she hated war. She hated all wars, and worried about them constantly. She was certain that war was not essentially part of human nature and was caused by imperialism and big business, by arms and armaments manufacturers, by warmongers in the Western World, and by greed and exploitation. Exploitation was one of her favourite words. She had worried greatly about the war in Zimbabwe. She denied ever calling it Rhodesia and claimed she had from the very first insisted on calling it Zimbabwe, and was unceasingly vigilant and on the lookout for those who did not. She was unconvinced that a solution had been worked out in Zimbabwe, for she could not believe Tory politicians capable of working out anything for the good of other people.

Yet somehow she was convinced that all those struggles had been won, and would be won, and would always be won, and that all political struggles would eventually be won by the good and the just. It all went to show that the world could be changed and that good would win in the end. She was an appalling, asphyxiating, overripe, optimist.

She worried also about her looks and her figure and keeping thin.

What she didn't worry about was work or money or her job, she'd always found these easy. And she didn't worry about boyfriends; she always had one, and found getting another one the easiest thing in the world.

At the moment, as she sat on the bus ready to object instantly and raise a fuss (inwardly she prepared a withering look - she was a great one for what she imagined were withering looks), if the man next to her did not offer his seat to the woman carrying a baby about to get on at the bus stop, the biggest thing that she worried about were her nicknames. She'd always called herself Liz, and she had been called that most of her life in most of the company she found herself, except for her mother who called her Elizabeth. But now her colleagues, led by her fellow reporter on the news desk Cill Weaver, had started playing around with her name. Sometimes they would call her Tin Whistle; sometimes Tin Lizzie; sometimes Thin Lizzie; sometimes Tin Liz and Thin Liz; sometimes Liz Whiz and Tin Whiz; and sometimes even Tintin. She didn't like any of them. They were all too flippant. They didn't take her seriously enough. There seemed an essential absence of respect in these nicknames, and in the underlying attitude behind their invention. It was perhaps just as well that she had no idea yet that behind her back some of her male colleagues had also taken to referring to her as Tin Tits.

Of them all, if she were forced to choose, she liked Tintin the least worst. It was less flippant and not abusive, and at least connected her to a famous reporter. A strange reporter, it was true, because Tintin never seemed to file any copy, nor wrote any stories, and actually didn't seem to do any work at all. He seemed to exist solely on Captain Haddock's largesse. Not bad if you can get it, she thought. Although she also thought that living like that would actually bore her stupid.

She hadn't taken to Cyril Weaver at all. For a start he called himself Cill, as in window-cill, instead of Cyril. He claimed this was what he'd always been called in his family as a kid because his little sister couldn't pronounce Cyril. But Liz reckoned he just thought Cyril was a bad name and had come up with something better. Either way, Cill it now was.

And apart from twisting his own name, he didn't appear serious enough. He seemed to hold nothing sacred. He didn't seem to worry about anything serious in the world at all. She was sure he'd been a hippy in the early 1970s. He had come up with most of these nicknames, to the delight of their other colleagues, and for the time being most of them had stuck. And short of showing her extreme distaste for them publicly, or by making some embarrassing statement of disapproval, she didn't know what to do about it.

She'd responded by calling Weaver CW, but he seemed to like that. So she'd tried Cilly, which at least had the verbal advantage of being almost an anagram of his real name. But he seemed to like that even better, so she'd stopped, but not before both of them had caught on.

She'd held back from the obvious next stage, which was to try Cilla, as in Cilla Black. She had an instinct that would be a name too far and would reveal her distaste for her own nicknames. And she had a deep fear of being revealed.

And anyway she also had a feeling Weaver would object humorously not on the grounds that it was clearly a women's name but more on the grounds of it being associated with such a god-awful singer. And then everyone would laugh and the point and object of her thrust would be diverted and dissipated.

Anyway, it would be a bit mean, she always thought. And whatever she was Liz Tintwistle could never be accused of being mean.

Liz Tintwistle stared a little forlornly out of the bus window, part of her mind wondering which nickname it would be today, while another part watched the shop fronts mechanically, taking in the names and the shop wares as the number 11 bus lurched its way down Victoria Street in its stop-start fashion, a metaphor Liz thought for the British economy in general.

Another part of her mind listened in to the conversation being acted out by the two young women on the seat behind her. Yes, she thought, acted out was right, because they didn't really exchange views or elicit information in their conversation, instead they related events like a verbal strip cartoon. Neither party took in at all what the other one said, just supplied a primer every now and then to keep the verbal flow issuing forth. Liz listened.

"So e goes: 'What djer wanter do that for?' An I goes 'Well we never do nuffin do we?' So e goes 'Course we do'. An then e goes 'All righ we'll go then'. An I was wearin like jeans an a tee-shirt. An me nanna goes 'Put summin else on yull catch yer deff.' An I goes 'Tswarm nuff tseated.' Then e goes 'Is motor's on the blink,' or summin, an we're goin like wiv is mate Steve and Chelle in theirs. An I goes..."

Liz withdrew her attention from the talk, now starting to have the same effect on her as the squeaking squealing sound of a polystyrene beaker sliding across a desk, and focused out of the window, looking at the shop windows and the streams of people on the street, but patches of the talk behind her still intruded occasionally:

"An this old bloke goes 'Old on sunshine.' An is mate Steve goes 'What's wiv those parked there?'..."

Liz watched the rivulets of people on the wide pavement of Victoria Street. There seemed two main streams moving quite easily and freely against each other in the middle of the pavement. Then there was a fast lane right at the kerb edge where the high-speed movers bobbed and weaved in and out of the lamp posts and big free-standing green litter bins, and in the road sometimes, in both directions. There was a subsidiary lane along the shop-front line, but this was moving the slowest, with people constantly being halted by shop-window gazers or by having to dodge others issuing out of the shops, the newsagents, and sandwich bars into the stream.

Everyone was dressed in clothes for work; the men in universal suits of shades of blue or grey. This observation reminded her of something Weaver had said in the office once: that the American Civil War had never finished, in fact was still being fought out on the streets of London, where everyone male was dressed either in Confederate grey or Federal blue.

War. That was another reason she didn't like Cill Weaver. He was always talking about war, and without any discernable disapproval. Images, lifted entirely from cowboy films, of how she visualised the American Civil War chased each other across the open unfenced range of Liz's mind.

In fact she despised cowboy films, though she had seen some, such as *Butch Cassidy and the Sundance Kid*, and *High Noon* of course, and *Gone With the Wind*. But she had refused to go and see *The Wild Bunch* - it just glorified violence - with her boyfriend of the time, and couldn't imagine what everyone thought was so good about Spaghetti Westerns. That relationship hadn't lasted very long. In cowboy films the women's roles particularly were stereotypical and underdeveloped, she stated frequently.

Liz was certain which side she would have been on in the American Civil War, she had no worries on that score. She had a strong suspicion, a certainty, that Weaver would have been a Confederate, a Rebel, a slave-owning arrogant ignorant narrow shallow Secessionist.

For Liz Tintwistle the greatest evil under the sun was to profess yourself unconcerned with human rights, and Cill Weaver didn't seem to care about human rights at all.

The bus made the three-sided loop round Parliament Square; between the statues of Abraham Lincoln on the left and the back of Winston Churchill on the right. The Houses of Parliament were black with over a hundred years of smoke and dirt and pollution, the soft limestone sucking up the airborne filth like a paper filter on a cigarette.

Liz looked across at the neo-gothic pinnacles and wondered whether the House of Commons was on this side or on the river side. She didn't know, even though she had been in the public gallery a few times. She couldn't seem to work out the inside layout on the outside. She focused on the tower of Big Ben and saw that the time on the clock face pointed to 9.29. Late again Ms Tintwistle, she thought, and then plotted ahead in her mind the time against the progress of the bus. Get to work maybe 9.50. Not bad. I'll go up the back stairs. If I leave my coat downstairs with Lydia I might be able to pretend I've been in earlier and have just been to the loo. See how it goes.

Liz repeated the words Ms Tintwistle to herself a few times

to see how it felt. Liz was a Ms. She definitely thought of herself as not a Miss; and she wasn't a Mrs. She was a Ms. She believed that the women of the world were the downtrodden majority. They had abilities equal to men, if not superior, but not the same rights, nor the same rewards. Liz was incensed that there were many companies and careers and wage structures where women were paid less than men for doing exactly the same job. She was infuriated by what was obviously a cattle market labelling where women were either a Miss or a Mrs, but men were just Mr.

Liz believed devoutly in women's rights. She believed that quite soon the world would come round to her way of thinking. Women would win. In fact she was a firm believer in the proposition that a ms was as good as a male.

The bus passed the entrance to Downing Street. Liz peered to her left up the street. Traitor, she thought, feeling personally let down and betrayed by the fact that Mrs Thatcher was a woman.

As the bus made its way round three sides of Trafalgar Square, Liz craned her neck to make out what show was being promoted at the National Portrait Gallery. She thought art was important. Billboards proclaimed an exhibition of faces from the Queen's collection. Liz thought that wasn't so interesting. Faces and portraits weren't real art. Interesting in a minor, historical, sort of way; but not real art.

Liz Tintwistle had strong opinions on most things she encountered in her life, or read about, or saw on television, or heard about from other people; and once engaged these opinions stuck as fast and solid as concrete and set as strong.

In her views and opinions she was utterly conventional yet was convinced she was the exact opposite. In the pub with a group of them once Weaver, after a number of pints, had said to her "Tintin one of the troubles with you is you have a clonial mentality." Liz thought he'd said "colonial mentality" and laughed scornfully because she knew she wasn't in the least that. Then she realised Rex Spurgeon was engaged in making a noise somewhere between a snigger and a titter in delight at the pun, and she'd had to ask Weaver what he meant.

But despite Cill Weaver's comment, and probably in some ways because of it, she was adamantly under the delusion that in her thoughts and her way of thinking she lived her life right at the sharp end, up front, uncompromising, pushing the envelope, riding on the piercing laser beam at the heart of Edge City. Had anyone contradicted this deeply held almost religious view of herself, such as Weaver in another drunken moment one lunchtime in the Printer's Devil, say, and accused her of being the epitome of conservatism and straightjacketed thinking, she would with absolute honesty believe him to be mad. She was at the front edge. She did live in Edge City. She knew. She felt it.

She began to count the dossers in the doorways along the Strand. Four, with evidence to judge by bulging tatty plastic carrierbags, of two others. The down-and-outs were moved on when the buildings began to open up in the morning. Dossers were one of Liz's prime worries. Not that she actually did anything to help them; she just worried about them. She blamed society in general and the government in particular for their existence. If only society was changed for the better, there would automatically be no dossers, that was plain. The one led to the other, clearly. It was more important to solve the problem rather than tackle its effects.

The bus passed the old BBC headquarters, and still home of the radio's World Service, followed very soon further on in the Aldwych by the Indian embassy. These institutions were two of Liz's most favourite places.

As a child she had been brought up to believe that one day she would work for the BBC. It was natural. And she had always been fascinated by India. She had read a lot about Gandhi and the struggle for Indian independence. Her romantic nature was fired with the story of the march to the sea to make salt; and the notion of only allowing a country's industries to be founded on what was pre-industrial and cottage-based seemed to Liz's mind not only totally workable but also just, right, good, and far better than the Western approach, and surely the only hope for the future of mankind. In some strange romantic union in her mind it seemed totally apt that the BBC's Bush House and India House should be neighbours on the Aldwych.

Now the bus had penetrated to the edge of the City of London and in a phase-change made the quantum leap between the Strand and Fleet Street, between the City of Westminster and the City of London. Liz's spirits sank a little. She stood wearily and made her way to the back of the bus and waited on the Routemaster doubledecker's open platform gripping the white pole for the next stop. She stepped off the still moving bus, hefted the strap on her bag to a better position on her shoulder, wondered whether to make a detour to pick up a coffee from the sandwich shop at the bottom of Dunstan's Court, decided against it, and with wandering steps and slow ascended the alley towards her office.

She pushed firmly against one of the pair of glass doors, and tutted audibly and pulled her face when she discovered it would not move. She had pushed on the one that was always left locked. Why could she never remember which was the unlocked door? She tried again on the other door.

She smiled sweetly but absent-mindedly at the receptionist who was holding the phone to her ear as though it was a flaming barbed-wire hosepipe with a look of utmost distaste welded to her face. Liz had no time for her. She thought she was an empty-headed bimbo whose world revolved around men, and therefore hardly a real woman. Then she noticed the bandage round each wrist.

Oh dear, she thought as she passed the lift area and headed for the back stairs, poor Lydia hasn't slashed her wrists again?

4. MEETING

"News meeting in ten minutes!"

Janet the self-important narrow-minded earnest busybody who was editor's assistant cannoned round the large open-plan office informing the journalists of the impending compulsory gathering. Janet McLing originally had the job of editorial secretary, but somehow in her journey up the pothole-ridden road of office politics had managed to achieve and enweasel for herself the grander title of editor's assistant, which in turn required that a new person had recently been hired as editorial secretary.

Weaver groaned quietly and bitterly and pulled a face, biting his lower lip, grating his teeth, then puffing out his cheeks and expelling the air with a sound of impatience. He glared at Janet with a look reserved for informants, stool-pigeons, Judases, toadies, arse-lickers, brown-nosers, sycophants, quislings, fellow-travellers, Benedict Arnolds, and fifth columnists. He knew that one of Janet's jobs first thing in the day was to peer remorselessly and vulture-eyed out of the editor's office window and make a note of the times the journalists passed into the building through the front doors two storeys below. As a result she regularly spotted Weaver coming in ten minutes after the regulation 9.30 start.

"Scrap-metal merchant," he murmured abusively, out of her hearing. "Davidov. Penguin-fancier. Seaweed virago." Plus, as always, his favourite: "Mac-Quis-Ling." In Weaver's opinion Janet McLing was the original wall that had ears.

When Janet turned to look at him he tapped the concrete column next to his desk a few times with the end of a Bic and said in a loud voice: "Well we better watch out for this one then, hadn't we?" He did it deliberately; he knew it would confuse her. There was no way on earth that Janet McLing would have worked out the column by Weaver's desk was the fifth one along from the wall.

She looked blankly at him, and made a dismissive noise somewhere between a snort and a tut, implying that his behaviour was childish, churlish, uncouth, and unworthy of response, and moved on to the next clump of desks, the features section. She thought Weaver was a time-waster. She had caught him once doing the crossword in the office. She disapproved of him loyally on behalf of her boss the editor with a righteous and powerful disapproval.

Weaver knew what Janet thought of him, and played up to her opinion. He did this out of a feeling of superiority. He felt superior to her because he did not take his opinions from someone else, he reckoned, and made his own judgements, and was loyal or deferential to no one. Sometimes he wasn't sure that he wasn't deluding himself about this self-satisfied independence of mind and for a day or so became all timid and quiet and reclusive. He hadn't yet worked out that this was the time his friends liked him best.

He looked around to see how the others were reacting. Everyone seemed to be hiding what Weaver was sure were their real feelings and presenting an unconcerned look to the world. God, toadies in all directions, he thought.

Weaver knew that every office needed a scapegoat, a receptacle for the collective guilt and sins of the office, and suspected that many of his colleagues had him fitted up for the slit eyes, shaggy coat and horns; to be followed by a ritual driving out and a solo sojourn in the desert.

<<HORROR OF FAMILY PET'S DESERT SOJOURN. VET CALLED TO PUT DOWN LARGE CUDDLY FURRY ANIMAL WITH HORNS. RSPCA CONSULTED. KENNEL CLUB REJECTS PEDIGREE CLAIM>>

Finally Weaver sighed and began to look for his notebook on a desk that resembled the first day on the Somme about the time the pals of the East Lancs regiment were gaining their six VCs before breakfast. The magazine's Monday morning ritual was about to begin.

"Once more unto the breach," Weaver began. "After me lads over the top, dear friends. It is a far, far better thing that I do. It is a far, far better place that I go to. Someone kick a football ahead of us please! You couldn't have done that with a mere-smear magazine!" he said gently, sadly, and obscurely. Everyone within hearing nearby concentrated on ignoring him.

The main strategic event in the week for a weekly news magazine is the news meeting. In this meeting, usually held on a Monday morning, the news editor goes through his news list and outlines the stories he intends to include in the news pages for that week's issue of the magazine. Reporters are allocated to these stories. All the resources of the magazine are put into the news editor's hands to give him the best chance of beating the paper's rivals to the best news coverage of the week. Yet, contrary to what might be imagined, the most important thing was not to break the best news stories, or to unlid a desperate cover-up, or to inform the readers with the magazine's wide-ranging and interesting coverage. No the most important thing was to beat their rivals to an important story. Of course "important story" was by nature self-defining: it was invariably one which the rivals had missed, important or not.

The senior journalists trooped towards the editor's office - a glass box set in the corner of the open-plan floor with a desk, table, sideboard, bookshelf, and most important a drinks cabinet, set about it. Though only Weaver was prepared openly to admit it everyone else also but secretly hated these meetings; but they were also a mark of seniority in the office; only the senior journalists were invited, and there was a divide, a subtle pecking order, between those who were deemed senior or important enough to attend and those who were not. All section heads were included: news editor, deputy editor, chief sub-editor, managing editor, features editor, art editor; various important correspondents - business, political, and foreign; and assorted review editors - arts and leisure, science and technology - and a number of senior reporters and writers. The editorial secretary was also present at the meeting. Her function was to take notes.

"Did you see Lydia's wrists?" Liz Tintwistle said to the young woman walking beside her across the office. This person, Carmen the editorial secretary, had a lean pretty face surrounded by a mass of black hair cascading in curls to her shoulders like a waterfall of slender writhing slugs.

"I know," Carmen said. "Why does she do it?"

"Because she's a daft cow," a deep voice said from behind them. "God knows."

"Thank you Eddie for that pearl of wisdom," Liz said in what she was sure was a withering tone. She was a great one for what she imagined were withering tones.

Eddie Osmoe, the chief sub-editor, grinned and said no more, but looked triumphantly unwithered. Eddie Osmoe was forty-four, fat, frequently fatuous, but a ferociously fast and falcon-eyed sub-editor. He exuded an air of superiority because he had not been to university. Unlike all the other journalists, reporters, sub-editors, section heads, and columnists on the magazine, Eddie Osmoe had been trained as a journalist on a local paper in Lancashire. "Come up the hard road" as he put it, though with only a trace now of his native accent, a hard zed on the end of the word us, and a fixed belief that the chip butty was the food of the gods.

He fostered the popular but unproven hypothesis that all reporters trained as sixteen-year old school leavers on local papers were somehow, invisibly but certainly, better reporters than all university types and degree holders. One of the struts of this hypothesis was that university types had no idea of the real world, and therefore no ability, he claimed, "to get their foot in the door". The remarkable thing was that the university types and degree holders working on *Front Page* magazine appeared not to demur at this slur on their abilities, so endorsing Osmoe's hypothesis by default.

Carmen was upset at the thought of any woman as serene, beautiful, elegant, and superior as Lydia being described as a "daft cow". She pinched her lips in mild dismay and little dimples appeared on her cheeks.

She ignored Eddie and spoke to Liz.

"She was all bright and happy last week. She's got a new man. A surveyor with a Porsche. He sent her flowers every day."

"Personally I can't imagine any man being worth slitting

your wrists over," Liz said in a determined voice, mainly for Eddie's benefit, and any other man in hearing.

"That's not, I trust, yet I fear the worst and that indeed it must be, a chartered surveyor, is it?" Osmoe said. "Or rather I should say, less in jest than you'd think, a char-turd surveyor, is it?"

Both women tried to ignore him, embarrassed by the scatological pun. Eddie Osmoe wasn't surprised: long ago he had discovered to his own satisfaction one of the Last Great Truths Of The Universe: that the world is divided into men and women, and men find jokes about shit and piss and arseholes and farting funny, and women don't. He was inwardly pleased to see the reaction, and so reveal to his further satisfaction the underlying essential true reality of another of his hypotheses.

"Maybe there's been a strike in the bulb-gardens of Holland. Perhaps the lad pulled his finger out of the dyke" - Eddie smirked with glee at the double entendre - "and the tulip fields are all inundated by tempest and flood. Cry havoc in the bulb fields of the Low Countries."

"Actually Eddie for your information you're wrong. It was red roses," Carmen said, forgetting her resolution to having nothing to do with Eddie that day. "Every day last week."

Now Eddie did indeed look triumphant.

"Red roses! For God's sake. In fact red roses, ye gods! I'm not surprised the poor girl's slashed her wrists. I'd slash my wrists if someone sent me red roses every day."

I don't think anyone ever will Eddie, Carmen thought to herself.

Then to Liz's and Carmen's relief they saw they had arrived at the door of the editor's office and further conversation was prevented by their proximity to The Presence, their closeness to the Sublime Porte.

Here there was a parting of the ways: Eddie and Carmen passed on through the doorway, but Liz turned aside and made for the coffee pot on the filing cabinet next to a window. Liz was not yet considered senior enough to be invited to the news meetings. Carmen of course was the most junior person in the office - apart from the two career-study work-experience school leavers presently attached to the staff - but her function was to take minutes of the meeting.

SA - "Essay"- Moriarty sat behind his curved desk waving everyone to seats. "Sitting there like Piffy on a rock-bun" as Eddie Osmoe once aptly described him. Pictures of previous editors adorned the walls of the office.

Newcomers to *Front Page* magazine's editorial team often expressed bafflement that everyone called the magazine's editor Essay when it seemed clear and was also widely known that his name was something completely different. The reason was this: Moriarty had long ago while still not yet a teenager in Glasgow decided that his given names were a total embarrassment.

He had been christened Scipio Africanus Moriarty.

Moriarty spent a lot of his childhood trying to adapt his first and second names to something less risible.

At home he was always called "Skip" and "Skippy". And those names were fine at primary school too. But by the time he reached secondary school he'd become much more wary. They had too many connotations of rubbish receptacles and Australian kangaroos.

So he'd managed to conjure "Rick" out of the second syllable of his second name. He called himself Rick from then on. As someone always moving into new environments, and so leaving people behind who knew him by another name, it was always possible to reinvent himself without too much social difficulty.

And Rick seemed adequate to him for the rest of his teenage years and into adulthood.

But soon after reaching London in search of his fortune he felt that Rick was now out of keeping with the heavyweight businessman and person of social significance he intended to become.

So he started calling himself by his initials. He even started by trying SAM, but pretty soon felt this lacked the necessary weight, seriousness, seniorority and sonorousness he was looking for.

So he switched to "SA."

And this in turn tended to be pronounced "Essay" with a weaker second syllable rather than the equal stress that SA required. And he was happy with that. So Essay he became. Moriarty also imagined his new name lent him some kind of real credibility by association as an essayist and man or letters. He didn't care that he wasn't either: he was happy if people thought he was.

Not that many people could tell what his real names were anyway, since all it said on his business cards was "SA Moriarty".

He always introduced himself by his initials to new people. He became like women writers over the centuries, like E Nesbit and PD James and PL Travers, who were wary of broadcasting, revealing or even acknowledging their female reality in case it put off male readers. They preferred instead the neuter and non-specific mystery of initials. So with SA Moriarty.

Over time SA morphed, not least in Moriarty's mind, to Essay.

The word Essay was printed on his latest business card. He made sure he named himself as this now to new introductions.

But it was a small world and word got around. He couldn't keep it a secret for long what SA really stood for.

And while Essay was now fully entrenched, and the name went with the face, people were surprised and taken aback when they found that his name was not Essay at all but really Scipio Africanus.

Unfortunately for Moriarty when this realisation did happen it had the effect of lowering him greatly in the opinion and esteem of the people he had introduced himself as Essay to, since it became clear immediately to them that here was someone who hadn't the bottle to accept the name he'd been christened with. They also felt that they had been lied to. They felt that Moriarty was a charlatan and not to be trusted. Strangely enough they were right.

In fact so lacking in respect for him was his current chief sub-editor that he was once heard suggesting the best thing everyone could do for Moriarty's given name was to call him by the last four letters of his second name. That would be the most apt name, he said. The same chief-sub also often referred to Moriarty behind his back as Skippy.

A second thing which surprised people about Moriarty when they met him was that he was Scottish when he clearly had an Irish name. This too worked against Moriarty in people's esteem. It might not be his fault, but it threw them, and the suspicion grew that Moriarty was not all he appeared to be. There might be a further charlatan element to him, in other words.

And a third thing about Moriarty that surprised people who met him was that he didn't have any kind of Scottish accent. This was even more surprising to those who knew him back in Glasgow, because he used to have a strong Glaswegian accent then. At some point between there and London he'd lost it. This had been done deliberately. He thought the accent would be a bar to his upward progress. After hours of practice he'd replaced his native voice with a kind of general-purpose received pronunciation. Most of the time his RP was serviceable and worked well enough. But occasionally the original phonemes would burst through like weeds in a prized allotment. And this too actually worked against Moriarty in people's esteem, because it would then seem to those who met him that not only didn't he have the bottle to keep his original first name, he had a surname that was geographically suspicious, and he hadn't the balls to hold on to his original accent. They felt that Moriarty was even more of a charlatan than they first thought.

The senior reporters, chief sub-editor, section heads, art editor, and correspondents entered the office in groups and one by one, each with an acknowledgement of some sort towards the editor. For some this was a cheery hello, for others a mock-cheery hello; others again merely offered a grunt. Still others offered no salutation apart from a brief nod or a twitch at the side of the mouth. Eddie Osmoe refused even to look in the direction of the head of the long table where the editor sat. Osmoe thought his editor was a twat, a prat, a great Scotch fairy, and worst of all no journalist. Weaver was envious of Osmoe's disdain but found the nerve lacking to emulate him. He said good morning Essay in what he hoped was a neutral and not too toadying a tone. Essay Moriarty smiled and nodded in turn, enjoying the deference and acknowledgement of his power, position and authority.

Carmen sat down in the chair at the editor's left hand. Colin Cuddleigh-Cook the deputy editor, an ancient white-haired hack who had once been news editor back in the mists of time, beyond living memory it seemed, when lead news stories consisted of the colour of the Queen's dress at Ascot and the launch of aircraft carriers, sat down in his customary position in the chair to the editor's right. Jerry Carter the present news editor took his seat at the far end of the long table facing the editor. Everyone else scrambled for seats at the table or in chairs along the glass walls of the office.

"Is everyone here that's coming that's coming?" Moriarty said to the room at large.

When Moriarty said things like this no one knew whether it was meant as a joke, a kind of humorous levity of phraseology, or whether it was the way he always spoke and didn't know any better. It was always said in a serious tone of voice. It sounded mock-Irish, but there was a feeling that Moriarty didn't know it sounded Irish, that he'd just picked the habit up from somewhere and continued to run with it for no apparent reason. The general consensus among his staff was that Moriarty would have been better suited to a career as a television game-show host.

Everyone seemed to glance at everyone else in feigned calculation. There was always a strong subliminal urge to be seen to be useful.

Carmen answered, indeed she was the only one present who had any idea of the answer.

"Bill sends his apologies. He's covering the er..." she scanned her notepad professionally "...the Falklands land ownership story. He's left a note for Jerry."

She offered to pass a folded piece of paper down the table towards the news editor. Moriarty intercepted it, read it, refolded it, and passed it on. The absent Bill was Bill Roadhouse the business editor.

Watching the note progress down the table from his vantage point against the glass wall Weaver pondered on the delightful possibilities of a game of Chinese whispers in written form and the consequences for the news pages. Send three-and-fourpence to the Falklands indeed!

"All right if that is everybody that is everybody, let's make a start," Moriarty said.

He looked towards Carmen: "Could you..?" he said inclining his head towards the door. Carmen got up from her seat just as Weaver shut the door. Carmen sat down again.

"All yours, Jerry," Moriarty said. "What have you got that you've got for us?"

Jerry Carter began scanning across his clipboard. He pushed his brown tortoise-shell glasses back up to the bridge of his nose with the middle finger of his left hand. Weaver saw the gesture and wondered, not a wearer of glasses himself, whether the move was a rude but disguised offensive gesture by the news editor aimed at Moriarty. Weaver made a mental note to ask Jerry about it over a pint sometime.

"There are various Falklands options," Jerry Carter began in a high-pitched earnest voice. He was new to the news editor's job and wanted to do it well. "While the Task Force is sailing we've obviously got one week, perhaps two, to do some background stuff on the conflict."

"What's the lead? Is there a lead?" Moriarty asked.

"Maybe Bill's piece on land ownership down there. See how that pans out," Carter replied, then carried on quickly before Moriarty could ask anything else: "We're looking at the military options. I'm going to get the views of some of the Sandhurst or Camberley lecturers, or maybe an ex-Nato bigwig, or a retired field marshal or two."

"Or as well," the editor said.

"Indeed as well. Cill will you get on to that?"

"Right." Weaver made a note. His widely-known interest

in and knowledge of war had made Weaver effectively senior reporter on the Falklands situation, even though he was technically still a relative junior. Liz Tintwistle for one certainly resented his recent rapid elevation into the sacred grove of the editor's office at news meeting time.

"The other major aspects are the American connection and the so-called Peruvian peace proposals," Carter carried on. "Haig's going to be hurtling about making a lot of concerned noises now and for the next week or so."

He noticed that Judy Bodkin the features editor sitting on his left had written down "Botcher Haig" on her notepad. Carter almost laughed aloud, but managed to carry on without pause.

"The news team's working on these now. And then we ought to look at this historically. Take a dispassionate view..."

"What about this darned ship?" Colin Cuddleigh-Cook interrupted Carter. The deputy editor used words like "darned" and "bally" all the time. Listeners to his conversation felt themselves transported by some sort of mysterious time-warp into another epoch. A time when there was such a thing as the "Commonwealth", and "Dominions", often inhabited by "natives". Such "natives" often showed a lot of "pluck", particularly according to Cuddleigh-Cook it seemed on the cricket and "rugger" fields.

Carter looked up blankly from his clipboard.

"Which ship?" he asked. "The Argentineans seem to have only two: one named after an old warlord generalissimo, some old American cruiser, and an antiquated aircraft-carrier that appears to be named after a date. Which one Cu-Colin?"

When he was in a good mood, which was seldom, Cuddleigh-Cook didn't mind being referred to as "Cuddles" by his colleagues. But never in news meetings.

"The 25th of May. That's what the date translates as," Weaver spoke up.

"What happened then?" Rex Spurgeon the literary editor asked.

Weaver shook his head. "Dunno Rex. Independence from the Spanish, I'd guess. I'll find out."

"No, no, dammit, not their blasted ships. Our bally ship," Cuddleigh-Cook insisted peevishly.

"What ship's that Colin?" Moriarty asked.

"The ice-breaker. What is it? Come on, you're the news editor. The *Terra Nova*? The one that started it all. *Discovery*, that's it," Cuddleigh-Cook ended triumphantly. With the mention of the two most famous British ships to have operated in Antarctic waters over the previous 80 years, the deputy editor had effectively exhausted his knowledge of such matters.

"*Endurance*? That's a bit old now that story Colin surely?" Carter said, less decisively than he wanted to be.

"Oh I don't know about that. Withdrawing that ship sent all sorts of wrong messages to the Argentineans. Might be worth a piece on HMG's whole Antarctic policy. What do you think Essay?" Cuddleigh-Cook appealed to the editor to back him up.

"Might be worth a look Jerry," Moriarty said.

"Right." Carter made a note on his clipboard.

Rex Spurgeon, sitting next to Carter's right hand, saw he'd written down "Fucking Terra Nova!!!". Seeing out of the corner of his eye that Spurgeon had noticed what he'd written, Carter carried on writing: "What now? A reprise of Scott of the Arse-antic? He'll be asking us next what we plan to do on the search for Franklin." Spurgeon coughed to smother a giggle. Spurgeon then wrote on his own notepad so Carter could see: "Arctic turns!"

"Apparently according to the tabloids the Forkbenders call them 'Argies'," Eddie Osmoe said.

"Yes, I noticed Eddie," Moriarty said. "That we used the word 'Argentines' last week. We don't want to use that again. They're Argentineans. The place is the Argentine. Okay? Can we get that in the House Style, Eddie?"

"Yes. Of course," Eddie said. He had no intention of doing so. "I was hoping to get 'Argie-bargie' in somewhere this week," Osmoe responded.

It was clear to everyone else in the room except Moriarty and Cuddleigh-Cook that Osmoe was taking the piss out of the editor. Jerry Carter quickly moved on to defuse the situation.

"We need to get hold of any Falklanders actually here at the moment, if we can find any. Get their views. Human interest."

"How do we do that?" Moriarty asked.

"Apparently someone threw a tin of corned beef through the Argie embassy window last night," Osmoe said with a laugh. "It said on the *Today* programme."

This information was greeted with a widespread splash of laughter round the table.

"Is that relevant Eddie?" Moriarty said with an attempted put-down tone of voice.

"Was it Fray Bentos?" Weaver asked amid general laughter.

"I expect it was. That would be the point wouldn't it," Osmoe continued pedantically. "Argentinian corned beef, though naturally the BBC didn't specify the manufacturer, just said 'Argentinian corned beef' in that prissy tone of voice everyone at the BBC has. And I think it is relevant," he pushed on before Moriarty or Carter could interrupt him, "What about doing a piece on the damage this conflict is likely to do to our trade with South America? Not just Argentina, but the whole continent."

"Yes, I like that," Carter made a note. "I'll discuss it with Bill when he gets back."

"Actually I think Fray Bentos is Uruguayan," Rex Spurgeon said. "The corned beef. It's a town in Uruguay."

"Mmm," Eddie said. "It gets better. Someone threw a tin of corned beef through the embassy window. What we're assuming was Fray Bentos corned beef – because what else corn beef is there? And I bet the person throwing it thought it was Argentine anyway. So now, does the designated abuse work if the mechanism is wrong? The perception might be right, but the actuality is wrong. Interesting one. Do the Argies take offence if the corned beef is not theirs? I doubt they do. In fact they're probably laughing heartily at Anglo ignorance."

"Getting back to what we were talking about," Moriarty said with an attempt at a decisive manner, then immediately sidetracked himself: "By the way apparently the Falklanders are known as 'Kelpers' by the Argentineans." Reacting to the blank looks this caused, he carried on: "Because of the seaweed. Place is covered with it. Perhaps you might get that in somewhere this week, Eddie."

Weaver wondered where Moriarty had gleaned this piece of information. Probably over lunch with some "well-placed source". Moriarty was a great one for lunches, always with what he invariably called a "well-placed source". In fact all his staff knew that no genuine stories ever resulted from these three and four hour lunches. And as for the "well-placed source" it was much more likely to be a reference to what the main course had been cooked in or poured over the plate in some £60-a-head restaurant rather than to any useful mine of information for possible stories. Since it was widely known among his staff that their editor was searching hard for a mention in the New Year Honours list - certainly for an OBE and perhaps even higher - for "services to journalism", it was always assumed that Moriarty's frequent and lengthy lunches were either with an amenable MP, a venal civil servant, or a "captain of industry" (another of Moriarty's favourite phrases), all of whom might well be expected to further Moriarty's increasingly desperate search for an award in public recognition of all his efforts to raise the standard of British news journalism, as he himself put it to whomever he might be lunching with.

"Perhaps the Falklands embassy -" Judy Bodkin the features editor began.

"High commission, I suspect," Rex Spurgeon smoothly corrected her.

"The Falklands whatever-they-have-in-London could help with locating some Falklanders here?" she finished.

"No we've tried it. Everyone's tried. They won't talk to the press. I gather they've been told not to talk to the press," Carter said sadly. "Can't even get pics of the place. I haven't got the foggiest notion what the place looks like."

"Maybe some merchant seaman who go there might have taken some shots. It must have some seaborne trade? Or perhaps we can find someone who's been there for a holiday," Weaver said. "Unlikely I agree, but what about putting an ad in one of the papers, anonymously, with a box number? We could get it into tomorrow's *Standard*."

Weaver could see this idea was falling on stony ground. Too obvious, he realised, for journalists that one.

"To get hold of their holiday snaps. Or maybe some round-the-world yachtsmen perhaps, in those ocean races, maybe they call there," he explained, more in hope than certainty that any-one would take up his suggestion.

"Not sure about that Cill," Moriarty said in dismissal.

"One thing we do need," Carter continued in a facsimile of decisiveness. He was news editor and he was supposed to be running the news meeting. "Is a good map of the islands. Any ideas anyone?"

"We've got *The Times Atlas*, surely?" Cuddleigh-Cook said.

"Yes indeed, but it's not enough for something like this," Carter countered.

"Damn it all Jerry, I seem to recall you wanted us to get that atlas. Cost us an arm and a leg. Now it's no use!"

Jerry Carter began to look a little harassed. He looked around.

"I agree," Weaver spoke up nervously in support of the news editor. "Um, we'll need to know every headland and bog, every hamlet, every mountain top, every kelp-covered possible landing-place. I reckon we'll be certainly needing the most de-tailed map of the islands we can get."

"You think so, do you?" Colin Cuddleigh-Cook said aggres-sively, as though talking to some insignificant worm. Cuddleigh-Cook gloried under the fixed but totally erroneous impression that news coverage had become easier since his day, and that his successors, all of them, had it easy. Weaver could supply an im-aginary ending to this sentence: "Didn't need a fancy blasted map of the darned Falklands when I was news editor". Weaver didn't reply for a moment or two, wondering which way this dialogue was going to end up, and stared out of the window at the glass-covered building being built opposite. Then he pressed on.

"Yes I do. I also think we should get detailed Admiralty charts of the whole of the South Atlantic," he said.

"Oh, why?" Moriarty asked, also beginning to become fearful himself of the cost implications, and not knowing what was involved in 'Admiralty charts'.

"What happens if there's a naval engagement out in the Atlantic somewhere and we've no idea where it is or what it's near?" Weaver responded. "What happens if one of the carriers goes down and we've no idea where - no idea where the nearest land is and whether air cover could have been provided by land-based fighters. We'll have no way of showing it apart from some general schematic lifted from the atlas. I say we need the maps. I volunteer to go to Stanfords at lunchtime and see what they've got." Weaver sank back in his chair, conscious of all eyes watching him after such an impassioned speech.

"Another thing," Carter said, gaining in confidence, "Yes, and we ought to get them before any of the nationals get hold of them and clean the place out. And we ought to get the maps pretty sharpish in case the government tries to put a block on access to maps. You never know. It's the sort of stupid thing they've done before."

Cuddleigh-Cook muttered something. Exasperated, Carter imploded, inwardly seething at the deputy editor, taking the muttering for a criticism of the way the news desk was being run. His anger surfaced, his cheeks went red.

"What was that Colin?" he said.

Colin Cuddleigh-Cook hesitated and glanced at Moriarty before replying.

"I said I didn't think it mattered a damn," he said dismissively.

"That's it! You've got it! I do believe you've got it, old man!" Eddie Osmoe broke in excitedly, doing a passable impression for some reason of Professor Henry Higgins. Osmoe waited a moment for the whole room to focus on him and wonder what the hell he was talking about, then went on, his voice rising in apparent excitement and mock-Archimedean revelation.

"That's it! Send them a Turd-a-Gram!" He said, and explained in a loud stage whisper to his neighbour Spurgeon the literary editor: "'Mattered a damn'; turd-a-damn; turd-a-gram. See? Geddit?"

Horrified at the cheek and effrontery, Spurgeon pretended he hadn't understood, but Weaver nearby let out a high pitched squeak of delight.

Osmoe tilted his chair forward to the ground from against the radiator where he had been leaning and staring out of the window. The impetus threw his long black greasy hair over his eyes. He swept it back.

"Yes, let's send a Turd-a-Gram to the Argies," he cackled loudly.

Now everyone round the table began to get the full impact of the scale of Eddie's joke. Carmen smirked in the direction of her notebook and bent her head down. Her shoulders began moving silently up and down. Moriarty made a noise somewhere between a cough and a splutter and banged the table with his 24-carat gold-nibbed Mont Blanc fountain pen, aware that he was losing control of the meeting, but still not aware of what the hell it was that Eddie Osmoe was talking about.

"You know," Osmoe went on right in the thick of it and carried along on the force of his own verbal glee, "like a Strippagram. You send someone a Turd-a-Gram. Someone's having a 21st party, or it's the office Christmas do, and you think what can we do to liven it up, and you look in Yellow Pages and see Turd-a-Gram, so you phone them up and order one, and along they come and someone parks a tiger on the dance floor, or maybe better still does requests with a Pyrex plate!"

The whole room erupted in laughter. Carmen was completely appalled at the disruption to the ordered universe represented by the news meeting, and wasn't sure whether she should be taking notes of what had been said. Her hand was shaking too much with laughter to do any writing anyway. She gave up the fight and started openly laughing. Weaver was enthralled at Osmoe's performance and felt himself in the presence of a Master.

Spurgeon was unsure. He laughed, certainly, but quietly and was ready instantly to assume a straight face when and where necessary. Carter, though delighted at the put-down of Cuddleigh-Cook, was annoyed that his control of the meeting should be usurped in such a way. Moriarty was still banging the table with the end of his pen. Cuddleigh-Cook said "Oh really!" in an exasperated tone of voice. Judy Bodkin laughed loudest, she actually found the convoluted pun funny, as well as the hilarious prospect of sending Eddie's Turd-a-Gram round to the Argentinian embassy. Everyone else in the room laughed both at the joke and the discomfiture of the editor and deputy editor.

Finally Moriarty quelled the uproar and said angrily to Osmoe.

"Eddie if that's the only contribution you can make to this important news story you better leave the room. Forthwith."

Eddie Osmoe gathered his things together and stood up.

"Come on SA, it was only a joke," he said, making sure he used the double-stressed version of Moriarty's name. He passed a look to the room at large which said: anyone who used the word 'forthwith' when 'now' would do must be a proper dickhead, and left the room amid total silence.

"Right Jerry, back to you," Moriarty said. "Where were we? What have we got that we've got?"

Moriarty would have loved to have sacked Osmoe months ago. He resented his stature among the journalists, but oddly didn't have the nerve to do it. In the last resort Moriarty felt comforted in the knowledge that Osmoe would be around to sort out any mega-cock-ups that often and regularly occur in the operating life of a magazine. If the cock-up was big enough - as it sooner or later might be - only Eddie Osmoe would be capable of sorting it out. Moriarty knew that only Osmoe had the requisite skill, experience, and capability to troubleshoot a cock-up at an early enough stage to prevent it becoming a disaster; and if one were to develop to be able to intercept it and close it down before any serious damage was done. He knew that if his magazine gained a reputation for cock-ups, as editor he could kiss goodbye to any prospects of an OBE.

The departure of Osmoe dampened the spirits of everyone round the table and the rest of the news meeting passed quickly and uneventfully. Each senior correspondent and section head went through their lists of business and outlined to the editor what they expected to be carrying in their columns in the coming week. It was to be expected that much of the column space of the magazine would be devoted to things Argentine.

Much of the remaining time was given over to a discussion about what would go on the front cover. Robert Blynde – universally and naturally known as Rob - the art editor came to the fore at this point. Rob thought a cartoon on the latest aspects of the Falklands crisis would work best. He would brief the main cartoonist – a freelancer, but held on a substantial retainer to preclude him working for any other similar publication – on a melange of secretary-of-state Haig, the Peruvian peace proposals, the Argentinean embassy and Fray Bentos corned beef.

One thing that had not yet been finalised was the leader, either its topic or who would write it. The leader was the column under the magazine's logo alongside the listing of main personnel, the masthead as it is known. It was the main place where the voice of the magazine was expressed, its voice and opinion on weighty matters of importance. It was clear that the leader that week would be on some aspect of the Falklands crisis, but as yet there was no one theme or topic that suggested itself. It was assumed that a theme would emerge over the next two and a half vital news days before the magazine closed its pages at Wednesday noon, ready for printing. In theory any member of the editorial team could write the leader. In practice it was either the editor, the deputy editor, or one of the senior columnists. It was decided that a special meeting to discuss the leader would be held briefly on Tuesday afternoon.

In little less than another threequarters of an hour the meeting was over and the journalists rose and stretched and ambled out of the editor's office.

5. LUNCHTIME

It was lunchtime. Or close enough to it to make no odds to a hardened pub-seeker like Weaver. He toured the clumps of desks in the open-plan office enquiring whether anyone fancied a drink.

"Anyone want to join the party searching for El Dorado?" he asked one group of desks.

"Who or what is Elder Ardo?" Judy Bodkin asked. She nearly added when it's at home but decided against it as she couldn't add anything overtly ironic to the cliche.

"Is there a Junior Ardo? A member of the hoon-ta perhaps?" she pronounced the word slowly and deliberately, stressing it ironically with an exaggerated H sound.

"Dor-ardo. It's a new lager. Highly potent. It's brewed in the Seven Cities of Cibola. Creates a whole New World inside your head," Weaver outlined with a degree of historical accuracy regarding the names but also a large degree of implausibility.

"CW what on earth are you talking about?" Judy said, mystified, and not sure whether there was some sort of joke or pun involved here or whether Weaver was being straightforward.

"Sounds like a load of old Malvinas to me!" she said.

"I think he's talking about an ongoing lunchtime liquid down-throat scenario," Bill Roadhouse said. Bill had just arrived. He unloaded a Sony Pro tape recorder and a spiral-bound notebook onto his desk, draped his jacket around a wooden coat hanger and suspended it from a light fitting.

"If you are," Roadhouse now addressed himself to Weaver. "Then mine's a Guinness."

"Right. See you there. At the Tipp."

"Ooh-er matron, hold on though. Second thoughts, nay and thrice nay." Bill Roadhouse said, picking up a note on his desk and reading it.

"I better chase this ownership story up. Sorry." Roadhouse began to roll up his sleeves.

It being Monday and thereby a day when news stories had

53

to be hunted down, written, checked, rewritten and then handed to the news editor, most of the reporters did not go for a long liquid lunch. They would go to the pub at the end of the day instead. Weaver realised there were going to be no takers for a lunchtime visit to the Tipperary. Strictly sandwiches at the work-face for the troops on news days. He sighed sadly.

He turned towards his own desk and sat down. He opened a drawer low in his desk and pulled out a battered black note-book, held together by a broad elastic band. His contact book. A vital supply line, secret and unavailable to any of his colleagues except under the most exceptional circumstances. He began to wonder whom he might know who might know someone who might have a contact at the officers' training school at Sandhurst or the Army Staff College at Camberley.

He found a name in the folds of the contact book. He was reaching for the phone when he remembered he had rashly of-fered to go and search in Stanfords map shop for what they had on the Falklands.

<<SEVEN CITIES OF CIBOLA FOUND NEAR FALK-LANDS. FABULOUS LAND DISCOVERED BY REPORT-ER: "I FOLLOWED LAGER TRAIL">>

He pulled on his mac and rushed off towards the stairs, intent on making his way to Covent Garden, reciting quietly to himself as he went the words:

"Twas on the ship Malvinas,

By God you should have seen us.

The figurehead was a nude in bed,

Sucking the captain's penis."

At the clump of desks in the centre of the room Liz Tintwis-tle was talking to the news editor. She hadn't yet really got into the thick of the action on the Falklands and wanted to, desper-ately. She was also concerned at the way the news coverage of the crisis was being presented.

"Look Liz don't worry about it," Jerry Carter said in his high-pitched voice, pushing his glasses back up his nose. "All the reporters are going to get a chance to get involved in the Falklands, one way or another. It's the biggest thing."

"But Jerry are we actually taking a pro-war stance or what?"

"We're not taking any stance at all. There isn't a war yet. Actually."

"That doesn't stop us warmongering!" Liz Tintwistle filled the word with the deepest hate and loathing.

"For God's sake Liz give it up. Get with the programme. Give over. It's a fucking big story. Tintin you've got to decide whether you really are a reporter or instead some sort of constant bleeding heart commentator. This is the fucking biggest story any of us has ever fucking seen - apart from maybe our white-haired old wunderkind of a deputy ed there," he jerked his thumb over his shoulder in the direction of Cuddleigh-Cook's desk in the far corner of the room.

"Cuddles probably got sent to Munich with Chamberlain and like as not thought he was there to cover the fucking beer-fest," Carter raised his voice and almost shouted at her, then re-lented. It wasn't her fault he was feeling harassed. Liz was a good reporter, he knew.

"Okay, okay, look Liz, see what you can get on these latest mediation efforts from Perez de Cuellar. The Per-u-vian peace proposals," he rolled the alliterative phrase round his mouth with an ironic stress.

"To the rest of the world they're the UN peace proposals. But to us they're just referred to as Peruvian. Why is that?"

"Right. Thanks Jerry," Liz said gratefully. She returned to her desk.

Carter sat down in his own chair and began scanning his clipboard. He sighed. So much to do. So little time to do it.

6. FIVE THOUSAND

Eddie Osmoe was correcting some copy, his red biro speeding across the galleys like Fangio's Ferrari at the Nurburgring. However he wasn't concentrating particularly on the job in hand, there was something else on his mind. Osmoe had developed the hypothesis that the best thing that could happen if the sailing of the Task Force actually led to large scale fighting with Argentina was that Britain should lose the ensuing war. 'May you live in interesting times', indeed. The trouble was, how could he swing the magazine over to accepting this view?

Rex Spurgeon approached. For some days he had been conducting much of his conversation in a fake cod-Spanish accent in which every word containing a CH or a J was pronounced as though it were a guttural H sound. Thus the town Chichester had become "hi-hester", and Charing Cross station "h-aring cross". This had caught on for a while with some of the more impressionable among his colleagues until the whole of the floor echoed with "hi" this and "ha" that and "ho" the other.

Most recently Spurgeon had taken it a stage further and now said almost every initial letter as though it were a Spanish H sound. So he now said "hub" when he meant pub, and he talked of travelling on the "hube" across London. As yet none of his colleagues had ventured with him into these linguistically uncharted waters. In fact most of them were now hoping the whole thing would die out very quickly.

Spurgeon tended to develop these word-play notions and use them until they had spread like viruses into the minds of his colleagues, and then he'd move on to the next while they were still playing with his last one. He was the first to admit however that some were better than others. Seeing the effectiveness and spread of his word-games often gave him more pleasure than anything else. As a critic and literary editor he'd had some pretensions towards writing himself but had never to date converted the pretensions into published reality. He'd had plans and a strong wish, but never seemed to have the ideas or the commitment or the time. He now knew, or at least a part of him did, that he never would be a writer himself, though yet still another part of him had not yet fully come to terms with this and his mood would fluctuate accordingly. At the present his creative urges were temporarily satisfied by word-play, and particularly at seeing how everyone else took up his word-ideas.

"Heddie," Spurgeon said approaching the chief-sub.

Eddie Osmoe was talking to Billy Ayk about copydates and deadlines. He broke his talk and turned to Rex and raised an eyebrow.

"No, no problem Heddie. Hi'll come back. Nothing vital," Rex said, moving away.

Eddie turned back to Billy Ayk.

This was Bill Aykroyd, the production editor. There were two Bills in the office, Bill Roadhouse and Bill Aykroyd. Roadhouse had been there longer, and was more senior, and had always been called Bill. When a second Bill arrived naming became a little more problematic. Much of the time it didn't matter that two "Bills" might be called across the *burolandschaft* office floor as it would be obvious which one was being addressed. But sometimes it wasn't so easy to differentiate, such as in The Printer's Devil, say, or The White Hart in New Fetter Lane, when both Bills were standing at the bar.

So over the months secondary parts had been added to Bill Aykroyd's first name. It started off as "Billy A". And this naturally led to "Billy Ayk". For some reason this was never stretched or metamorphosed into "Belly Ayk". Though it was sometimes taken by the more imaginative of his co-workers into the dark realm of "Willy Ayk", but that one never really hardened, as it were, and caught on. Instead the name was shortened into "Ayk" – which was imagined by most of Billy's colleagues to be spelt as "Ache", or sometimes expanded into "The Ache" when being referred to out of his hearing.

Then after a while it was realised that a solution had been staring everybody in the face all along: Bill Roadhouse stayed as Bill, and Bill Aykroyd became Billy. But he was still called "Ache" and referred to as "The Ache" quite frequently. That was because, when all said and done, Billy Ayk was a pain in the neck.

That was because of his job. The job of production editor is liaison. And the focus of the production editor is time. All publications regulate themselves to a certain beat of time. The person most tuned to this timebeat is the production editor. For any publication the production editor is in charge of time.

For a weekly publication this means that every day of every week has things that take place – have to take place – on that day of the week and no other day. The key day for a weekly like *Front Page* was the day the magazine was printed. Everything worked backward from that date and forward to that date. The person in charge of this weekly clock was the production editor.

Front Page was printed on Wednesday allowing it to be published on Thursday where its physical presence would be visible in newsstands in station forecourts, newsagents, kiosks, and other outlets for papers and magazines. Those people who laid out cash and bought the magazine could do so at these outlets from Thursday onwards.

For those who subscribed to the magazine, a publication date of Thursday allowed it to be posted and arrive at their office or at their home on Friday. Either buying the magazine on a Thursday or having it arrive in the mail on Friday, the implication was that buyers and subscribers would be able to read *Front Page* over the weekend. In that way, the owner, publisher and editor of *Front Page* were confident that their publication could and would compete with the Sunday papers.

"The dailies will tell them what's happening. But we'll tell them what it means."

This was one of the famous quotations by the founding editor Thomas Telford Thompson, later Lord Ironbridge, back in the 1930s when the organ was launched.

"Analysis. Analysis. Analysis," was another of Tom Telford Thompson's nostrums about the key to performance success of his new publication. He'd been asked in a radio interview by a BBC earnest-worthy to outline the three ways his title would beat the opposition.

Another one was: "Unlike my famous but unrelated namesake the engineer, I don't want to build bridges: I want to tear them down."

This was thought to mean that Tom Telford Thompson's new organ would not necessarily uphold existing social or political structures. Nor would it be scared of undermining the foundations of any hidden hierarchies within the establishment. And wouldn't hesitate to attack the bastions of entrenched opinions or old-fashioned values. No one in authority would be safe if they weren't totally upright, forthright, humble and honest.

For subscribers in central London there was also a service where copies of *Front Page* were physically sent by bike or van to the subscriber's office or home. As a consequence large numbers of the magazine would arrive at the company's post room early on Thursday morning, ready for despatch round London.

Something else, equally important, also used to happen to the magazine on Thursday morning as soon as the stacks of that week's issue arrived at the post room.

Vanloads of the issue were driven round London and dumped.

This was due to the necessity to maintain the fiction that the magazine had a circulation of over 500,000, or "half a million" as the magazine's editor, advertising manager and publisher preferred to say.

This was down to the need to impress the revenue sources of the magazine.

All magazines have three revenue sources: sales; display advertising; and classified advertising. Sales is one thing, it's fickle, and may fluctuate depending on the contents of any given week. But advertising revenue is far more important. And classified advertising revenue is far more important than display advertising – crucial as that is.

The difference between the two types of ads is: display is about products; classified is about jobs. Or another way of looking at it: display advertising is about lifestyles; classified advertising is about lives.

Big glossy full-colour ads about travel or vodka or cars or clothes might look splendidly expensive – and they are, a back cover or an inside front cover might cost £20,000 – but the total revenue brought in to the magazine in any week by these display ads is well short of the total revenue brought in by the dull-looking black and white job advertisements at the back of the book. The job advertisements are known as classified. The key to financial success of a magazine in any field is to become the main recipient of job ads in that field.

Clearly a magazine that has a larger proven circulation than a rival magazine could claim to be a better recipient of both display and classified advertising. What then stops a magazine just inventing a circulation figure to impress prospective advertisers? The essence is the word "proven".

A monitoring organisation called the Audit Bureau of Circulation checks the veracity of a magazine member's circulation claims by checking its print runs. Although membership of the ABC is voluntary, a magazine that has its circulation audited by the ABC body will have greater credibility than one that doesn't. Hence most reputable magazines are accredited to the ABC.

The editor, advertising manager, publisher and owner of *Front Page* magazine felt it vital to the credibility of the magazine that its ABC-accredited circulation figure should always be above the half million mark. Five hundred thousand sounded good. It sounded weighty and serious. It sounded like it reached a lot of people. It sounded like it reached a lot of the right kind of people.

In fact *Front Page*'s circulation was nowhere near 500,000. Sure its print run was still that high. But its total circulation had been dropping for a number of years and was now nearer 495,000. Four hundred and ninety-five thousand doesn't sound anywhere near as good as five hundred thousand, and nowhere near as good as half a million. So the magazine's print run was still maintained at the artificial, false and unrealistic level of 500,000 copies. It was, in fact, a lie.

Printing more copies than could be sold meant that every Thursday morning, very early, 5,000 printed but spare, unsold and unsellable and non-subscribed copies of the magazine arrived from the printer at *Front Page*'s despatch and post room.

The very first job of the post room's van drivers therefore early every Thursday morning was to drive round central London and dump 5,000 copies of *Front Page* magazine on street corners, in litter bins, on building sites, behind hoardings, and on waste ground. This operation was known as Feeding The Five Thousand. It took one trip each for *Front Page*'s five white vans to dump the 5,000. Only then would the vans return to the post room and stock up with the copies of the magazine that were to be driven to subscribers' homes and offices.

And everybody was happy. ABC was happy because it vetted and audited the print-run which showed 500,000 copies of each issue being printed. The editor was happy because he could claim the circulation of his magazine was over half a million. The figure was printed on the magazine's masthead, just above the ABC logo. The publisher was happy. The owner was happy. The display advertisers were happy. And the companies, employers and recruitment agencies placing classified job ads in the magazine were happy. They all thought they were reaching half a million people.

The result of Feeding The Five Thousand was as miraculous for *Front Page* as the original Feeding The Five Thousand was for the crowd at Bethsaida on the shore of Lake Galilee. In fact Jesus and his five loaves and two fishes wasn't a patch on *Front Page*'s five white van drivers. They kept *Front Page*'s circulation above the magic half million mark.

In fact because of the multiplier effect the magazine could claim - and did - that it was actually being read by five million people every week.

The multiplier effect was based on research and opinion polls that showed how many copies of a particular week's issue of the magazine was read by how many people. In *Front Page*'s case, surveys showed the multiplier was ten. That is, an average of ten people read each copy of the magazine. Only one person may have bought it, but an average of ten people read it. Hence the claim that each issue had a readership of five million. For advertising purposes such numbers were gold dust.

The only people who weren't so happy about Feeding The Five Thousand were the van drivers. They had to get to work even earlier than they should have done on Thursdays in order to first dump the five thousand.

Feeding The Five Thousand wasn't exactly a secret. It was just one of those things no one talked about. It was the kind of thing that everyone hoped no one outside the magazine would ever ask a question about. Certainly no one from the ABC organisation ever asked about it. Nor did any of *Front Page*'s advertisers.

The editorial staff at *Front Page* were mostly ignorant of the weekly Thursday morning ritual of Feeding The Five Thousand. It happened well before any of them got to work for a start. They all thought they worked for a magazine with a circulation of over five hundred thousand.

But Billy Ayk knew all about it. He knew a lot about the physical creation and backroom operations of the magazine. That was his job.

7. FLATPLAN

Billy Ayk was also responsible for setting the weekly clock that all the journalists on the magazine worked to.

This is known as the flatplan.

Producing a magazine or any publication requires two major and distinctly separate operations: filling it and printing it. Printing was printing. But the filling side was further subdivided into two operations: "editorial" and "advertising". Editorial involved writing stories and features; and advertising involved fielding and placing the two types of advertising. The flatplan is the hinge between these operations.

All newspapers and magazines are published according to a ratio between advertising and editorial. Basically whether journalists like it or not the advertising pages pay for the editorial pages. As a rule of thumb this ratio will vary and oscillate between 70:30 and 60:40. That is to say if a magazine works to a 70:30 ratio and has one hundred pages, then 70 of them will be advertising and 30 of them editorial. The higher the ad:ed ratio the more profitable the publication.

Currently, probably because of its coverage of the Falklands crisis, *Front Page* was enjoying a boom in over-the-counter sales. That meant its current ad:ed ratio could move from its traditional 70:30 towards a more editorial-heavy 65:35.

Another rule of magazine publishing that needs to be understood is that advertising pages take precedence over editorial pages. In other words advertising gets first choice of page numbers. Editorial makes do with what's left.

Another rule of thumb is that right hand pages – the odd numbers in a publication – are more preferred slots for advertisers than the left hand, even pages. This is down to the belief - probably extrapolated from the fact that 90 percent of the world's population is right-eye dominant - that readers notice things more on the right hand side of two pages than they do on the left. In many publications the right hand pages are given over totally to advertising.

Because of its strong over-the-counter sales *Front Page* could to a certain extent waive this rule. Its over-the-counter sales freed it to a certain degree from the iron grip of the requirements of advertisers.

So a normal *Front Page* issue in 1982 would consist of editorial and advertising on both odd and even pages.

Aside from the odd-even rule, there are a number of prime slots that advertisers are thought to desire and which therefore come at a premium. These are the front cover, the inside front cover page, the back page, and the inside back page.

Front Page's front cover was spoken for. This page was not available to advertisers, nomatter how much they were willing to pay. It had an editorial front cover. This was often a cartoon of some sort.

But apart from the front cover advertisers could take any page in the magazine they desired. This meant that those pages were not available for editorial.

This needs to be stressed. Aside from the front cover advertisers had first call on any page in the magazine. In other words, adverts first, editorial second. As legendary founding editor Tom Telford Thompson used to say: "We're in the publishing business, not the reading business."

Does a magazine or newspaper succeed because it has huge over-the-counter sales because readers want to read its editorial pages? Or does a magazine succeed because it is the market leader in terms of receiving orders for advertising space? Does one create the other? And if so, which creates which? Which way round does it go?

Each side believed it was more central to the success of the title than the other.

The editorial team believed its pages created huge demand for readership. The advertising sales team believed that the quality of editorial content rested solely on the money-stream created by advertising sales.

The real precedence in page choice of advertising over editorial led to a tensile stress between the two teams. Both those who wrote the editorial pages and those who sold the advertising space had a belief central to their working existence, which was, that each was more important than the other. Yet at the same time both sides paid lip-service to the central mythology, that editorial was more important than advertising. This was the definitive founding and operating creative myth of newspapers and magazines. But it simply wasn't true.

The difference between the two sides was that editorial believed the myth, while advertising did not.

In essence the tension created by the founding myth led to the editorial side devoutly believing it was superior in every way to the advertising side. And at the same time the founding myth determined that the advertising side should continue to let editorial believe it was superior to advertising.

Yet at the same time advertising felt it was secretly superior to editorial because it knew about the underlying bedrock of reality beneath the myth.

Editorial believed the myth. Advertising knew it was a myth but let editorial continue to believe it.

The prime task of a good editor and a good advertisement manager was to keep their teams believing their own mythology without upsetting the base mythology of the other team.

Telling the editorial team which pages had been taken by advertising was one of the first and primary functions of the flatplan.

Every Thursday morning, the day of publication of the current issue, Billy Ayk would talk with Don Phurse the advertising manager to find out which pages in the next issue had been claimed by display advertising.

Classified advertising, the job ads, was always at the back of the "book" – as the magazine was called by those who worked for it – so this never presented any problem for Billy when he was laying out the flatplan. The last ten or even twenty pages in the book every week would be taken up with classified advertising. It was just the balance between editorial and display advertising spread over the first threequarters of the book he needed to sort out and lay down the pagination on the flatplan.

After his conference with Don Billy would return to his desk and begin to form the next flatplan.

The next consideration he had to take into account was the physical requirements of the printing process.

Printing is governed by what is known as "signatures". A signature represents 16 pages in an A4 size magazine. This is to do with the way the original paper roll is printed, folded, cut and bound by the printing, guillotining, gluing or stapling, stacking and baling, and paper working machines to make the finished publication. The printing process is governed by the length and size of the rolls of paper that are fed through the printing machines. The number 16 is crucial to the printing process. And printing is done by signature units, that is by the number of 16 pages-at-a-time that can be printed.

In terms of time, then, the printing house needs to receive "copy" - that which is produced by the editorial team - in batches of 16 pages at a time. One group of 16 pages is one signature.

A magazine with 32 editorial pages will, in printing terms, consist of two signatures. These two signatures will have two different copydates.

Billy Ayk outlined the editorial pages falling into these two signatures onto his new flatplan. Signature printing dates tend to work from the back of the book towards the front. The first signature, sig A at the back of the book would have an earlier copydate than sig B at the front.

Everything on the flatplan was governed by the signatures – or "sigs" as they were known.

News pages at the front of the book fell under sig B and therefore had a later copydate than Rex Spurgeon's review pages nearer the back under sig A. Judy Bodkin's features pages fell between the two sigs. Some of her features had to get away early; others could go two days later.

This was all controlled by the flatplan. And Billy Ayk produced the flatplan.

In essence the flatplan was a graphical representation of an issue of the magazine showing what went on which page and what its copydate was. What page went where and what was on it and what date it had to be filled and sent to the typesetter and when to the printer.

The typesetter was installed at an in-between stage between writing copy and printing it. By the early 1980s preparation of copy for printing had arrived at an intermediate stage between the centuries old metal-letters-in-a-frame rolled in ink method of printing and the futurist completely computerised digital method. For a short time, less than a decade, independent small typesetting companies set themselves up to cater for this halfway house in the production process. A halfway house between age-old William Caxton and the fully digital age.

The typesetter had a special photographic machine that took photos of the made-up pages. It was this series of photos – a "film" – that was sent to the printer. The printer printed the magazine from the page images on the film produced by the typesetter. The film was physically taken by motorbike messenger from the typesetter's office to the printing house. The typesetter could be in London and the printer in Bristol. The messenger would deliver the film from one to the other.

The typesetter made a film of the finished pages. The film was taken by messenger to the printer.

The filmed page images were printed into the finished magazine by the printer.

Every aspect of this whole process was controlled by signatures. The signatures ordered the placing and the printing priority of the pages.

Billy Ayk's whole working life was governed by signatures. Billy didn't care about editorial or the quality of the editorial. All he cared about were the times and days of copydates on the flatplan.

He constantly had to cajole and threaten, persuade and wheedle, order and complain at the journalists to make sure all his flatplan times were met. It was always a close-run thing.

Because if flatplan items and copydates were not met, the

printer could claim extra money. And if the printer claimed compensation for unscheduled printing operations, Billy Ayk would get the blame.

Billy Ayk was, therefore, the main pain in the neck to the editorial team during their weekly working lives. Billy Ayk was essentially that fat bloke in the leather jerkin at the back of the galley beating the drum that governed the rowing speed of the oarsmen. For the galley-slaves in the editorial team it always felt like Billy Ayk's drumbeat was always insisting on nothing else but ramming speed.

Rex Spurgeon often self-consciously referred to the editorial team, Evita-style, as "We, the galley slaves." He did it to show both his knowledge of history and his knowledge of the printing process. But Cill Weaver suspected it was just because he'd seen *Ben Hur*.

Billy's flatplan was usually completed ready by Thursday afternoon, ready to be photocopied and handed out to the editor, deputy editor, art editor, leading correspondents and section heads. Everyone who needed to know what went where and what its copydate was would receive a copy of the flatplan.

8. COPY

The typesetter also now stood in at another intermediate stage in the printing process: the creation of galleys. Galleys were the first stop on the printing process of representing the words produced by the writers. The printed pages ultimately derived from the stories and written words produced by the journalists. These sheets of paper typed by the journalists and reporters were known as "copy". Copy was written by the journalists on sheets of paper in typewriters. These typewritten sheets had a special box at the top righthand corner in which instructions were written as to how the written words should be "set". That is, how they should appear in print. The instructions included what font should be used to form the words, what print size the words should be, how wide a column they should appear in, and whether the column edges should be "justified" or "range left".

Thus for a *Front Page* news story, the instructions might read:

9/10 pt x 10 ems Times Roman unjust.

This meant that the copy should be set in the font known as Times Roman, at a size in points of 9 on a leading of 10 points, across a column width measuring 10 ems; and it should be set unjustified, that is range left, ragged right, not justified.

9/10 pt x 10 ems unjust is read as "nine on ten point by ten ems unjustified." So 9/10 point means a type size of 9 points on a leading of 10 points. And "leading" pronounced "ledding" is the size of the white space upon which the black ink is printed. In this case it meant that the size of the letters was 9pt, and they would be set in a larger white space of 10pt. Leading is required so descenders of letters on one line don't actually touch the ascenders of letters in the line below. The words would appear in a column width of 10 ems. An em is an ancient printing measure. Magazines generally use a 12 point em. That is to say the em measures 12 points from side to side. Points themselves are mostly considered as a unit of type size in which there are 72 points to the inch. Supposedly it's called an em because M is the widest letter in the alphabet.

And the instruction for a *Front Page* feature story might read:

10/11 pt x 13 ems Times Roman just.

"Ten on eleven point by thirteen ems Times Roman justified." Features pages in the magazine were everything else in it that wasn't news. Interviews, profiles, in-depth focus and analysis and reviews were all features. News stories in *Front Page* were set as four columns to the page. The features pages were set across three columns to the page, hence the larger em measurement. Features pages used larger type set in a larger leading than news pages. The columns for features were set justified. That is they had a level and unbroken edge on both the left and right hand sides. In justified setting, words at the end of lines were hyphenated and broken to create the smooth right hand side. The news page columns were set range left, unjustified, or ragged right. They all meant the same thing. They meant that the left hand edge of the column was smooth, but the right hand side would be formed purely as the words fell, so would be randomly indented. Words in unjustified copy were not hyphenated and the lines ended naturally wherever a full word would fit the available space.

There were three other things that were essential for the marking up of good copy. Its "catchline"; the phrases "more-to-follow" and "ends" on each page; and its page number.

The idea for these things went way back. They were a solution to the problem of a story containing more than one sheet of paper and passing through the hands of more than one person. In the days when sheets of paper were passed physically from the writer to the printer, it was absolutely necessary that each story be clearly, consistently and sensibly identified. The same held true right into the era when sheets of paper were faxed to the printer or typesetter. Identity was still everything.

The catchline, or catch, was the name of the story. This was always in a shortened handy version, invented by the writer. It was a convenient and unique label for a story. So the first story by Cill Weaver on the Harrier jump-jet or his third story on the Sidewinder missile, for example, might be called "falks-harr1" and "falks-side3". It was written on the top righthand corner of the topsheet, and repeated on every subsequent sheet.

As for the phrases "more to follow" and "ends", there was a sub-editing rule, perhaps no more than a custom, that a sheet of paper should never end mid-paragraph. If there wasn't room for a complete paragraph towards the end of the sheet, the paragraph instead was taken to the start of the next sheet. Then in the white space at the end of the sheet the abbreviation "MTF" or "MF" would be handwritten. Both "MTF" and ""MF" stood for "More To Follow" – meaning the story continued on to the next sheet. When the last sheet of the story had been reached, then the word "Ends" or "End" would be written at the foot of the page.

In the same cause of clarity and identity each page was numbered. Numbered not simply as 1,2,3…. and so on, but 1/4, or 2/4, and so on. Meaning first page of total four, second page of total four. Identity and clarity were everything.

Before the pages of raw copy were sent to the typesetter they passed under the eyes of the sub-editors. On the subs' desks the copy was "subbed". This meant the copy was corrected and adapted and cut in various ways in the cause of consistency.

Corrections of spelling and consistencies of grammar were obvious necessities. But copy was also changed and adapted according to the strictures of a mysterious beast known as the "house style". The sub-editors were the guardians, administrators, marshals and foot-soldiers, keepers and unleashers, of the house style.

Unlike with French, say, with its ruling body the Academie Francaise, there is no ordained, commanding or controlling priesthood of English. The language has no one waving a big stick over grammar, usage, or spelling. English has no commandants of correctitude.

But, as with clarity and identity, consistency is all.
So how is consistency throughout a publication ensured?
By means of the House Style.

This is a document containing all the agreed options and usages for the English used throughout the publication. The document attempts to be as universal and comprehensive as possible.

Every publication in English has its own House Style. It provides answers to whole series of questions.

Do we use Latin plurals or add an S? Do we say *auditoria* or *auditoriums*?

Do we use the ugly *datum* or use *data* as a singular as well as a plural?

Do we write *percent* as one word or two? Or use the % symbol?

Do we write *government* and *minister* with upper or lower case?

Do we write numbers as *one, two, three, twenty*, or *1, 2, 3, 20*?

Do we write *ICI is* or *ICI are*? Are companies singular or plural? And what about partnerships?

Do we write *inquiry* or *enquiry*? Do we make *enquiries* at an *inquest*?

All these and many more were listed and a judgement made in each case in the House Style.

Front Page's House Style had rulings on all these issues and more. And it was the four sub-editors under Eddie Osmoe's command who were the assault troops, the enforcers and arbiters, the scouts and guides, the sheriffs and marshals, the long-stops and goalkeepers, the umpires and referees, the consultants and specialists of the magazine's House Style.

When copy was marked up, corrected and cut (or rarer, expanded), and made consistent with the House Style by the subs, they did it using the centuries-old proof correction marks.

These were a series of hand written marks on the copy showing where changes would be made, and what sort of change was indicated. Proof correction marks were instructions to the typesetter and the printer to make changes in a certain specific way to what was typed on the paper.

Among the most used of these were the caret mark which

meant "insert at this point" (and which Eddie often thought of as looking like an upside-down carrot); and the "delete mark", which was shaped like the Greek character *delta*. Among Eddie's favourites was "*stet*". This was the Latin for *let it stay* and was written in the margin when required. He often used this when he changed his mind about some copy. His first instinct was always to change and cut and correct. And so he sometimes over-corrected and over-cut. *Stet* came in useful when he changed his mind and had to backtrack.

Another part of the sub-editors' armoury was a good knowledge of how many words there were to a page in *Front Page*. The wordcount to a page of news was different to a page of features. A two-page feature might total 1800 words when printed. If the feature copy presented by the writer totalled 2000 words, then the sub would have to cut 200 words from it to make it fit the available space. And so with news.

A golden rule for the subs was that it was easier to cut copy than expand it.

As Eddie kept telling all the writers and reporters: "Easier to cut than create. Bear that in mind fellers." In other words, it was always better to write more than necessary than write less.

After subbing the copy was finally ready to be sent to the typesetter. The typesetter received all the typewritten pages of copy, now covered in multiple proof marks and changes and corrections by the sub-editors. They were not physically sent to the typesetter's office, as they had been in the old days of barely a few years before, but were faxed.

In these early days of faxing it could not always be guaranteed that a fax line could be opened, or if once opened it would be sustained without breaking off. To ensure an opened fax line could be used continuously without interruption, the sheets of copy were sellotaped together, end on end. Once the fax line had been opened, with that characteristic sound of a shrieking banshee gargling underwater, the initial sheet would be fed into the fax machine. The connected sheets of twenty or even thirty or more pages would snake in a straight line from the fax machine across the office. The snake would gradually diminish as the sheets arrived one by one at the gurgling gargling machine for their turn to pass through the maw.

From the faxed copy sheets the typesetter would create galleys. These were sheets of A3 paper with the copy set and printed in columns according to the instructions written on the sheets. The galleys were not printed by traditional ink-and-metal means but by a primitive but effective proprietary computerised system, usually comprising some sort of laser, daisy-wheel or dot-matrix printer. Computer printing could be done for a small limited batches of pages. It could produce galleys but could not as yet print whole issues of newspapers or magazines. Or if it could it would be prohibitively expensive.

But this ability to photograph made up pages and print galleys allowed typesetting houses to exist. For a short time between the hot metal days and the full computerised digital age.

Thus it was that photographic typesetting began the revolution that broke with the hot-metal stranglehold of Gutenberg and Caxton and Aldus and not far into the future broke the printing industry altogether.

The galleys printed by the typesetter from the writers' copy were faxed back to the fax machine at *Front Page* editorial team's office. They could then be taken to the art department to be made up into pages. It was the job of the person sitting at the nearest desk to the fax machine to announce to the general floor that a fax was coming through. Those expecting a fax would go across and inspect the incoming fax to see if it was theirs.

Making up the pages was the next stage in the printing process. The journalist responsible for the particular section, the section head or desk-head, would take the galleys, plus any photos, to the art department.

The desk-head and the graphic artist between them would decide on the layout of a page. There was a general rule at *Front Page* that any page should contain two photos. That wasn't the rule in the old days, in Tom Telford Thompson's day, say. Then printing of photos was out-of-the-question expensive. Black and white was feasible. But colour was not on. Nowadays the primitive computer photography systems and colour separation printing had vastly reduced the cost of colour printing. To produce a full-colour image, the image was photographed three times in three different colour filters that were combined together, with a fourth run for black, to make a good facsimile of real colour. These three and four passes were known as "separations" and were named by their colours: magenta, cyan and yellow - or opposite-red, opposite-green and opposite-blue. So while words - copy - could be photographed for print in one go, it took four runs to photograph a photo for printing.

In his day Tom Telford Thompson had dismissed colour printing as a pricey gimmick. "If God wanted us to see photos in colour we'd be born with cameras in our eyes," he said, somewhat illogically. In Thompson's day he went as far as allowing one black-and-white photo on a page.

"One photo might be worth a thousand words," he said. "But it's not worth a thousand quid."

Things had moved on since Tom Telford Thompson's day.

The desk-heads decided on the running order, the prominence, of their stories on a page, and gave the galleys and photos to the artist. The layout artists then designed the page. They cut up the galleys into strips with scissors and pasted them into position onto a dummy layout sheet using a special glue called Cow Gum. They decided where the photos would go and resized or cropped them to suit and fit the space available. They left spaces for captions under the photos and a space across the top of each story for headlines. They informed the desk editors of the number of words or even letters that would fit into the headline spaces.

The layout sheets for each page in a signature were then sent to the typesetter. He printed out the layouts into page proofs. These were sent back to the magazine, sometimes by fax if printing deadlines were approaching, or physically by bike messenger if time allowed.

The page proof is a facsimile of the final printed page in the magazine. It includes the photos which too have been photo-produced by the machines used by the typesetter.

Each page proof was read by two people. They were looking for errors. Not just for spelling mistakes but to make sure the right photograph had the right caption; and even if the photo was the right way round. It's surprisingly easy to get photos the wrong way round. Sometimes the only way to be sure if a photo is correctly oriented is to see which side of the road any traffic in it are driving on. If the traffic is on the right and the photos is about an event or news item in England, then you know the photo has been laid out and glued down for the page proof the the wrong way round.

For instructions back to the typesetter, the correctors made corrections using the centuries-old printer's proof marks. On completion they added their initials and a date to the top of each proof. The page proofs were faxed or biked back to the typesetter. On occasion for some critical pages there was a second proof stage. This was to ensure that all the corrections made on the first proof had been incorporated.

When page-proofs were read by two readers, each reader initialled the top right hand corner of the page proof.

The page-proofs were thus okayed for printing.

Finally they would be sent back to the typesetter for filming.

Finally the pages would be printed from the film.

9. PRAIRIE

Judy Bodkin caught up Weaver in the ground floor lobby where he was talking to one of the display advertising salesmen. They approached the glass front doors together.

"You going to Stanfords CW?"

Weaver made an affirmative noise, more of a grunt.

"I'll come with you if you don't mind. Is that all right?"

Weaver didn't mind.

"Just going down to get a paper first." The *Evening Standard*'s early edition would be out. "Shopping, Judy The Obscure?"

"Not really. My building society's over there."

Out on the streets the rain had stopped, as Weaver thought it would. They threaded their way through a thickening matrix of people. Some were outdoors in search of food, others in search of shopping. Some clearly were out and about in an instinctive and probably futile attempt to benefit from the air, or at least get out of their offices for an hour or so.

They walked down Red Lion Court. As they passed the junction where the alley issued into Fleet Street Weaver walked over to the newspaper stand on the corner. A sturdy galvanised iron box held copies of the *Evening Standard*. A rudimentary grille on the front retained and supported a rapidly reproduced flyer teasing out the paper's front page story. It said:

<<HAIG FLIES IN>>

Next to it stood an elderly lived-in dwarfish man clenching more copies of the newspaper under an elbow, while at the same time shouting out almost unintelligibly the name of the newspaper.

"DANDRUFF!"

Weaver had heard it too often before to be surprised by the outburst even though it was bellowed in a high and loud but ailing sergeant-major parade-ground sort of shout only two feet from his ear as he approached. He stopped and bought a copy and scanned the front page. The Task Force had called in at Ascension Island. About halfway there.

"DAN DARE!" the vendor shouted on a falling note at a group of young women passing by.

They looked at each other with a tame surmise, then giggled together, bending forward hiding their mouths with their hands, defining their own universe by this mechanism and thus to their own satisfaction immune to an apparent exhortation to read about a 1950s radio and comic serial sci-fi hero.

Weaver wondered why he didn't try really shouting "Dandruff!" He might as well. On the other hand perhaps that's what he was shouting. Who could tell?

"LEPER!" the man shouted, getting into his stride.

"NEW-LEPER!"

Weaver led the way towards Long Acre, the main street in the Covent Garden area. "I know the quickest route," he said decisively, not giving the features editor much option: follow me or go your own way.

From Fleet Street they made their way along the Strand towards the Aldwych, heading west, and crossed Kingsway north of Waterloo Bridge just where the old tram tunnel portal spews forth traffic like the vomitorium intermission at a Roman banquet.

The crowds swelled as they approached Covent Garden, the flurries of shoppers mixed increasingly with injections of tourists - Americans in white macs and tennis shoes; Japanese in expensive designer jeans and black dresses; Europeans in leather, assorted jackets, and light anoraks - attracted by the fame of the recently refurbished Covent Garden market hall and piazza.

Once the focus of London's fruit and veg industry, the market area was now the lair of upmarket "retail units", restaurants and cafes, many of them spilling white cast-iron tables and chairs onto the pavements and streets in pathetic imitations of a received but entirely mythical image of life in Parisian faubourgs.

"Look at this place," Weaver said, waggling a hand in the air at the expanse of brick paving. "It's absurd. The whole complex has been done up in the totally erroneous fiction that London can be made to imitate an Italian piazza. People are supposed to be able to sit out here and pass the time of day drinking Grappa and Martini under a sweltering sun and think of hot sweaty sex under single sheets beneath immense starlit skies. It's ludicrous."

"Ooh I don't know. I think it's nice," Judy said, trying to give the impression that hot sweaty sex under single sheets was an entirely plausible notion even in England. "Sweltering sun and starlit skies? Can't be both."

"The architects and town planners think it can. Simultaneous. What? This nice? Come on. It's ridiculous. England can't be Italy. England is alleyways and ginnels and backs and dark entries and outside privies and abandoned warehouses round silted-up canal basins and rendezvous on street corners, not piazzas. England is indoors. Firesides. Inglenooks. Captain's chairs. Leaning on mantelpieces and warming your toes on the chimney breast. It's too wet and windy in England for large open spaces. I mean look at them, it's summer and people are scurrying about desperately trying to get out of this hurricano'd brick-paved prairie as quickly as possible. This sort of thing becomes a windswept steppe in England not a pretty piazza. It's just..." he petered out. He smiled sheepishly at Judy and turned the corners of his mouth down self-consciously. They continued in silence.

The two journalists weaved and wove, dummied and dodged, jostled and jinked their way through the broad crush of bodies on Long Acre.

Near the Covent Garden tube station Judy Bodkin spotted the last remaining vestige and evidence of the market's former life, like the white residual scars of chicken pox left long after the epidemic has gone its way: a fruit barrow nestling against the tube station wall and blocking half the pavement.

The rest of the pavement was obstructed by the barrow's proprietor attracting custom. The youthful barrow-boy bawled out his ranges and prices in cod-cockney, his patter clearly exaggerated for the benefit of tourists. The result was identifiable as residing somewhere between Eliza Doolittle and Dick Van Dyke.

Have you seen the Muffin Man? Weaver thought idly. I think they done her in. Oranges and lemons said the bells of

St Clements. Come and buy an authentic piece of Old London Town and pay through the nose for the privilege.

"Must just get some oranges Cill," Judy said. "Won't be a mo," already crossing the street and talking over her shoulder. A reluctant but otherwise neutral Weaver followed her across.

Judy Bodkin assessed the ripeness and quality of the oranges with the simple technique of poking them with her finger. Has she seen that on telly? Weaver pondered. Or imitated from her grandmother?

<<GRENADE DISGUISED AS FRUIT BLOWS OFF SHOPPER'S HAND. MUFFIN MAN SOUGHT>>

Judy asked the price of the ones she had selected with such tactile expertise, and grimaced at the figure quoted, but nevertheless delved in her large floppy embroidered shoulder bag for her purse.

Then a thought seemed to strike her. She held one hand fingers up and palm outwards to ward off the brown paper bag of oranges being proffered by the barrow-boy.

"Just a minute. Um. Are they South African?" she asked with a ready-to-be-justifiably-indignant tone.

"Dunno lav," the barrow-boy had clearly had enough of such questions. He caught Weaver's eye and then looked up to the sky, but, aware that his professed ignorance about the origin of the produce made a worse impression than admitting where they came from, decided to be brazen.

"Yeah, I spose they are. Could be," he said, extending the bag towards her again.

"Oh then I'm sorry," Judy Bodkin said firmly. "I'm afraid I don't want them then, thank you." She dropped her purse dramatically back into her bag with finality.

The barrow-boy began unpacking the oranges and replacing them in their display carton. Weaver and Judy moved away.

"Can't blame ya lav," the barrow-boy said, calling after them.

Judy turned back to look at him, surprised to have her anti-Apartheid stance supported by someone with whom she had refused to do business on that account, and further intrigued to hear why someone who blatantly sold the products of that vile regime should also be critical of it.

"Yeah," the fruit seller continued in a commiserative tone, "You never know what black ands've bin andling em do ya!" He cackled doggedly in imitation delight at his own wit.

Both Weaver and Bodkin smiled as they walked on.

"I should have known," Judy said. "Never tangle words with a cockney."

"What cockney?" Weaver said dismissively. "That was Dick Van Doolittle."

"True," Bodkin said. "But he sounded the part, surely? Didn't he?"

"God knows," Weaver replied with a shake of his head.

They walked on a little further before splitting up and heading for different local destinations.

Glad to be on his own Weaver let his thoughts turn with excitement to the coming weekend and the concert. The concert. The gig. The pop festival. Two of Weaver's great heroes, Bob Dylan and Eric Clapton, were going to be present at the all-day open-air rock festival at Blackbushe aerodrome along with a supporting cast of minor stars.

Weaver had never been to an all-day open-air rock festival. He didn't like organising things and he didn't like crowds and going to a festival felt too much like a combination of both those. In this instance a group of his friends were going and they had organised the tickets and he was glad to be included. He was glad to have been to one before the golden age passed.

Everyone likes to be able to say "I was there" or "I experienced that" and to have listeners fall silent who had not been there or not experienced whatever it was. Weaver called it the St Swithin's Day effect.

Weaver often daydreamed not of being in authority exactly but of being respected and heeded and admired, whereas in reality he spent most of his time being none of these things and couldn't understand why not and anguished himself greatly with wondering how he could make himself more respected, more heeded, more looked up to and admired.

10. AFTERNOON

It was afternoon in the office.

Front Page's editorial team took over the entire third floor of the office building. It was an open-plan office – *burolandshaft* was the technical term, as it was after all a German idea – with clumps of desks grouped together in sections like islands in an archipelago. The news team took over one wall by the side window like a reef of jagged rocks. The four sub-editors Eddie Osmoe, Margaret Hardman, Peter Bowling and Kate Clore were grouped in a sandbank of desks in the centre of the room. The business editor and review editor were together in a dock of desks by the window on the far side of the room, near the double doors giving on to the lifts and stairs. Judy Bodkin and the assistant features editor Mike Philbert were in a reef between the subs and the news desks. A large space on from the features desks, a marina reaching nearly all the way to the back wall of the office floor, was occupied by the layout artists, Rob Blynde, John "Enver" Hodger, Caroline Clipper and Kim Sook and all their extra accoutrements and equipment. Near them was the department of the two editorial photographers, John Smigley and his assistant Cathy Wight. They had their own dark room. Behind them taking up the whole of the rest of the floor was the library, run by librarian Alison Wong.

Weaver often expressed delight that the office he worked in had both a Wong and a Wight. He once asked Ali Wong whether she had a sister. In which case if she had, were they then capable of reaching the levels of excellence achieved by Cathy?

Did, in other words, two Wongs make a Wight?

Alison Wong, a graduate from Hong Kong, laughed politely, using a hand to cover her mouth.

Cathy Wight, a graduate from Manchester, told him to piss off, using a hand to signal a vee-sign.

Back the other way, the secretary's desk and the editor's assistant occupied two desks outside one side of Moriarty's office door like breakwater moles to a harbour, while Cuddleigh-Cook had a much larger quay-like desk on the other side of the doorway. There was a closed off glazed room next to the editor's office, known as the quiet room, which could be used for larger editorial meetings, or for interviews when a certain amount of privacy or quiet was required.

This room's glass walls were now covered with Weaver's maps of the South Atlantic. There were large scale maps of East and West Falkland, and of South Georgia. There were also broader scale maps of the whole of the South Atlantic, from Ascension Island down through to St Helena and then Tristan Da Cunha right down into the Southern Ocean, Bouvet Island and Antarctica.

Everywhere across the entire large open space between quiet room and editor's office on one side of the floor and Alison Wong's library on the far side of the floor, there were mesas and buttes of grey steel filing cabinets standing in discrete clumps like beached whales.

The quiet room was vital to the interviewing business of the magazine because noise was the essence, key and nature of the space.

Noise came from telephone conversations. Noise came from discussions within and round the islands of desks, and between the desks among colleagues in an island. Noise came from people shouting from one desk-island to another across the space, rather than getting up and walking across the office and having a quieter conversation face to face. But above all noise came from the striking and smiting, the clanking, cranking and spanking, of scores of typewriter keys in a large room full of heavy manual typewriters.

Each desk had its own typewriter. Big heavy manuals with names like Olivetti, Adler, Remington and Olympia written in large gold letters on the back. The machines were so big and heavy and so dominated the desk that the journalists not only pushed them away but tilted them up on end when not in use to create desk space when they had to mark up copy or check page proofs; and even to make sufficient space to place a notebook on the desk when doing a phone interview.

The only electric typewriter in the room was Carmen's the editorial secretary. She had an IBM Golfball. But though as high-tech as high-tech could be, and state-of-the-typewriter art, it was just as noisy as the manuals on all the other desks.

The IBM Golfball was the wonder of the office. People came to look and stare at it when Carmen was typing a letter for Essay. There was something alien and unworldly spore-like in the way the letters were carved round the surface of the jumping sphere. And wonder of wonders, you could actually remove the metal sphere, the golf ball, and replace it with another one with a different font. It was magical. It was beyond first principles. It was the future and it was here now. It inspired wanting and envy. And when working, oh rapture. The way it lifted and spun at electric speed and stamped down on the right letter on the paper on the remarkably unmoving platen. Always with the same pressure, and so always leaving the neatest and most consistent of ink marks.

What was so wondrous and interesting about it was that after a hundred years of typewriters with keys and mechanical levers and arms someone had finally come up with a different design to do the same job. And most wondrous of all it was a typewriting machine where QWERTY was no longer queen of all she surveyed. Because there were no arms to tangle, you didn't need to separate out the most commonly used letters, and so could choose any arrangement of keys, QWERTY if you so wished, but alphabetical too if desired.

But it was just as noisy as any of the other typewriters.

The building itself was a brick-built office block put up in the 1950s. It had steel window frames pioneered and manufactured by the Crittall company. It was a six-storey structure with a flat roof with a brick parapet round the roof area. You could get access to the roof and take the air up there. Some of the women smokers went up there for a fag break. But there was no view of anywhere: no view of the river or Fleet Street, or St Paul's. Nothing but the bare brickwork and windows of surrounding office blocks.

Because the steel Crittall windows were now so old and knackered in a number of places they no longer closed tightly and so let in air and even rain sometimes. So a system of interior windows of double glazed units had been installed. This left a broad space between the outer and inner windows where plants and flowers could be displayed. Janet McLing frequently brought in bunches of flowers and displayed them in the space between the windows. She placed them in various window-spaces throughout the office. But she never placed them in either of the two windows by the news desks. Weaver assumed it was because Janet didn't like him.

Not to be outdone by such vegetal displays, and to give the news desks a floral display of their own, Simon Ridge another junior reporter on the news desk with Liz Tintwistle, brought in a plant of his own and placed it in one of the window spaces behind his desk.

It was about two feet high, was green and had long thin leaves. It never changed colour and never grew any flowers. To all observers it didn't appear to change from one day to the next, or one season to the next.

To anyone who asked Simon said it was a cannabis plant.

They laughed and went away, smiling at Simon's youthful prankish rebelliousness. And they never believed him.

But it was true. It was a cannabis plant.

Weaver thought it could well be a cannabis plant. Like everyone else, he had never seen one and did not know what one was like. And like everyone else he had seen plenty of cannabis product, but never a plant. He just thought he'd take Simon's word for it until proved different.

11. PHILOSOPHY

Everyone at their various clumps of desks was getting on with the work in hand.

On the news desk the reporters began to follow up stories they might have begun to work on on Friday. Or they might be assigned new stories to follow as events developed over the weekend. Each one would be assigned to the task by Jerry Carter. Periodically he would check with the reporters under his direct command how certain stories they were working on were shaping up, and whether they might make a page lead, or deserve a lesser position, or might be fizzling out altogether down to no more than a brief.

He would also go and check with the journalists not under his direct control, such as Bill Roadhouse, Rex Spurgeon and Judy Bodkin, who though not news reporters may have been assigned a news story to follow up as a result of the deliberations in the news meeting.

It was a prerequisite of news that an exclusive story should always have priority over non-exclusive stories. That is, *Front Page* would not slavishly follow and publish the stories that all the other main news outlets would be covering. It didn't matter to a great degree whether the exclusive was a major story or not. What mattered was that *Front Page* had it first.

The great aim of Jerry Carter's news desk was that they should break a story. All the other news outlets would then be following them.

It was a matter of debate to what extent *Front Page* should cover the news stories that the other outlets had covered. Or even whether they should cover them at all. Some felt that if something was on *News At Ten*, ITV television's leading news programme, then *Front Page* shouldn't cover it at all. Others thought that because something was on *News At Ten*, then it should automatically also appear in *Front Page*. Others felt that *Front Page* had a duty to give its readers the full round-up of the main news stories of the day. In other words, if you read *Front Page* you didn't need to get your news from any other source.

News editor Jerry Carter was somewhere in between these three camps. Deputy editor Colin Cuddleigh-Cook was firmly in the camp that *Front Page* need be the only news source for its readers.

"Look Jerry, for god's sake; there's no way we can compete with *News At Ten*," Cuddles would say. "I agree with you there. But that doesn't stop us doing news. All the news. So we ought to give our readers a round-up of everything that's going on in the news."

At that time *News At Ten* was the leading news outlet in Britain, and quite possibly the world. Every news organ, whether it be print or radio or TV, judged their own capabilities and performance by the yardstick of *News At Ten*.

"We can't cover everything Colin," Carter responded. "There's no way we can go down that route. We might in some ways compete with a half hour news programme, whether it be telly or radio. But there's absolutely no way we can compete with daily newspapers for news."

And while I'm news editor, Carter thought, no way will we even try to go down that road.

Instead what Carter intended was that *Front Page*'s role model for news coverage would be the Sunday papers. In particular *The Sunday Times*, *The Observer* and, to a degree, *The Economist*.

What that meant Carter decided was that they would cover news stories where appropriate, those that fell within their weekly time frame, but for major but older ongoing stories they would take a more analytical approach. They would, under Carter's news editorship, provide news plus analysis.

"We won't just tell our readers what's going on," Carter said. "We'll tell them what it all means." Tom Telford Thompson would have approved of that, he thought.

Cuddleigh-Cook didn't like it.

"That's not the way we've always done it before," he said. "TTT wouldn't do it that way." Cuddles had an annoying habit of constantly referring to founding editor Tom Telford Thompson as TTT.

"That's how we'll do it while I'm news editor," Carer said with finality. And Tom Telford Thompson can kiss my arse, he thought but didn't say. He thought as well, but couldn't be absolutely sure, that in fact Cuddles had got it completely wrong about how Thompson would have done things. As if it mattered now. But that was the trouble, he thought, in many ways it did matter now. Crawling out from under the heavy shadow of Tom Telford Thompson - Lord Ironbridge, ennobled for services to journalism - was a fiendishly difficult business.

Cuddleigh-Cook didn't respond. He just made a harrumping sound and stalked off.

There seemed constant arguments now with Cuddles, Jerry thought. It was getting him down. But there was one plus point: Cuddles was coming up to sixty-five and would be retiring sometime this year. Jerry couldn't remember when the date was, the middle or end of October possibly, but he couldn't wait.

Carter knew he had for the moment editor Moriarty's backing. But he also knew that was a fragile, friable and inconstant reinforcement to depend on.

Jerry Carter sat down and went through his new plan for the next issue. Things were shaping up.

12. DRINK & SMOKE

Weaver had a can of lager on his desk. It was a large can of Foster's. Australian lager had started making its way into England. The two frontrunners were Foster's and Touhey's. You couldn't get either of them on draught yet. The draught lager in the Tipperary for example was the Swiss lager Hurliman. But they were available in cans from off licences. The advantage Foster's had over Touhey's was it came in a monster pint-sized can. There was an off licence down near the bottom of Fleet Street just before Ludgate Circus. Weaver wandered down there on his way back to the office from Stanford's, his map sheets of the South Atlantic islands under his arm.

Weaver was the main drinker during office hours. The others would occasionally place an order with him when he went down to the off-licence – usually after lunch – but he was the only one who regularly had a can of beer on his desk.

Weaver placed the can down next to his glass ashtray. He fished out his Gauloises cigarettes, his Colibri lighter and a pack of chewing gum from a jacket pocket. The jacket was draped round the chair back. Sometimes he used the coat stand that was conveniently placed by every clump of desks, and sometimes he forgot and just draped the jacket over the back of his castor-wheeled office chair.

This week Weaver was smoking Gauloises. He varied between Gauloises, Disque Bleu and Gitanes. Occasionally he would try a pack of Gitanes Maïs, the ones with the yellow cigarette paper made out of maize. But mostly it was Gauloises or Gitanes. But it was always French cigarettes with the classic "black tabac". He never smoked anything else.

He was only an occasional smoker at work. No more than a couple of fags a day. That was because he was almost entirely a social smoker. He smoked mostly in the pub after work. He tried not to inhale much when smoking. That was the main reason he smoked French cigarettes. It was easier not to inhale the rough smoke from them than it was the smoother Virginia tobacco of

English and American cigarettes. So over a pint of lager after work he would puff away regularly on his black tabac, tasting rather than inhaling. He found it satisfactory enough.

In any case there were fewer smokers in the office than there used to be. A couple of years ago there had been a permanent smoke haze in the office. The smoke seemed to hover just above head height. In summer they would open the windows on both sides of the office, and outside the office on the landing by the lifts, to try to generate a through draught across the office to dissipate the smoke.

But gradually people were opting out of the smoking game. And the ones who hadn't given up were either trying to or had cut down on their frequency.

Nowadays it was a couple of the men and most of the women who smoked. All the women in the office smoked apart from Carmen Siguenza and Alison Wong. But among the men the only smokers were Weaver and art editor Rob Blynde. While Weaver was very much a social smoker, Rob Blynde was almost a chain smoker. He rolled his own cigarettes and constantly tried out new brands of rolling tobacco. Every few weeks there would be a new and different pungent smoke wafting across the floor from Rob's desk. And just as the floor had got used to the smell, it would change and a new stinky cloud would come puffing from Rob's vicinity like smoke signals from a butte.

A couple of both the men and women would regularly accept a cigarette from Weaver in the pub after work, but they never bought their own. Some of the women would actually take a fag break and go up onto the roof and smoke outside when it was warm enough.

Carmen Siguenza had tried to get a vote going to ban smoking in the office. The vote had been lost by a small majority. She would let the smoke settle and dissipate she thought, then she would try again.

13. LEADER

Bill Roadhouse was writing the leader.

First thing after lunch Bill had been called to a meeting with Essay, Cuddles and Jerry Carter in Essay's office. The topic for the leader obviously was the Falklands and the crisis between Argentina and Britain. But it was Bill who had suggested the angle. So it was agreed that he would write it.

Bill came out of the editor's office and sat down at his desk. He pulled up his sleeve cuffs a little to tighten them on his wrists. He looked down at the keyboard on his typewriter and began to poke the keys.

In essence what Bill wrote was this.

Assuming Britain won the looming war with Argentina over possession of the islands, things would still have to change in the Falklands.

It couldn't go on being a neglected forgotten embarrassment. Everyone was aware now, Bill said, that the government had sent conflicting messages to the Argentine junta about Britain's commitment or otherwise to ownership of the Falklands. That was a mistake now well acknowledged. There would have to be far greater defence spending on the islands, come what may, Bill said. A permanent military airbase would be a good start. Second there need to be a permanent research icebreaker working in Antarctic waters, if not two, based in the Falklands. If one was replaced through age it should immediately be replaced by a new one. There must be no more hints in the future that Britain was abandoning such a vessel and had no further interest in the South Atlantic.

Then Bill got to the nub of his piece. Something that as yet he was certain had not been picked up by the dailies or TV news. Bill pointed out something he had learnt quite recently: that ninety percent of the total land area of the islands was owned by a single company, the Falklands Island Company. That couldn't continue, Bill wrote. Whatever the reason for this near-monopoly of land ownership, an enquiry should be established to understand the situation and recommend ways of remedying it.

As a clincher to tug the patriotic heartstrings of his readers, Bill finished by noting that during the Second World War the Falklanders gave more per head than anyone else in the Commonwealth to Britain's war effort. They had paid for a Spitfire.

He didn't have to spell out the obvious conclusion. In the light of the Spitfire given to Britain in its darkest hour, didn't then the islanders deserve something from Britain in return in their darkest hour?

Both Moriarty and Cuddleigh-Cook would read it, and in effect okay it before Bill could send it to the typesetter. Bill knew that the clincher about the Spitfire would go down well with Moriarty. It was most likely the only thing he would notice or remember about it. And would okay it on the strength of that.

As for Cuddles, Bill Roadhouse didn't care what he thought.

Colin Cuddleigh-Cook was a natural blustering bully.

While nearly everyone working at the magazine who had dealings with Cuddles had no respect for him either as a journalist or a deputy editor, it was only Bill and Eddie Osmoe who were the only two people on the staff who regularly stood up to Cuddles.

Bill wasn't frightened of him and thought he should have his job. He thought he would make a far better deputy editor than Cuddles. And Cuddles for his part was actually fearful that Bill might indeed make a better deputy editor than him. He felt strongly that he deserved to be deputy editor because he had been at the magazine for so long. He knew all about the title's traditions and heritage. Tradition and heritage were important words to Cuddles. He'd read TTT's autobiography, and other books about the legendary editor, while he was sure no one else in the news room had. He had actually worked for TTT for a few months when he started at the magazine over twenty years ago. That was back in the 1960s, just before TTT, despairing of the written word as a force for change, turned in a new direction and resigned from the magazine, from journalism, and took up his seat in the House of Lords as the Labour life peer Lord Ironbridge. As the only person currently on the staff who had actually worked on the magazine under Tom Telford Thompson, Cuddleigh-Cook thought that alone deserved a mountain of respect. But he also feared he only got the deputy editor job because Essay Moriarty wanted a complete yes-man as his deputy. Cuddles didn't think of himself as a yes man, far from it. He thought of himself as the custodian of the values and traditions and heritage of the magazine, come what may, and felt himself to be the spokesman of those values to the current generation.

As for Eddie Osmoe, he knew that Cuddles couldn't do his job as chief sub-editor. Eddie thought he could do anyone's job. But the difference between Bill and Eddie was that Eddie was content to be chief sub. He didn't want to be deputy editor.

Jerry Carter was still a little scared of Cuddles. He tried not to be. And he tried to stand up to him. But he had not been in the job long enough to be certain of the strength of his position. He also naturally hated confrontation and went out of his way to avoid it.

14. YEARS

Each section, each group of desks, worked in sometimes similar sometimes different ways. Some could start clattering on typewriters at a relatively early stage. And on Judy Bodkin's desk she and Mike Philbert had features to write or to commission when they weren't working on news stories. So either or both of them would be typing or talking on the phone.

On the news desk, some of the easier one-source stories could be got out of the way on the Monday. So Weaver and Liz and Simon Ridge clattered through a series of briefs and lower level stories, especially ones that weren't too date sensitive. They also rewrote minor stories from press releases sent in by government ministries, departmental organisations, other news outlets such as Reuters and Agence France Presse, and public relations companies on behalf of their clients. They'd be typing away, and occasionally getting on the phone to verify a quote, or check a fact.

Over on the far side of the large space, behind her high shelves of books and files and photos and folders of cuttings, Alison Wong fielded enquires suitable for her position as librarian and archivist. Most often it was a reporter getting some background on a story or feature they would be working on. They might want to know the ins and outs of a scandal say, or a long-ago story that somehow had new relevance. They might want background information on a politician or info about the CV of a leading business figure.

Ali Wong would supply all that.

One of her main jobs was filing clippings. She put files together of all the contents of each week's issue in indexed and cross-referenced form. She was also the custodian of back-issues.

She was also very pleased that she got to write something too. She wrote a small column every week. It was based on extracts from the magazine from 20 years ago and 50 years ago to which she would add a commentary. Admittedly it was invariably a comment that was wise after the event, but still. It was always interesting, she thought, to see how some critics and commentators could see the future clearly, while others had no idea, lost in the contemporary fog of their own time.

The 20 and 50 years ago extracts were chosen by her but vetted by Cuddles. Like Jerry Carter, Alison Wong found Cuddles to be a pompous pontificating prancing prat, an interfering incompetent ignoramus, well capable of making absolutely wrong decisions when it came to choosing what to publish in the 20 years and 50 years ago slots.

For 1962, in some of the 20-years-ago slots, Alison often wanted to publish a series of extracts from the reviewer columns of the day about popular films and music. She thought readers would be especially interested in how good or bad reviewing critics of the time thought the new pop groups just emerging were.

But Cuddles would have none of that. He insisted she published extracts from the main news story of that equivalent week 20 years ago, however uninteresting or irrelevant it might be twenty years on.

And for 50 years ago, 1932, the year the magazine started, she thought readers might be very interested in what *Front Page*'s news and opinion pages of the day thought about the rise of the Nazi Party in Germany, for good or ill.

But Cuddles would have none of that either. He insisted, as with 20 years ago, that the 50 years ago column should just publish whatever it was that was the main news story of that week despite often striking no chord with readers twenty and fifty years on.

Alison Wong felt frustrated sad and unhappy. But she never let it show.

She wondered how she could by-pass Cuddles's input. She wondered if she could approach the editor. But had an instinct it wasn't something he cared about and would automatically back Cuddles. She began to wonder what to do.

But like Jerry Carter, Alison was consoled by the fact that Cuddles would be retiring soon. And like Jerry she couldn't wait.

15. CRITICS

Rex Spurgeon was putting together his review section for the week. His section reviewed the arts in general which included music, films, books, theatre and telly programmes. Some he did himself, particularly films and television, and he kept an open brief for himself to cover anything not reviewed regularly, such as painting and museum exhibitions. But he also had a bank of regular correspondents who acted as specific critics and reviewers.

Some of these were famous names in their fields. The deal was they would write exclusively for *Front Page*, and were paid a retainer for their trouble. They were also paid for their columns. Retainer and column returned a tidy whack to each reviewer. The exclusivity agreement only applied to direct competitors which obviously meant the daily papers, the Sundays, and other weekly printed news outlets. They could however ply their trade in other mediums; on TV and radio. As some did. Indeed they achieved greater publicity, or notoriety, through their broadcast programmes than they did through print. Hence some of them, Rex felt, let it go to their heads and could all too easily forget their main requirement was to write review columns for *Front Page*.

It was a chicken and egg argument. Was the reviewer famous and well-known because he wrote a column for *Front Page*? Or was an already famous critic adding his aura to *Front Page*? But *cui bono*, as Cicero, and Rex, often said: *who benefits*? And as far as Rex was concerned a critic who thought himself bigger than the magazine was trouble. More trouble than they were worth. When *Front Page* no longer benefitted from their presence it was time for them to go.

Whenever Rex got the feeling that one critic columnist or other was getting too big for his boots he would look into ways of getting rid of them. They were after all expendable. There were plenty of other names out there in the great ocean of publicity-hungry reviewers, pundits, commentators, critics and writers. And plenty among these who would relish the chance to write a column for Britain's leading news weekly.

One of the things Rex was aware of was the necessity to ensure his bank of writers and critics had sufficient age spread to be able to comment credibly on their chosen cultural field. It was no good for example to have someone in their fifties or sixties commenting on the wave of Punk music that had emerged a few years before and now looked well-established. That needed a younger stance. So Rex was constantly on the lookout for new faces and new voices.

Rex himself often appeared on review programmes on television, participating as a critic and commentator on films and TV programmes.

He had not yet been offered a position as the anchor of any of these existing or proposed arts programmes, but he lived in hope.

16. COLUMNS

Judy Bodkin too had a bank of writers that wrote regularly for her section. She also had a budget to commission other writers – some of whom might be regular, but could also be one-offs.

She was also the in-house liaison for the magazine's two fortnightly writers. These alternated with each other in the weekly issues.

The first of the fortnightly writers was the law column. This was written by celebrity barrister Bartholomew Gonner, Queen's Counsel and head of his chambers in Lincoln's Inn.

As well as being paid to write a fortnightly law column Bart Gonner was paid a substantial retainer to act as legal consultant to the editorial team.

Coming out as a practising, lively and buoyant homosexual as early as his university days, Gonner had been nicknamed "Rear Gonner" at Oxford. In time over the course of becoming a high-profile barrister specialising in libel and slander he had become known to most of his enemies, and to many of his friends, as "Gonner Rear".

While Judy Bodkin was the liaison with Gonner for his regular fortnightly column, the person in the editorial team who had first call on Gonner's professional expertise most of the time was Jerry Carter the news editor.

Part of the deal in paying Gonner a large retainer was that he could be reached at any time of the day or night, any day of the year, to express an instant legal opinion on the libel quotient in a story the magazine was intending to publish. Occasionally Carter had literally pulled Gonner straight from the main course of a high-profile dinner, or the rostrum at a speaking engagement, black tie and all, to express an opinion on a story that Carter would read to him down the phone. Carter was in awe of Gonner's ability to think fast, accurately and unfailingly helpfully while on his feet. Very often it was Gonner rather than Essay Moriarty who gave the actual go-ahead for a lead story.

Jerry for one was very glad they'd caught Gonner Rear, and

he was on their side.

The other fortnightly column fielded by Judy was the political column.

This was written by Derek Goodbread, Member of Parliament. Goodbread was MP for Melton Mowbray in the English midlands. He was a member of the Social Democrats and was the party's spokesman on Europe and on foreign affairs in general.

The reason why the law and politics columns were fortnightly and alternated with each other was twofold. Firstly it was thought that both top lawyer and high politician would be too busy to write a good quality column every week; and their performance would deteriorate if asked to write on a weekly basis. And secondly it was felt that *Front Page*'s readership might well be bored if it were exposed to both law and politics on a weekly basis. "Little and less often," was how Tom Telford Thompson put it when he first established the law and politics columns over twenty-five years before and gave instructions to the original columnists.

Derek Goodbread also acted as political advisor and consultant to the editor and to the editorial team. He was paid a huge retainer for this service. What the service consisted of was for Goodbread to advise the team about the "thinking in Westminster" as he put. He would give the lowdown on what was going on in the committees; what was brewing in legislative terms; what the general feeling among MPs and ministers was on various topics. He would in short act as *Front Page*'s ear to the ground in Parliament. There was also an unspoken but implicit understanding that Goodbread would give hints in a nods and winks kind of way of any impending legislation that might affect the publishing industry in any way.

Goodbread was earning his money during the current Falklands crisis. Mainly he kept the journalists informed on how strong the will to go to war with Argentina was in Parliament: how much was bluff and bravado and how much was real. He admitted that the instinct of most MPs was only to go as far as a bit of classic gunboat diplomacy and if necessary a bit of sabre-rattling. With Margaret Thatcher however it was the real deal, and they would most likely go to war. But Goodbread was convinced this was a mistake and the whole affair would turn out to be a "horrid embarrassment for Britain" he said. Goodbread particularly thought the British armed forces would be defeated. "That would be a huge loss of face for us. We're not ready. It's too far away. The Argentines are too well set," he said. "And it will be all Thatcher's fault."

On the side Goodbread was also advising Essay Moriarty in a private, but paid, capacity as to the likelihood of the editor being awarded an OBE in the next Honours List. And to what extent he might be able to conjure himself onto the list by whatever manoeuvres, journalistic or otherwise, he might come up with to facilitate that end.

Front Page always had a policy of appointing its political advisor from the opposition parties in Parliament. With a Conservative administration currently in power and its prime minister metaphorically steaming full ahead for the Falklands, the choice of the magazine's political insider would usually have come from the ranks of the Opposition, in this case the Labour Party.

But Moriarty was convinced that Labour was doomed. A future post-Conservative government – in all probability not the next but in the next-but-one election, particularly if Britain won the coming conflict in the South Atlantic - he thought would be more likely to be Social Democrat than Labour. So he broke with the long tradition initiated by Tom Telford Thompson and appointed a political columnist from one of the other non-governing parties in Westminster rather than the Official Opposition. Colin Cuddleigh-Cook, as the in-house guardian of TTT's legacy, was shocked and felt badly let down by this. But didn't say so.

Goodbread often had private lunches with Moriarty at his club, The Reform in Pall Mall. He also was a guest at a regular monthly lunch held in *Front Page*'s own dining room on the ground floor of the office block. The high-standard food itself plus waiting staff was provided by outside caterers. And the lunch was hosted by Cuddles as deputy editor, though in practice news editor Jerry Carter raised most of the issues with the MP. The lunch involved the whole of the news team plus the main correspondents, all getting wisdom about goings-on in Westminster from a horse's mouth.

In reality the MP was more of a horse's arse, Jerry Carter thought. This was because of a conversation he'd had with Goodbread at one of these lunches a few months before. It was in fact Jerry's second such lunch.

The Channel Tunnel was again looming as a political topic. And this time there seemed to be good chances of it actually getting out of the ground and given the go-ahead. Or rather into the ground, Jerry thought. The auguries for it looked good.

Jerry asked Goodbread if he was for or against the Channel Tunnel? MPs as like as not would be voting on it at some point.

"Oh most definitely agin it," Goodbread replied. "Agin it." His vehement tone of voice suggesting how could he possibly be otherwise?

This naysaying surprised Carter as he hadn't heard any valid argument against it apart from the one from some decades before when field marshal Montgomery had expressed a somewhat ludicrous and hysterical worry about foreign invaders swarming out of the tunnel portal to overrun Kent. Though in retrospect Carter later realised the MP's absurd use of "agin" was something of a giveaway.

"Oh really? How come?" Jerry asked.

"I'm MP for Melton Mowbray," Goodbread replied, as though enough said. Again his triumphant tone implied that was all he need say to demonstrate his opposition to the Tunnel.

To Jerry Melton Mowbray seemed a curiously long way from the Tunnel for its MP to be so strongly against it. What was it, 180 miles away? It seemed far-fetched to Jerry.

"So?" Jerry said. "Why does that make you against it?"

"Pork pies," Goodbread said. His look of complete disdain in Carter's direction suggested he was the dimmest, most lacking in insight, most benighted, and most obtuse person Goodbread had ever met.

Jerry still didn't get it. For a start he just didn't get the adverse connection between the Tunnel and a small Leicestershire constituency town slap-bang in the centre of England, famous for, in Jerry's opinion, a very nasty delicacy.

"Sorry," Jerry said. "I just don't get it."

"You don't?" Goodbread said. He turned away to speak to a neighbouring chair. The Channel Tunnel conversation it seemed was over.

Jerry was completely mystified. Other people around him had all heard the conversation. There was a shared array of blank looks. Even a few smirks at the quirkiness and weirdness of their political insider.

Goodbread, razor-sharp to contrary body language and possible slights, immediately turned half back to Carter and said over his shoulder with utter disdain and finality:

"Rabies."

Finally for Carter the penny dropped.

This idiot MP was against the construction of the Channel Tunnel because he was MP for a place that was famous for making pork pies. He was scared that once dug a rabid fox would be able to scamper helter-skelter through the Tunnel. The fox would somehow make its way all the way to the centre of England, 180 miles away. There it would bite a pig. And so rabies would get into Melton Mowbray's pork pies.

Jerry was utterly stunned. It was beyond absurd. It put a whole new complexion on the word "porkies". Was this then the calibre of people who entered parliament? Jerry felt decidedly anxious and slightly short of breath. He was seriously worried for his country.

He vowed he would try his utmost to be elsewhere every time this clown was invited to meet the editorial team for lunch. If necessary, like Oscar Wilde, he would plead "a subsequent engagement." He'd stay away and get Cuddles to brief him afterwards on any political insights and gems the MP might have passed their way over lunch. He had a feeling that Cuddles thought the sun shone out of this MP's pork pies. As often as not Jerry managed to stay away from the Goodbread lunches. And usually when it turned out Cuddles couldn't remember if anything interesting had come out of it, one of the news reporters could fill him in.

One lunch that Jerry was sure he would attend was the correspondents' lunch. This was a twice-yearly lunch date when all the magazine's external columnists, critics, reviewers and feature writers were taken out for a slap-up lunch at *Front Page*'s expense, as a thank-you for their efforts over the previous six months.

Editor, deputy editor, and the various section heads joined the external writers at the correspondents' lunch.

It could be held in *Front Page*'s own dining room, as was sometimes the case; or it could be in a private room in a top-class restaurant in town. The venue usually depended on which day of the week the lunch would be held. Getting top lawyers and busy MPs and assorted minor and big-name celebrity columnists and critics together for lunch was a tricky business in pinning down an agreeable date. So though not recommended the lunch might have to be organised on one of *Front Page*'s news days. In which case the venue would be the in-house dining room. If it turned out to be arranged for a Thursday or Friday, then the venue would be in town.

Wherever it was and whenever it was Jerry always tried to attend. It was evident from their first meeting that QC and MP couldn't stand each other. Jerry was delighted by the ease with which Gonner Rear verbally took Goodbread down at all and every opportunity without his really realising he was under attack. It put Carter in an excellent humour for the rest of the day.

17. JUNTA

The afternoon moved on. Copydates were pressing. Each individual in each section got their head down and got on with work for the rest of the day.

The week days went by. Some evenings most of the team would go for a drink after work.

Nine-thirty to five-thirty were the official work hours. Most people arrived and were at their desks by quarter to ten. Some didn't stroll in till ten o'clock. But most of the staff were well into their work by around ten o'clock.

At ten-thirty the tea and biscuit trolley came round, pushed by Betty, an elderly lady with pink-rinsed hair. This was an antiquated arrangement. Quaint but antiquated. The tea-lady called everyone "love" She served the six office floors with tea and biscuits between 10.30 and 11.30 every day. Everyone took either tea or coffee from the two large steel containers on the trolley, and were allowed up to two biscuits each. Some favoured Garibaldis, the famous "squashed flies"; others went for "jammy dodgers"; others dived in for the digestives; others preferred those rectangular ones that were a bit like digestives but nicer. Most of them were dunked in the tea and coffee.

End of the working day was five-thirty. Some got up and left the building immediately, but most finished what they were doing, or brought it to a natural halt, before deciding either to go to the pub or go straight home.

One advantage of going to the pub for a couple of pints was it let the rush on the tube die down. There was a much greater chance of getting a seat in a tube train at six-thirty than there was at five-thirty. Hence it was actually normal for nearly everyone to go for a drink straight after work. For some, like Weaver, it was because he wanted a drink; for others it was just to pass time while the tube crush lessened.

Either way most of the editorial team were installed in the Printer's Devil, perhaps, by six in the evening, most days.

A group of them were sitting on stools round one of the low

circular tables in the Devil.

One of the reasons they all liked it was it was a manager-trainee pub for the brewery so you always felt you were instantly being served as soon as you set foot through the door by trainee managers desperate to impress their assessors.

Liz threw a copy of that day's *Sun* on the table.

"That's just awful," she said.

The headline

<<STICK IT UP YOUR JUNTA>>

blared out aggressively from the top of the paper.

"What's the matter with it?" Cill Weaver said, in a tone that suggested he was ready to defend the indefensible.

"These are peace proposals," Liz said, bending down to sip the froth off the top of her pint of bitter. Liz was one of the few that drank bitter rather than lager. She felt it was more authentic: if you're going to drink beer, then drink proper beer, not "eurofizz" as she'd once heard lager being referred to. She thought bitter better suited the identity of herself she wished to portray. Someone distinct and distinctive: someone almost uniquely capable of cutting through the marketing crap. "From the UN," she continued. "You just can't be so flippant about that."

"I like it," Judy said. Then carried on in explanation when everyone round the table stared at her. "Not least because it does go to show that our fellow hacks at *The Sun* think the word is pronounced with a J and not an H," she said.

Rex nodded. But everyone else round the table looked blank.

"Junta not hunta," Judy explained. "It has to sound like 'Jumper' doesn't it? Otherwise the pun, the joke, doesn't work. Can't be hoonta either, for the same reason. So junta with a J and a short U it is."

"It's a good point, Huudy," Rex said.

"But they shouldn't be making a joke at all," Liz was angry and passionate and let it show. "It's serious. There could be war. And they're saying: bring it on. That's terrible. Totally irresponsible. People will die."

"I guess it's deliberate," Bill Roadhouse said. "It's not really a joke, is it Tintin, for them. They're trying to become the paper that gets behind 'our boys'," Bill waggled two fingers on each hand in the air. "And be more patriotic than *The Mirror* or *The Express*. They think – and are willing to bet with headlines like this – that patriotism sells papers."

"Patriotism. Nationalism. They're bad enough. But this is neither," Liz said, digging in. "It's beyond that. This is jingoism. Deliberate callous chauvinism."

"Maybe it is," Bill agreed. "But remember, circulation isn't a joke for Murdoch. So this isn't a joke at all. It's deadly serious. It's war. it's a war in another way. War carried on by other means. A circulation war."

This self-evident wisdom stopped the argument in its tracks. The discussion became more light-hearted.

"Talking about 'our boys'," Judy said. "I can take this deviant levity," she pointed to the headline. "But at least we'll be spared that pompous clown from the Pathe newsreels in the Second World War who spoke about something being 'That's one in the eye for herr Hitler, as our boys cross the Rhine.' That kind of thing. Woeful how someone with such a plummy voice thought he could be chummy. And it's so weird to be rude about someone and still use the polite 'herr'."

"Bob Danvers-Walker," Rex said. "That Pathe newsreel voice from the war was Bob Danvers-Walker."

"Everyone in those days seemed to talk like him. They all sound like they're talking through a duck's arse," Judy said with feeling.

"I guess that would tend to mangle your vowels a bit," Rex said spluttering into his pint. He looked up with a grin. A drop of beer froth covered the end of his nose. He wiped it away with a beer mat.

"I agree Huudy. I prefer Dad's Army's 'mister Hitler' to Pathe's 'herr Hitler' every time," Cill said.

"Yes weird how newsreels and papers used to use the foreign word for 'mister', like 'herr' or 'monsieur'. At least we don't do that anymore," Eddie Osmoe said. He'd been silent up to now following the debate with interest. "Or at least I hope we don't. I better check with Cuddles tomorrow and swamp, stifle and stamp on any intentions he might have of digging out 'senor' for any of these Argies. There's going to be no 'Senor' Galtieri on my desk."

"But surely you'd be happy to use 'general'?" Liz said. "As in General Galtieri?"

"Oh yes. I'd be happy with that. I've no problem with that at all. No reason not to give all three members of the junta" – he pronounced it with a J – "their military titles. Or anyone else. Ranks and titles is fine. It's this ludicrous untranslated politeness using herr, and monsieur and senor I can't stand."

"It actually makes them seem more undemocratic and fish-out-of-water too, doing that," Cill said. "Using their ranks in their names."

"As in military men have no business in politics?" Rex said.

"Exactly. Shows in verbal terms what we're up against. How alien, different, and nasty they are. So please do Eddie. Go ahead. Get in all the generals and admirals and air force big cheeses you can. I like it."

"What's the Spanish for 'big cheese' Rex?" Judy said.

"Not sure, *grande queso*, or *gran queso*, something like that, why?"

"Well if the junta was French we'd be able to refer to them as *grands fromages* wouldn't we?"

"So Galtieri is *El Grande Queso*?"

Everyone laughed.

Liz frowned delicately. She'd thought it an essential politeness to use the titles and ranks of their potential enemies in their coverage. But she could see Weaver's and Eddie's point.

She was beginning to realise that her adamantine views on the world might need some mild tempering.

18. BLACKBUSHE

The weekend came.

Blackbushe city limits, Weaver thought.

He lived in Crouch End, on his own in a first floor flat in large terraced three-storey house that was divided into flats. It was north of the river.

His girlfriend Sarah Deeds lived down in Clapham in a similar house that wasn't yet converted to flats, with a several other friends, all women. They'd all been at university together and all rented a room in the house. They had a communal kitchen and two bathrooms. It was all very chummy and satisfactory for the women, but not for their boyfriends. It was south of the river. Sarah was a trainee producer at the BBC.

Once by mistake, feeling all warm and effusive towards her, Weaver asked Sarah to move in with him. Fortunately she refused.

It was fortunate because there was no doubt that Cill and Sarah were drifting apart.

Weaver had begun to develop the feeling – he didn't know where it came from – that Sarah was secretly seeing someone else at the same time as going out with him. He felt he was in some kind of triangle. He couldn't be certain, and knew he couldn't be more concrete or pin the feeling down. It was perhaps no more than an observation that Sarah seemed somehow more detached lately; as though her mind was elsewhere; and she was just going through the motions with Cill; beginning to assess their relationship, and view it dispassionately from a distance or through the bottom of a glass.

But what clinched it for Cill in his own mind was that Sarah was disagreeing with him nowadays. She was disagreeing with him a lot.

When they first went out he felt he had never met anyone who saw the world in exactly the same way he did. So much so that he was certain they were soul-mates, and in some impossibly romantic way they were supposed to be together. They had the same views on politics, on books, on history, on people, on places, on humour, and on music and films and TV programmes.

Cill never quite got over the excitement he felt when he realised he'd met someone who saw the world exactly as he saw it. He felt the excitement that comes with the realisation that from now on, on any level, he would never be alone.

But now all that had changed. Things had shifted. And yet the difference, the shift, wasn't something he could put his finger on. After all, Sarah still agreed with him on many things. But just occasionally now she differed. Occasionally she expressed a contrary view to Cill on a telly programme they'd just seen, or a film they wanted to see. And gradually at first, then suddenly, Cill convinced himself that this was because she was now exposed to someone else's views and opinions; someone whose views she was inexplicably taking very seriously. More seriously, in fact, than she was now taking Cill's opinion. It wasn't anything to do with the relative value of the opinions, Cill was sure. It was purely he felt Sarah wanted to support the other person in her mind against him. And she could do that without giving anything away by supporting a contrary opinion.

It was complicated, and very unsteady in its foundations, Cill knew. But he was convinced Sarah was seeing someone else.

This other bloke then, Cill was sure, also worked at the BBC with Sarah. That was ominous enough on its own. It was well known that BBC people got off with, went out with, and married other BBC people.

Weaver felt hurt and betrayed by this. But he didn't confront Sarah with the accusation, nor tried to find evidence. He dreaded the outcome of such a confrontation, dreaded the positive outcome of his suspicion.

The character Sykes in *The Wild Bunch*, at the end of the film, says to Robert Ryan's character Thornton: "It ain't like the old days; but it'll do." And Cill thought that too. It wasn't like the old days, but it would do. Things were different, but they were still okay. And who knew? Maybe the old days would come back. If he waited. And was patient. And gave her time.

He'd rather carry on in a nether-world of uncertainty rather than have the proof positive revealed, and have a new world order ensue. Better the status quo, he felt, than a status without quo. So he just carried on the relationship, carried on with the suspicion that Sarah was seeing someone else, and carried on feeling a little hurt and betrayed.

But this weekend, this Saturday, today, come what may they were all going to Blackbushe.

Bob Dylan would be there. And Eric Clapton. Joan Armatrading. Graham Parker & The Rumour. It was an all-day open air music festival at an old Second World War aerodrome at Blackbushe. It was southwest from London out along the A30 down Hampshire way.

There were eight of them in their party. Cill and Sarah Deeds and Bill Roadhouse and his girlfriend Esra Oz were going in one car, Cill's Renault 4. And there were four other friends, a friend from Sarah's house, Molly Stelfox, and her latest boyfriend Christy Beeby, and another friend from Sarah's house, Eva Malone, and her boyfriend Philip Flagstone. They would travel in Molly's ancient Wolseley 15/50 saloon. The two cars would travel in convoy out to Blackbushe.

Weaver knew all the girls well, apart from Esra who he'd only met a few times, and he knew and liked Phil; but had never met and didn't know Christy Beeby at all. Cill understood that Christy worked at the BBC, like Sarah did. But no BBC-on-BBC alarm bells rang because he'd been told by Sarah that Christy was Molly's new boyfriend.

"He's nice," Sarah said. "He's a correspondent. Maybe not your type though."

Cill had no idea what "a type" meant, so he just smiled and shrugged.

"So he's a co-respondent then?" he said.

Sarah laughed, a little shrilly, he thought. Then he thought no more about it.

Early on Saturday Bill and Esra made their way on the tube to Weaver's flat in Crouch End. Sarah had stayed the night there.

The four of them then drove down to Clapham to rendezvous with the other four. Bill was in the passenger seat next to Cill who was driving. Sarah and Esra were in the back.

Sarah had seemed both very jumpy and unusually grumpy that morning, Cill thought. He had no idea why. Maybe it was because she didn't like the fact it made sense for her to sit in the back, and Bill with his longer legs sit in the front. He had also volunteered to map read. But apart from that Cill couldn't fathom it. He assumed the jumpiness would settle down, and or, she would vent her wrath on him at some point – probably when they got back home – and all would become clear. But until then he shrugged mentally and thought no more about it.

As they drove over Waterloo Bridge Esra let out a squeak of disappointment from the back seat, where she was sitting next to Sarah.

"Oh! I thought perhaps we would be travelling over the Tower Bridge."

Esra was new to London, and hadn't yet travelled around. Clearly there were places she hadn't seen but wanted to.

Weaver knew she was American of Turkish extraction, and worked for an American bank in London. Bill once told him she had only recently qualified for American citizenship. Her English was an enticing and ludicrously erotic mix of American accent allied to a weird kind of schoolroom English vocabulary and grammar.

They pulled up behind Molly's decades old Wolseley at Sarah's house in Clapham. The others piled out of the house and they all congregated round the two cars. Introductions were made for those who were new to the party and unknown to the others.

Weaver was decidedly amazed by what Christy was wearing. While everyone else was wearing jeans, tee-shirts, and assorted lightweight jackets and tops, with trainers on their feet – and in Cill's case Timberland boots - and Molly who was wearing a Laura Ashley summer dress - Christy had on a tweed sports jacket, what looked like cavalry twill trousers, tan oxford brogues on his feet, and a light pale-blue shirt that badly needed a tie to stop it drooping askew at the collar. Weaver wondered where he'd been throughout the 60s and 70s to wear what he was wearing now.

<<CHRISTY RUMPLESTILTSKIN SLEEPS TWO DECADES WAKES IN 1982>>

He even had a parting in his hair. Weaver wondered to himself the last time he'd seen anyone under the age of thirty with a parting. Then again, maybe everyone at the BBC still had a parting?

They piled into the two cars and set off towards the southwest, Weaver leading in the Renault. It was a warm sunny day, and getting hotter.

Bill in the passenger seat was map-reading. They made easy progress and joined the queue of traffic alongside the long hedge skirting the venue as marshals directed the cars to parking places inside the huge grassy aerodrome. It was ten-thirty. Already there were hundreds and hundreds, perhaps thousands, of cars parked in neat rows in the vast parking area.

As they emerged from the cars and took food, drinks, blankets, and spare clothing from the back of his hatchback, Weaver noticed that his two front wheels were parked on grass and the two rear wheels were parked on concrete. I guess that's the old runway, he thought, and we're parked right on the edge of it. He wondered what had been stationed here during the war? Fighters or bombers? He had a feeling that bombers had all been stationed further north on the flatlands of Lincolnshire. So maybe this was a fighter squadron? Did it fight in the Battle of Britain? He didn't know.

They made their way towards the massive flat open concert space and sought a good spot to make their base. Already there was a vast crush of people near the elevated stage in the distance to their left. Then in the other direction the same sort of distance away to their right, there was a huge bank in a semi-circular array of temporary structures, large tents, stalls, forty-foot containers and portacabins. The whole area was a parallel universe of guy ropes and pegs. Here would be lavatories, food outlets, souvenir stalls and knickknack kiosks and first aid posts; probably St

John's Ambulance Brigade as well, Weaver thought.

They chose a spot midway between the temporary stage in one direction and the temporary support village in the other. They spread their two blankets on the ground and made a compact base on the grass for the day. It was getting hot.

They chatted and basked and drank and dozed in the sun. The hours passed. The music began. The figures on the stage were tiny. Christy produced a pair of binoculars which he passed round. When you looked through the binoculars there was a definite delay, a mismatch, between what you saw being played by the act on the stage and the music multiplied and passed on by the relay masts dotted around the huge space.

At one point Molly produced some cocaine, while Bill lit a joint which he inhaled deeply on then passed round. Phil triumphantly lifted a bottle of port in the air with a da-daa sound. Esra brought some champagne out of her bag; as did Eva. Cill and Sarah stood four bottles of red wine on the borderland between their two blankets. And Christy clinked together two bottles of white wine he had been carrying.

Molly dug out a mirror and a strange metal container from her large loose leather bag hanging on a shoulder. Unstopping and tilting over the bronze container formed in the shape of the Roman god Priapus, complete with huge out-of-proportion phallus, she tipped out a line of white powder three inches long on the surface of the mirror. Then she sniffed hard on the white line through the clear plastic six-sided tube of a Bic biro, bereft of its inky insert, and making sure to place her thumb over the small airhole pierced in the side of the biro about halfway up. The white line vanished up the tube and into her nostril as she moved the tube like a miniature handheld hoover, like a nasal magic wand, from the bottom of the mirror to the top. Sniffing slightly she handed over the vial of Priapus, the mirror and the Bic to the next person.

Cill took goes both on the cocaine and the joint, as did Bill, Eva, Phil and Molly. Sarah snorted only a line of cocaine and refused the cannabis joint. Esra refused both – "I think it's very silly" - was all she said and laughed. Her demeanour suggested that while she would not indulge, she had no problem with anyone else indulging. Christy on the other hand refused both and looked shocked and affronted that anyone should ask him in the first place, and at what was going on around him.

Weaver thought it strange to say the least that Molly's boyfriend seemed to be the only one present who wasn't aware how famous Molly was within the circle of her friends for all and any kind of hedonisms. Well, judging by Christy's shocked and thunderous face, that relationship won't be lasting long, he thought. He noticed too that while all the other couples were sitting or lying next to each other, Christy and Molly were well apart. Christy was alongside Sarah, next but one from Cill; while Molly was on the far side of the second blanket, horizontally across from Christy.

While the snorts of cocaine perked the party up, the alcohol and cannabis made them more soporific. As the day wore on the alcohol and cannabis trumped the cocaine and eventually six out of the eight were lying full length on the ground, half asleep. Only Christy and Sarah still sat up, talking quietly to each other.

Weaver had stopped trying to watch the stage in the distance. It was pointless: they were too small. He lay on his back in the sunshine and listened to the music. He looked up sightlessly at the blue sky.

Suddenly the blue blurred and the sky darkened slightly. A pair of legs had stepped right over him. They belonged to a young woman. She had legs like Pompey's Pillar, he thought. She had legs like chopsticks to a grain of rice. She had legs like telegraph poles, they seemed to reach the sky. Or at least to the line of her white panties glimpsed as she stepped over him. Cill Weaver looked right up between her legs. He could see her white panties quite clearly, aided a little by the light from below, and more so by the light that penetrated the thin light summery material of her long skirt.

She must have seen the confused expression on his face as she looked down at him. She grinned a dazzling grin in his direction as she stepped over him, understanding his apologetic look at what he must have seen, and moved on. Cill sat up and watched her back as she moved away. She was heading for the lavatories at the back of the vast flat arena, stepping over bodies as she went.

Afterwards Cill Weaver was never quite sure whether it was the vision of the girl with legs like Pompey's Pillar that caused it or not. But whatever it was, by dawn the next day Cill Weaver and Sarah Deeds had broken up.

It was nearly dark when Cill Weaver realised his relationship with Sarah Deeds was over. That was when he saw Sarah and Christy Beeby kissing in the queue for a temporary WC.

But that final shock and the later row were some short time yet in the future. In the meantime there was a hot summer's day, some fantastic music, and a lot of drugs and alcohol to enjoy.

Cill sat up again and took in a bit more of his environment. He realised he must have been dozing and half asleep, daydreaming, until the girl with legs like Pompey's Pillar and the white panties stepped over him and startled him fully awake.

Bill had produced the latest in his unending supply of sleekly rolled joints. He lit it, took a long drag, and handed it to Eva on his left.

"Leeva?" he said, offering the joint.

She took it.

Cill was intrigued.

"Why Leeva? Why did you call her Leeva?" he asked. "I've not heard that one."

Bill grinned. "You haven't? Eva Malone. Leave 'em alone. Leeva Malone. That's what Phil calls her."

Beside him Esra giggled in delight at this play on words in a language not originally her own. And beyond Eva, Phil nodded and grinned in encouragement. Weaver smiled. So Eva was now Leeva. Just as in the current climate Judy at work was now Huudy. It was all good.

The bands played and the acts did their act. Afternoon became evening. Eric Clapton performed. Evening became night.

Bob Dylan performed. Then it was midnight and the Blackbushe Aerodrome Pop Festival was over.

They stood up and gathered their things together. It was pitch black. No one had thought to bring a torch.

"Where's the cars?" Molly said.

It was a good point.

"Um, that way I think," Cill said, pointing.

The others more-or-less agreed. Or at least there was no obvious dissenters. They moved off and found themselves in a huge thronging mass of people all heading in the direction where they all thought their cars were parked. The mass of people became larger, stretching forwards, sideways and backwards into the hidden dark.

They crested a small rise in the landscape. Beyond it there seemed to be a panorama straight out of a vision of hell; Pandemonium from Milton's *Paradise Lost*, or one of the concentric circles of hell in Dante's *Inferno* perhaps. Or rather, Weaver thought, more like a scene in one of the strips in *2000AD*, the comic he read regularly, which currently had a story about the devil escaping from imprisonment in a far corner of the galaxy and being brought to Earth where he was hellbent on turning it into a new hell.

Torchlight and the glare of burning fires illuminated the darkling plain. Small tents had been erected. People sat round makeshift campfires. Guitars were being strummed. Nearby a group of people lay curled up or stretched out in sleeping bags or blankets.

But there was no sign of the car park.

"Must be in another direction, Cill," Molly said.

"Yes but where?" Phil Flagstone said.

Grouped round him on the top of the little lump of a hill, Cill realised that they somehow expected him to know where he had parked his car.

Trouble was, he hadn't a clue.

Then suddenly Cill remembered something.

They had parked both cars side by side with the front wheels on grass and the back wheels on concrete.

"We need to find the runway," he said. He explained why. "If we walk along the edge of it, with one foot on concrete and one foot on grass, we'll find the cars."

"I saw the concrete," Sarah said. "Back over that way, when I went to the loo." She pointed into the dark.

For some reason he didn't understand, Cill noticed that this revelation of Sarah's brought a big smile to Christy's face. At the time Cill put it down to Christy being pleased they were making a kind of progress. He had no idea then it was a possessive and proudly proprietary smile.

They set off in the new direction. They now had to fight their way against the flow of people. The sharp sweet smell of marijuana emanated from a miasmic cloud hanging in the still night air above the throng. The crowd was still mostly intent on moving in the direction they themselves had first gone. Now they were moving against the traffic. It was slow progress in the dark.

Eventually Molly found the runway rim. She stamped her ankle boots on the concrete.

"Here it is!" she said doing a little tapdance.

"But what now? Which direction?" Christy seemed to be asking Sarah.

"Well I think we have to split up," Sarah said. "We can go this way, and you lot carry on that way."

Weaver couldn't fathom why Christy Beeby seemed to be included in the "we" while he was definitely bracketed into "you lot".

Cill looked at her in disbelief.

"That won't work. It's like the scenes in *Alien*," he said. "Disastrous. It's always a bad idea to split up. Anyway how does the group that finds the cars tell the other group they've found them?"

"I agree," Esra said. "We just have to follow this line along the edge of the runway. If we choose the right direction, then we are lucky. If we chose the wrong direction, and go the long way round, then that is unlucky. But whichever way we go, we will come to the cars sooner or later. And we must stay together. It is the only way."

What she said was so sensible there was no disagreement.

"So shall we toss a coin?" Eva asked.

"Well, I think we should go in this direction," Molly said, pointing.

No one thought the other direction had better credentials. They set off.

It took an hour. But they found the cars.

Three hours later they realised that finding the cars had been the easy bit.

Finding their way out of the aerodrome and back to the road was the hard bit.

They kept following the line of the concrete edge. Sometimes this was through lines of parked cars. Sometimes it was just grass and concrete. They kept moving. Quite a few times they were intercepted by parties moving in the other direction. They were asked if they had seen a particular car in their travels, a rumour on the road: a blue Ford, a red Vauxhall, a white Transit van? But they never had. Or had never noticed in their adamantine intent to seek their own cars. The blue Renault and the grey Wolseley.

They came upon them at last, just as Esra said they would. They were following a line of travel in the broad formed turning space between ranks of parked cars. The line on their right had all four wheels parked on grass; the line on their left had the front wheels parked on grass and the rear wheels on concrete.

It was nearly two in the morning as they came upon their cars on their left hand side parked amid a line of other cars. There were no spaces in the line. It seemed then they were the first in this line to find their car! And that had taken them almost two hours. Cill had a fleeting image of people still looking for their cars, forever. The Ford Purgatory. The Toyota Tantalus. The Vauxhall Styx. A fit punishment for a modern hell.

As everyone piled thankfully into the cars, Molly and Cill as the two drivers had a conference.

"Which way now?" Molly said. "Where's the way out?"

Cill looked around. Which is the way to Oldham? he thought. Over to the left in the dark distance he could see a line of moving cars, each car illuminated by the headlight beams of the car behind.

"Over there," he said. "They seem to know where they're going."

So they set off. It took longer than they expected. With a bit of manoeuvring and a lot of toing and froing, and some false turns that lead nowhere, they at last joined the line of cars, Cill leading and Molly behind him.

All the while the driver had to peer through the windscreen, eyes focused and concentrated on the ground in front. You had to be really careful you didn't drive over someone in a sleeping bag. It was exhausting work.

Just as they joined the tail end of the line it stopped moving.

Cill and Molly waited in the queue. After a while Cill turned his headlights off. Molly followed suit. After another while he turned his engine off. Molly turned hers off too. They sat and waited. The queue didn't move. After another while all the cars in the queue turned their lights and engines off. Time went by. In his car Cill noticed Bill beside him was asleep with his head against the window. In the back, Sarah and Esra were also asleep. After another while Cill got out. He walked back to Molly's car. She laboriously wound her window down as he approached.

"Not sure what's holding us up. I'll go up to the front and have a look."

"I'll come too," Molly said. "I could do with a walk."

Her arms were aching from turning the steering wheel of the heavy old car, and her left ankle and top of her foot were sore from working the clutch.

Cill noticed that Christy in the front and Eva and Phil in the back all seemed to be asleep too.

Molly and Cill walked past the line of darkened cars. He counted sixteen vehicles before they came to the front car, stopped on the crest of a low grassy rise.

On the other side of the rise, laid out right in front of the car was a dense thicket of tents and sleeping bags. A sprightly campfire burned in the midst of the tented area.

Which circle of hell is this, he wondered. The one reserved for sinners such as festival-goers?

There was no way through. This was a road to nowhere.

Beside him Molly burst into tears. She was dead tired and had had enough. She'd had enough of heaving the controls of the heavy old car; enough of the concentrated straining to make sure you didn't run over someone in a sleeping bag in the dark; enough of having to do everything herself while everyone else in her car slept; enough of going nowhere; and enough of not being able to get out.

Cill reached out and hugged her.

It was now getting on for four in the morning.

Looking over Molly's shoulder as her sobbing eased, Cill saw another line of slowly moving cars, illuminated by their headlights, going in a different direction to the line they were in. It may have been his imagination, but it seemed to be moving quite steadily.

Still holding Molly gently he pointed out the new line of cars.

They didn't say anything, just nodded at each other, and made their way back to their cars.

"How about swapping cars?" Cill offered as they came back. "That's a great car on the open road, but it must be a heavy old bastard to drive in these conditions. Mine's a lot easier to drive in this."

"No, Cill thanks, I'm fine. I'll give it another go. You keep leading and I'll follow."

"Mine does have a bloody funny gear lever you might not like anyway," Cill said. "A strange push-me-pull-you kind of affair."

Molly smiled tiredly. But she was grateful for his input. She felt less alone.

Again, with a lot of manoeuvring and twisting, turning, wheel rotating and space negotiating, the two cars made the hundred and fifty yards from the stalled line they were in to the moving line.

Just as they joined the back of this line it stopped moving.

Cill and Molly waited in the queue. After a while Cill turned his headlights off. Molly followed suit. After another while he turned his engine off. Molly turned hers off too. They sat and waited. Everyone else in both cars was sleeping soundly. The queue didn't move. After another while all the cars in the queue turned their lights and engines off. Time went by.

Cill got out of his car and went back to talk to Molly. She wound her window down.

"Shall we have a look?" he asked her.

"Might as well." She laughed bitterly. Cill cast her a quick glance, concerned. But he realised she was over the worst. She was holding her own.

Again they moved to the head of the line. Again the front car was stationary on the crest of a small low rise. Again, on the other side of the rise was a vast nest, a great tented expanse of canvas, sleeping bags, sleeping bodies and rudimentary fires.

What were they burning? Cill wondered. Did they actually bring sticks and firelighters? He realised that some people knew how best to attend pop festivals. He had no idea.

Someone somewhere in this tent-town was strumming a guitar.

"If I find him I'll wrap it round his fucking neck," Cill said.

"No you won't," Molly said. Cill shot another rapid glance at her, in case she was close to tears again.

"Not if I find him first," Molly said viciously. "If I do, that guitar goes straight on the nearest bonfire."

Then suddenly she exploded into laughter. Cill caught it, and the two of them laughed uproariously at the fading stars at the predicament they were in.

In fact as he threw his head back, expecting to laugh at the stars, Cill realised there weren't any stars to see.

It was getting light.

They both looked round. They hadn't noticed it before but it was definitely lighter. In fact they could see quite a distance now in the pre-dawn. Light and colour were coming.

Over in another direction Cill could now see there was the highest ground among all the low rising undulating spots and mounds in the area they were in.

"If we go over there and take a look we might actually see what direction we're supposed to go in to get out of here."

They made their way across to the hummock. In the new light they could easily see in the distance one of the aerodrome exits to the road. They could also see a relatively easy route through to it from where their cars were.

"Finally. A way out," Molly said. "I feel much better already."

They threaded their way back to their cars and set off again. As they walked Cill thought he better say something to Molly about what he had seen in the queue for the chemical closets. He was still trying to get a grip on it himself.

"Molly, I don't quite know how to say this, but how long have you been going out with Christy?"

Molly didn't reply. She just looked at him.

"I ask that because I saw him kissing someone in the queue for the lavatories." He didn't really want to admit yet even to himself that Sarah was the other one in the kiss.

"Cill, you need to talk to Sarah," Molly said.

"Yes. I think I do."

"I don't go out with Christy," Molly said, placing a hand on his arm as a kind of comfort. "I never have. Not my type at all." She smiled gently. "Talk to Sarah."

They moved on across the lightening ground. Cill particularly had a lot to think about.

And so around six o'clock in the morning the eight friends at last managed to find their way out of Blackbushe Aerodrome. It had taken six hours to leave the concert car park.

19. SPLIT INFINITY

They stopped at a roadside transport café on the A30 on their way back to London. Bacon and eggs and white toast and tea and coffee had never tasted so good.

For the first time since the end of the concert Cill managed to think about what he had seen in the queue among the temporary lavatories at the back of the concert space. Though he had attempted to tell Molly about it, to warn her about it in a way, Cill hadn't yet really come to grips himself with what the evidence implied.

As he drove, he thought back.

Darkness had come to Blackbushe. Joan Armatrading had finished her session. Eric Clapton would soon be starting. Many people took the opportunity to visit the lavatories, souvenir stalls and food trucks.

Cill needed a pee after numerous swigs of champagne and red wine straight from the bottle. He got up from the blanket and headed off to the temporary village service area.

He waited in line at one of the chemical closet cubicles. Good thing he wasn't that desperate he thought as he waited.

His turn came.

When he came out he glanced across to the multiple lines of stalls. Light came from arrays of hissing gas lamps and electric lights. The black electricity cables snaked across the grass in all directions. He thought he might check out the tee-shirts. He set off. Then glancing around his gaze fell on another queue for another set of chemical closets. He noticed the slender tweedy sports-jacketed back of Christy, distinctive in the queue. There couldn't be anyone else here today wearing that kind of outfit, he thought. An outfit from a time-warp. There was a brown-haired woman standing just in front of Christy. When Christy placed his hand on the shoulder of the woman in front of him, Cill wasn't particularly surprised. You could meet any old friends by chance in a place and space where there were reputed to be 120,000 people gathered together.

But he was very surprised when the woman turned round, lifted up her face towards Christy, and the two of them embraced in a lingering kiss. It was Sarah.

Cill reeled away.

His first instinct was to make sure they hadn't seen him.

His second was to wonder if somehow he hadn't seen what he'd seen.

His third was a realisation that it was the end of the world. A small world admittedly that consisted only of him and Sarah and their relationship; but ended it was.

He made his way back to their place in the arena space. For the rest of the night he carried on as if nothing had happened. He listened to the music. He lay on his back under the black sky. And all the while he kept a watchful eye on Sarah and Christy.

He didn't want to. But he found he couldn't stop. Consciously and unconsciously he was seeking more evidence of.... what?

Betrayal? Two-timing? Infidelity? Promiscuity? Over-familiarity?

The words seemed wrong somehow, they seemed to imply and involve too much accusation. There didn't really seem a word for what was happening. And what was happening, he admitted to himself, was this: his girlfriend had moved on to her next boyfriend without first breaking up with the previous boyfriend. Was there a word for that? Cill Weaver wasn't sure there was.

Normality? Usualness? Reality? Hedging-your-bets? Way-of-the-world?

That phrase was probably best: it was the way of the world. And he better get used to it.

He tended immediately to fortify himself with the rationale that he had seen this coming; he had known there was a problem; but had let it drift. He'd never asked Sarah what the problem was. And there had been a problem, he knew. Maybe he thought it would all blow over.

Well too late for that now.

He was the one that had been blown over.

125

What was an immediate necessity was for him and Sarah to talk.

When Molly said "talk to Sarah" Cill thought he knew now exactly what she meant. Now as he drove he knew for sure that what she meant was: "Sarah's moved on. You need to understand that. The best way of learning about it and moving on is to talk to Sarah."

So he would. The first chance he got.

After breakfast they headed back to London in a loose convoy. In Cill's car Esra and Bill were now in the back seat, chatting excitedly. Esra had been to nothing like Blackbushe in her life. She couldn't stop talking about it. In the front, Cill and Sarah were silent, both staring ahead through the windscreen; one looking at the road; the other seeing into the future.

At the house in Clapham everyone got out of the two cars and stood on the pavement outside the front door saying their goodbyes. Cill gave Molly a hug. Bill, Esra, Phil, and Eva gave Cill a hug. Sarah waited silently on the pavement by the car's passenger door. Christy came over and shook Cill's hand.

"It was very entertaining," he said.

That was a double meaning in itself, Cill thought. What was entertaining? The music? The festival? Or was it "very entertaining" to be involved in a threesome without the third person knowing anything about it? Cill suspected Christy leaned towards that understanding of the phrase. In his imagination Cill kicked Christy's cavalry-twilled arse.

Bill and Esra said they would make their way to the nearest tube – it was easier and more direct than hitching a lift with Cill back up to Crouch End. Molly, Phil and Eva, and Christy – which surprised Cill – trooped into the house.

That left Sarah and Cill standing on the pavement.

Cill assumed he and Sarah would go back to his place. Then they would talk. He moved into the road and pulled the driver's door open.

"I'm not coming Cill," Sarah spoke across the top of the car. "I'm staying here."

"I thought we might talk," Cill said, trying to keep any note of pleading out of his tone. Flatness was all. But all the while he felt a desperate shortness of breath. His lungs ached.

"There's nothing to talk about," Sarah said. "It's over Cill."

"So you're going in there to be with him? Sodding old cavalry-twill Crusty?"

"His name's Christian." Her voice was all misty for Christy and all swill for Cill.

"Jesus Christ even worse. Christian Beeby. He's so fucking BBC it's even in his name. Backwards, of course," he joked, trying to summon a smile from her, like he could in the old days. The old days of yesterday.

She glared at him, affronted, distanced, and committed to further distance. Now there was an invisible wall between them that would never be breached for the rest of their lives. Once they were one; now they were two; and would be for always.

They stared at each other over the roof of the Renault 4.

Then Sarah turned, stepped away, and headed towards her front door.

"Sarah," he called.

Sarah ignored him.

That was the last they saw of each other for a long time.

As he drove north across the river he reflected that for hundreds of years the poets had got it all wrong, Absolutely and totally wrong. Love and relationships had nothing to do with the heart. It was all in the lungs.

Love was in the lungs.

20. CHARITY

The weeks passed.

The Task Force headed south from Ascension Island, newly stocked with American missiles. It took up station to the southeast of the Falkland Islands. A 200-mile exclusion zone was announced. Any Argentine warship or plane found within the zone would be attacked.

The shooting was about to begin.

At *Front Page* the focus for a while fell on the Argentinean ability to fight and win. What in reality were the British armed forces up against?, it asked its readers. What exactly were they armed with? What damage could they really do to the Task Force? Were the two sides evenly matched? Were there going to be any nasty surprises?

Much interest then fell on the nature and capabilities and quantity of the French-made Exocet missile which some of the Argentine planes were armed with. Specifically how many did the Argentineans have? How would they be able to source more of them if and when required? What kind of shopping opportunities were there out there for this kind of thing?

When *Front Page* looked at the British side much talk and interest lay in the Harrier jump-jet. How good was it? Had it ever been properly tested in battle? Wasn't it deemed a little slow and pedestrian by modern standards? Was it really a world-beater? Or was it just another in a depressing line of quirky British failures? Was it a new battle-winning Spitfire, or in reality just a new sitting-duck Boulton & Paul Defiant?

No one seemed to know the answers to these questions.

Cill Weaver did point out at one stage in a news meeting that throughout history most planes were only as good as their armament; in this case the missiles they carried. And while the Argentineans did have the Exocet, the British had been equipped at Ascension by the Americans with the state-of-the-art Sidewinder air-to-air missile. That alone should make the Harrier more than a match for anything the Argentinean airforce had.

The Exocet on the other hand was a ship-buster, fired from the air or from other ships. No one seemed to know how dangerous it was. But the military contacts and experts that Weaver spoke to were very worried about it.

The magazine published diagrams of the battle array of both sides, showing planes and ships and weaponry and the balance between the two sides. Clearly the British had better ships. But the Harrier looked a little dated and definitely outclassed by what the Argentineans could pit against it, Mirages and Super-Etendards.

On paper it looked like this: if the British could use the advantages of the Sidewinder to destroy the Argentinean planes, then they would win the war. On the other hand if the Argentineans could use the advantages of the Exocet to destroy British ships, then they would win the war.

It was going to be a close-run thing.

For those working on the magazine it was an exciting time.

Downstairs in the lobby flowers were still arriving every day for Lydia Scant from the surveyor. Even Eddie was impressed by his constancy. In due course the bandages came off her wrists, the telephone became less of an unforgiving snake to be fought in a death struggle and more a docile tool of business, and she regained her smile.

Outside the editor's office, Carmen Siguenza still clicked away, speedily and ferociously, on the jumping-jack IBM Golf-ball electric typewriter.

Liz Tintwistle was beginning to enjoy herself. Jerry had asked her to focus on the human side of the coming conflict, specifically on the theme of "Those Left Behind". Bill was tackling business and economic angles. Cill was looking into the military detail. Now at last Liz felt valued and included at the front and sharp end of the magazine's news pages. Her brief was not just to cover the human side from a British point of view, but from the Falkland Islanders and even the Argentine side too. When Eddie Osmoe began to praise her copy, she felt valued and appreciated in the job for the first time.

One issue that had come up was whether the magazine should have a correspondent going to the war alongside and part of the Task Force.

There had been much debate about this between Essay, Cuddles, Eddie and Jerry. The Ministry of Defence had offered places aboard warships in the Task Force to all the leading print and broadcast media news titles, *Front Page* among them. It would be under certain conditions. There would be rules, of course.

The question was whether the rules and conditions of being part of the troops outweighed any disadvantage of not being present on the spot with the British armed forces when they went into battle.

In the end the four of them decided that there was no direct advantage for *Front Page* to have a correspondent travelling with the troops.

"We can't compete with the dailies for immediacy, and especially not with radio and TV," Jerry said. "We're not going to have anyone doing live broadcasts, or posting despatches for immediate publication."

Eddie agreed. "Our strength is in analysis and comment. That's always been the case. We won't benefit by having a man or woman on the ground."

"How about on the water?" Moriarty said.

Jerry couldn't tell if he was being serious. So he did what he always did when his boss said something either stupid or didn't add up. He ignored it.

"And not being there might give us a different kind of strength – it might help us with comment and analysis if we're seen and deemed to be more totally independent of the MoD and the government than the others," Jerry pressed.

"Might help with getting an Argie angle too, if we need one," Eddie said, ignoring Essay's frown at his use of Argie.

So in the end the MoD's offer of having a correspondent with the troops was turned down. The only one among the four who was in favour was Cuddles, who opined that since every other news outlet would be having a correspondent on the ships, they should have one too. It was superficially a powerful argument, but he was overruled.

Cill Weaver was touched by how everyone at work wanted to help him, look after him, get him through the time of his emotional damage. Bill Roadhouse and Judy Bodkin were particularly attentive. Carmen was also very solicitous. And even Eddie Osmoe softened his tone and commended Cill for the accuracy and adventurousness of his copy much more often than he had in the past.

Gradually his lungs regained their ability to fill with air properly. Slowly he started to enjoy work. He even cut down a little on his drinking. That was a surprise to everybody, including him. Everyone assumed with the emotional hit he'd taken he'd take to the bottle even more than he had before. But he didn't.

A big immediate difference everyone noticed was he no longer had a can of lager on his desk after lunch. He stopped his visits to the off-licence.

At first Cill Weaver wasn't sure either why he was drinking less and working harder. It definitely wasn't the old cliché about diversionary tactics - working more to recover from a broken romance. It was actually something earthier, older, fiercer, and more competitive.

He wanted to be better at his job as a journalist than Sarah and Crusty (as he now always called him) were at theirs. That was what drove him.

He noticed too he was doing far less of the imaginary headlines than he had in past. He'd almost stopped altogether coming up with headlines for any situation he found himself in. He wondered why at first, but eventually put it down to becoming less of a disconnected and detached observer on life; less of a commenting bystander. He was now fully immersed; doing his job rather than watching himself do it.

For a while he missed them and tried artificially to sustain them. But they didn't feel the same. After a while he wondered why he'd ever done it in the first place.

He also became more interested in the structure and ownership, and the politics, of the company that employed him. In a way for the first time in his working life he was becoming a company man.

Front Page magazine was owned by the Thompson family. It had been founded by Thomas Telford Thompson in 1932. It was part of News World Publishers, a family company set up by Tom Telford Thompson. The company was owned by the Thompson family, in particular Tom Telford Thompson's heirs.

With his new interest in the job, Cill Weaver began to learn all he could about News World Publishers and the family that owned it, the Thompsons.

This by default involved many hours talking to Colin Cuddleigh-Cook, usually over a pint or two (but not four or five as before) at lunchtime or after work. But one of Weaver's new rules was attempt to be nicer to Cuddles. So he was.

"He always called himself Tom Telford Thompson," Cuddles said. "It wasn't a double-barrelled surname. He just always used both his first names."

"Yeah, I can see why," Cill agreed. "I imagine Thomas Thompson sounded as parentally unimaginative and stupid to him as it does to everyone else." But then regretted it because the lack of respect seemed to pain Cuddles. Cill realised that Cuddles had a near hero-worship for his old boss.

"We always called him TTT," Cuddles said. "And TT often to his face as well." Cill imagined that Cuddles would prefer to be called CCC and CC in the same way in an echo of those old, gold, far-off times. Not going to happen Cuddles, he thought.

Cill learnt from Colin that the current head of the Thompson family was Dryden Thompson, aged in his late 50s. He was Tom Telford Thompson's nephew. Tom TT himself died twelve years ago in 1970 aged 80.

There were now two branches of the family.

Back in time, Tom Telford Thompson had a daughter, while his younger brother William had a son, Dryden. The daughter married. She, Rebecca known as Bex, married Major Sidney

Dudley. They became the Dudley-Thompsons.

Tom and William had had a serious falling out at some point just at the beginning of the Second World War. They didn't speak to each other for decades, and there had been no rapprochement right up to the point when Tom died in 1970. Before the break-up the two brothers had been close and Tom had offered shares in the company he'd formed to William and his children. They took up the offer. After the break all communication between them tended to be through solicitors and bank managers. William refused to attend the firm's board meetings. But his son Dryden did as soon as he reached 21.

Strangely, Dryden Thompson had moved closer to his uncle and was estranged from his father William. He too had chosen publishing as a career, much to his father's disgust. He'd had a relatively short professional career, however. Within a short time he could abandon the ratrace. The proceeds from the family firm allowed him to become something he never thought he would be. He was now a man of leisure and a country squire.

No one really knew what the falling-out between Tom and William had been about. There was a strong assumption it had been over a woman. But if true her identity was unknown. It was also rumoured, Cuddles said, that there was no love lost between the leaders of the current Thompson generation, Dryden and his cousin Bex. It was said they could barely stand the sight of each other.

That hadn't stopped both sides of the family benefitting hugely over the years and decades from the massive income stream that was *Front Page* magazine, wholly-owned as it was by the Thompson family.

Tom Telford Thompson's brother William belonged to a family tradition of naming their children after famous writers. William himself tired of people assuming he was named after Shakespeare and always went out of his way to inform them that he was actually named after Wordsworth. He named his son Dryden after the poet.

Dryden had a daughter, named Anna Aphra Thompson

who had recently completed a law degree, and a son. Colin finished relating the family history of the Thompsons by informing Cill that Anna Thompson's younger brother was Samuel Taylor Thompson, who was still at university in Durham, and was named after Coleridge the Romantic poet.

"So there are two sides now to ownership of the family firm?" Cill summarised, pinning it down in his mind. "The Thompsons in the shape of Dryden Thompson and his daughter Anna and son Sam; and the Dudley-Thompsons in the form of Bex Dudley-Thompson and her husband Sidney Dudley-Thompson?"

"That's right."

"Do the Dudley-Thompsons have any children?"

"No. They never did. And Bex is well past it now."

Back in the office after lunch Eddie Osmoe was standing with The Ache at the fax machine, as they often did when expecting a fax. They were chatting about the current and incessant incompetence of their new typesetter. This was a new outfit set up in premises on nearby Shoe Lane, so as to be close to *Front Page*. It was a joint venture by Moriarty and an old school contemporary, crony and horse-racing pal, Darien Macdaniel.

Darien Macdaniel was invariably known to those who had most dealings with him, Eddie and The Ache, as Darien Medallion. That was because he really did wear a bright gold or gold-coloured medallion dangling on a gold chain round his neck. He would come into the office to confer with Moriarty wearing blue jeans, a black blazer, a white shirt with the top three buttons undone, and a large medallion glinting and twirling on his chest like an ancient wonder of the world, the Pharos of Alexandria.

The typesetting company was named Macdaniel Type after the prime mover and joint proprietor, but it was naturally known to everyone in the office as Medallion Type.

At the time a hybrid intermediate stage had appeared in the printing process. Instead of placing metal letters in a wooden frame and inking them prior to printing them off, as had been done for centuries all the way back to Gutenberg, Caxton and Wynkyn De Worde, now a film was made. Typesetting now involved making a film of all the pages, the page proofs, that were going to be printed in an issue of the magazine. This involved photographing the pages full-size precisely with special photographic lenses and machines. The finished film was then taken by courier to the printer. The printing was done from the pages on the film.

The trouble with Macdaniel Type, the typesetters *Front Page* was obliged to use because the editor was joint proprietor, was they were totally and utterly incompetent. Eddie even suspected the typesetters working there making the film couldn't even read English.

"With that medallion he thinks he's the mayor of typesetting," Billy Ayk said as they watched Darien disappear into Essay's office.

"His typesetting's a mare all right, a total nightmare," Eddie agreed. "But then what do you expect from someone who appears to be named after the fucking Isthmus of Panama?"

"Not typesetters but trypesetters then?"

"Spot on Billy. Medallion Trype it is."

The fax machine clattered into life, a stream of special light-sensitive fax paper emerged from its secret and mysterious innards. The integrated guillotine at the mouth of the machine cut and snicker-snacked the fax paper roll into separate A4 sized pages. Unless they were intercepted the cut fax sheets curled up on themselves then dropped on the floor. Which was why Eddie and The Ache often stood by the fax machine when they were expecting one. Their first job was to roll the curled-up fax sheets back on themselves to straighten out the curl.

Eddie and Billy Ayk returned to their desks, Eddie armed with faxed galleys and Billy with the flatplan for next week he had faxed to Medallion Trype for comments. Eddie farmed out the galleys to the various desks expecting them.

A week later, about a month after the Blackbushe pop festival, Essay Moriarty emerged from his office and wandered in an oblique curve towards the news desks. He chatted a while with Jerry Carter after handing a sheet of paper to him, then wandered back to his office, stopping alongside Cuddles's isolated outpost for further chat.

Jerry came over to Cill's desk.

"Essay wants you to go with him to a charity function. Have you got a dinner jacket?"

"Is that a news story?" It didn't sound much like a news story to Weaver. "Doesn't he know there's a war on?"

Jerry shrugged. "Doubt it. He probably doesn't care if there is. This sort of diary thing is far more important as far as he's concerned. And he wants you and Cathy to cover it. There is a possibility of a Falklands angle," Jerry stressed the 'is'. If it was possible to make 'is' sound like 'if', Jerry had done it.

He handed Cill a photocopied sheet. "Better make another copy of that for Cathy."

It was an invitation to the Grosvenor House Hotel for a formal dinner in aid of various charities for wounded or homeless armed servicemen and women.

"It's the Thompson family's annual charity bash. This year it's soldiers. They'll all be there. The whole family. Essay said you don't need to RSVP. The Grosvenor House is reputed to have the largest dining space in London," Jerry said. "So if they're using it all, it'll be a pretty big do. Sandy Growler's going too."

"It's a bit previous isn't it? We haven't started shooting yet," Cill said.

"Making sure, I imagine, the charity coffers are full for when the shooting does start. It might be useful, might not," Jerry added as he moved back to his own desk. "Might depend on who's giving the main speech."

"I better check out Moss Bros then."

Weaver went over to the photocopier and then went in search of Cathy Wight.

He found her among the library shelves talking to Alison Wong.

Cathy exploded when he handed her a copy of the invitation.

"You can wipe your arse with that, CW. That's not a news

story."

"You took the words out of my mouth. It's something Essay wants us to do. He'll be there too, apparently, and I guess will brief us during the event what exactly he wants me to write about and what exactly you're supposed to take photos of."

"It's a waste of time. Even if we get anything worthwhile out of it, Essay only goes up in my estimation about a millimetre."

"That's a bit high, I suspect. Anyway Cathy it's this Thursday. The day after tomorrow."

Privately he entirely agreed with Cathy. It was a joke. And even if something did come out of it, wasn't SA Moriarty there anyway? Couldn't he cover the story and write it up himself?

Apparently not. One of the news desk lackeys had to be there to do it properly.

At lunchtime the next day he walked over to the other side of Covent Garden and hired a dinner suit from Moss Bros.

21. DINNER

The taxi dropped Cill Weaver off outside the Grosvenor House Hotel on Park Lane. He'd come straight from work. He'd showered, shaved and changed into his dinner jacket at the office.

His notebook under his arm, he entered through the large rotating doors and looked around the lobby for Cathy.

He couldn't see her anywhere. Then a voice behind him nearly made him jump.

"Took your time. The do's about to start, And you've not been introduced to the family big knobs yet," Cathy Wight said. She pointed over to the far end of the broad lobby.

"The moustachioed major is a grump, doesn't want to be here. The family head held my hand far too long. The bulky big-boobed bint definitely does not want to be standing anywhere near the head-honcho, the hand-holder. Not in the same galaxy if she can help it. Looks like she'd rather be visiting a slaughterhouse. But the younger one on the end is a stunner." Cathy grinned at him. "My, you do look quite good in a DJ, I have to admit."

He looked at her. No formal evening gown for Cathy, owned or hired. She was wearing one of her customary work outfits, a black trouser-suit and purple blouse. An expensive top-notch camera with a big light-gathering lens hung from a strap around her neck; a padded bag with spare lenses hung from a shoulder.

She saw him sizing her up and knew why.

"No way I'm wearing a sod-off ball gown if I'm working."

"Quite right."

"That's what I just told Essay. My tits would get in the way of the straps." She grimaced and shook the camera strap.

"Or vice versa. Did you tell Essay that?"

Just then Essay Moriarty spotted them and moved rapidly over to their side of the lobby. He'd been in close conversation with Alec – Sandy – Growler, the managing director of News World Publishers.

"Good you're here that you're here," Moriarty said as he came up to them. "Cathy-girl you take some atmosphere shots just now while I introduce Cill-boy to the family."

While he had no trouble with being referred to as Cill-boy, he very much doubted that Cathy would stand for Cathy-girl. But she just sneered behind Moriarty's back and sauntered off.

At the far end of the lobby Cill could see a rapidly moving queue had formed to be introduced to a standing panel of four figures, resplendent in expensive dinner jackets and ball gowns, complete with dull metal medals and sparky stone jewellery.

Weaver looked over. There were two older men then two women to be introduced to. There was no sign of the fifth Thompson, the younger brother. Then Cill assumed it was still term time at Durham and Sam Thompson had better things to do than attend a charity function in London. Ahead on Cill's angle of approach his view of the younger of the two women was obscured by the size of the older woman's bust.

It came his turn to be introduced by Moriarty to the four Thompsons. He shook hands in turn first with Major Sidney Dudley-Thompson, then Dryden Thompson, then with Bex Dudley-Thompson.

He noticed Cathy over to the left taking shots of the family and the line of introductions. Cathy's synopsis of the family had been pretty accurate. Major Dudley-Thompson, with his back as straight and upright as a factory chimney, murmured an inaudible how-do-you-do and stared over Cill's shoulder as he fleetingly shook his hand. Fortunately Dryden Thompson didn't hold his hand for too long as he had Cathy's. Bex Dudley-Thompson flooded him with a glowering leer that he thought was intended as a smile.

"So good of you to come," she whispered hoarsely with a voice like feedback from a Marshall amp, and shook his hand with both of hers.

Cill smiled agreeably. He could hardly say he had no choice.

This was a strange business, Cill thought. This dinner is to raise money. These four hosts expect the people coming to the dinner to get their wallets and purses out. And here am I ignoring all that in the hope that someone here is going to say something interesting, something newsworthy, because the dinner itself and the charity behind it just isn't newsworthy? News was a strange and ravenous, cold and calculating beast sometimes, he thought.

He moved on.

Then last in the line of four Thompsons was a much younger woman. A woman in her mid-twenties.

"Anna Thompson, let me introduce you to one of my team here that's here: stalwart reporter and journalist Cill Weaver," Moriarty said. He clapped Weaver on the back and ushered him forward. Confused slightly by the "stalwart", Cill extended a hand and looked into the woman's face for the first time.

He nearly froze to the spot. He felt himself going bright red.

The last time he'd seen her he'd been lying flat on his back on a hot summer's day and he was staring right up between her legs at a lengthy glimpse of her white panties.

To her credit, he was sure Anna Thompson recognised him too. But she didn't alter her stance or withdraw her hand. Her dark brown eyes held a speculative look and a slight smile played on the corners of her mouth.

Cathy was absolutely right about the fourth Thompson.

He and Moriarty moved on into the big dining room.

Just inside the entrance there was a seating plan.

"High table for me, for me," Moriarty said, and moved away. "Talk later," he said over his shoulder.

Weaver scanned the table chart. He found his name. Each table sat twelve guests. He made his way across the floor and stood behind his chair at the table.

He was stunned, his mind churning. He'd just met the girl with legs like Pompey's Pillar.

Soon the entire table had its twelve guests standing behind their chairs waiting for something, for permission to sit or for someone to say grace probably. Cill introduced himself to his immediate neighbours.

In his time as a reporter he'd already been to quite a few such functions as this. He was familiar with the pattern. They all had a similar way of doing things. A master of ceremonies with a booming voice would make announcements. And sometimes you got to sit next to interesting people and sometimes you didn't.

This time he was seated between a wounded soldier with an artificial leg and a female administrator for one of the relevant benefitting charities.

An artificial leg is a great starter of conversation.

The captain on his left had lost his leg in Germany, it turned out. But he was far too young for the Second World War, Cill could see that. While they were still standing behind their chairs, Weaver learned that the soldier had been run over by a tank, on manoeuvres, in Germany, in peacetime.

"Far more accidents with tanks than there are with cars," the captain said with a smile. "Relatively. You wouldn't think so but there are."

The master of ceremonies with the inevitable booming voice – with a possible Southend accent Weaver thought – invited the assembled guests to pray silence as grace was about to be said by the bishop of somewhere - Weaver had already lost interest – the right reverend somebody or other. He spoke in Latin, Weaver did notice that. An achiever of O level Latin himself, Weaver tried to follow and comprehend the formula, but got stuck on "Benedicat".

<<BENEDY CAT CREPT INTO THE CRYPT...>>

He started the familiar headline process, but it trailed away in his mind before completion. He tried to chase it down but his heart wasn't in it.

Then there was a huge rumbling sound as chairs were pulled back, the guests sat down and the hubbub began.

Each table place had a kind of printed order of service set before it. Cill opened it and flicked past the frenchified food courses and looked for information about the speeches. He found it on the back. Dryden Thompson was set to start, but the main speaker was a former head of the British armed forces, an ex-top soldier.

So that's why Moriarty wanted a reporter here, Weaver realised. He thinks the old codger, the ancient field marshal, is going to spout off for or against the Falklands crisis, and for or against the government's handling of it. Okay, good enough, he thought.

But either way his judgement on the crisis fell, Weaver could guarantee already that the field marshal would end his speech by claiming – without a shred of evidence to support it – that the British armed forces would be up for, and up to, whatever task their political masters set.

While nodding and seeming to agree with the two neighbours who now spoke right across him, his thoughts turned to the young stepping-over-bodies woman with legs like Pompey's Pillar who he now knew to be Anna Thompson.

He looked towards the far end of the room where the high table was spread out against the end wall. Instead of a circular table such as everyone else was seated at, the high table was a long rectangular affair set out like the Last Supper. Sixteen bigwigs, *gran quesos* Judy might call them, sat arrayed in a line along the far side of the table. Sitting just on one side of the table so they could all see the room and the room could all see them, Cill assumed.

The bishop of god-knows-where will love that, Weaver thought. He's at his own Last Supper. With three too many partakers of course. Well chuck in Mary Magdalene and another couple of freeloaders and hangers-on and maybe the original Last Supper had more than the statutory thirteen guests anyway? He'd always wondered why depictions of the Last Supper always showed the thirteen people arrayed along just one side of the table? It meant you had to have a table twice as big as necessary. And you could only talk to your neighbours on either side of you. It seemed like the definition of bad restaurant management to Cill. Very clumsy and careless catering. Much better if they'd had a big circular table like here, he thought. Then everyone could have talked to everyone else equally. But not so easy for artists to paint all their faces.

He could see Anna Thompson was the left hand seat – from his perspective - of the four Thompsons taking up the four central seats of the long table. There were six guests sitting to her right. Weaver noticed that the bishop of god-knows-where was sitting next to Anna Thompson in the first place on her right. On her left came Dryden Thompson, then Bex Dudley-Thompson, then next to her was her husband Major Dudley-Thompson, and next to him sat the field marshal.

The two senior News World Publishers figures, managing director Sandy Growler and editor Essay Moriarty, both sat among the six seats arrayed to the left of the major.

The assembled room began to move through the frenchified food as various courses were brought to them by whispering waiters.

Weaver turned down the offer of red or white wine. He decided if he was going to take notes of the main speech he better lay off the booze.

In conversation with the soldier-captain Weaver was delighted to discover he took a very dim view of the capabilities of the ancient field marshal. He didn't quite say "incompetent buffoon" but he hinted at it.

The woman on his other side looked shocked by the revelation. Perhaps she adhered to the school of thought that held that age and experience demanded respect, Weaver thought. He definitely wasn't in that school himself. For him, talking sense demanded respect, and only that.

Her perfume, or somebody's, was wafting about invisibly across the table like the crop-duster in *North By Northwest* on an industrial scale. Did Bayer or Hoechst or even JCB do fragrances? Cill thought not, but wondered which multinational chemical company was involved in the creation of this particular gas attack.

The shrimpy-saucy amuse-bouche had come and gone and the soup was being served. Weaver needed a pee, and he got up and wended his way through the maze of tables and out of the room. He followed signs to the gents.

On his way back he noticed a sign to the bar. On an impulse he decided a quick beer wouldn't do his note-taking any harm and changed tack to head in that direction.

He ordered a half pint of lager, and was just bringing it to his lips for the first sip when a voice spoke at his shoulder.

"I'll have the same as him."

He turned, surprised.

Anna Thompson was standing next to him a big grin on her face. The same dazzling grin she had used when she was stepping over him.

"It is you," she said. "Thought I recognised you."

"I saw you from a different angle," Weaver said. "A more intense, but also more life-affirming perspective, I have to say. I'd know you anywhere now," he added mischievously. "You looked almost as good from that angle as you do now."

Anna Thompson lifted her face and laughed loudly.

"Can't be helped what a girl shows when she's in a storming hurry and needs to be first in the queue."

"I guess not. Did you enjoy the day?"

"Fantastic. You?"

"How did you get out of the car park?"

"God don't remind me. We gave up in the end and slept. We couldn't even find our car till it got light."

"Took us six hours."

Anna whistled silently and took a gulp of her lager.

"So you work for the family firm?" she said

"Yes. One of the hired hands."

"Tell me about it. I'd like to know more."

"I'd like to. But unfortunately I'm working. I've got to note the speeches and write a news story about it. I better get back in." He paused. It was a big step. "Can we do it another time?"

She didn't hesitate. "I'd like that. Here's my card." She delved in a small clutch bag suspended from a bare and slightly tanned shoulder and pulled out a business card. "Call me."

They both bent their heads and sipped their drinks.

Just then a light flashed and Cathy Wight took a photo of the pair of them standing at the bar looking at each other over half pints of lager.

They both turned, surprised. Cathy waved and set off to snap other targets.

Weaver was looking at Anna's card. The address looked familiar.

"I work in Lincoln's Inn. I'm in Bartholomew Gonner's chambers."

"Gonner Rear!" he said.

"Yes Gonner Rear. I'm a junior barrister."

She moved away.

Cill looked down again at the card.

"I'll call you," he said, looking up, but she was gone.

Weaver went back in to the massive dining room. For some reason he felt his step was lighter.

Between the soup and the meat, the booming master of ceremonies, possibly from Southend, demanded silence. Dryden Thompson got up to speak. He had a pleasant slightly old-school received pronunciation accent. The old school long vowels in his accent, and a tendency to pronounce 'off' as 'orf' indicated to Weaver that much of the social revolution of the 1960s had entirely passed him by.

But nonetheless he spoke warmly and well – and briefly. He welcomed the guests and stressed how important to Britain its armed forces had always been. And how important it was that the aftermath of battle should matter as much as the planning for, and performance of, battle. The welfare of soldiers was paramount.

Weaver was slightly impressed, but nothing in what Dryden Thompson said merited a news story.

Then after dessert and over coffee the main speech came and it was a disaster. Just as the one-legged captain had prophesied, the ancient field marshal was hopelessly out of touch. He seemed to imagine a coming war in the Falklands with Argentina would be long and hard. It would even involve trenches and tanks. Wildly, he foresaw the necessity to send some kind of military column to cut off, outflank, besiege and starve out Buenos Aires. That, apparently, would precipitate an Argentine surrender. If it didn't, he reminded his audience that Britain had nuclear weapons and Argentina did not.

"One of the Falkland penguins would have done a better job," the captain muttered as the field marshal had them all up-standing to raise a toast to the queen.

Weaver had been talking at length to the captain about how he saw a war with Argentina. It was good. He learnt a lot. Trouble was none of it was publishable. He did hand the captain his business card before he left. The captain didn't offer him one in return. But he nodded and gave a strange kind of smile. A smile that said the card might come in useful, you never knew.

Then as he left the room to find a phone to talk to Jerry Carter about what the merits of the story were, he was intercepted by Moriarty. He had to spend a lot of words and a lot of time and effort having to talk down Essay Moriarty's wilder fantasies about the merits of the story.

In the end the only way Weaver could hope to make Moriarty leave it alone was to get Jerry Carter on the phone. Finally between the three of them and a phone it was agreed that the Thompsons' charity function would merit no more than a few of Cathy Wight's photos plus a caption. That would be the sum total of all that would feature in the magazine about the event. And it would all go in the *Diary* column. This was a couple of pages of rumour, titbits and celebrity gossip that had recently been incorporated into the magazine by Moriarty.

This was down to a bit of psychology on Jerry's part. He knew the *Diary* column was the editor's pride and joy. So though to him and Cill it was a downgrade to print the Thompson do story there, to Moriarty it was a triumph. It was a justification of his establishment of the *Diary* column. So everyone was happy.

Jerry had been waiting in the office specifically for Cill to phone in about what the story might merit. He was the last one there; everyone else had left for the night.

He tended to trust Weaver's judgment, he was after all senior reporter. Jerry was also aware of the reputation for the wholly out of touch and somewhat ludicrous entirely in-the-box thinking of the ancient field marshal and was in no way surprised by Weaver's judgment.

He wasn't at all surprised that Moriarty had a different view. He had been expecting it and had prepared himself mentally for the challenge of standing up to and if necessary diverting, if not overriding, the editor.

Just another day on the news desk, Jerry thought, as he switched off the lights.

22. FAX & PHOTO

Cill Weaver wondered how soon he could call Anna Thompson.

He reached round the back of his office chair and took her card out of his jacket pocket.

AAT it said along the middle.

Then under that: *Anna Aphra Thompson*, and below that a work address in Lincoln's Inn and a phone number.

He glanced up from the business card. Eddie was standing by the fax machine. He often did that when he was expecting galleys or page proofs back from Medallion Trype. Eddie and Billy's renaming of their typesetter had stuck. It was now Medallion Trype to everyone bar the editor, the deputy editor and Janet McLing.

The machine clattered into life. But it wasn't the multiple stream of pages Eddie was expecting. It was a single sheet.

Eddie leaned forward to inspect it as the paper emerged. Instead of intercepting it as usual, he let it curl up and drop on the floor. Eddie left it alone and stepped back, as if in deep thought. Then he picked it up and placed it back in the fax machine, balanced on the edge.

After a moment he called Bill Roadhouse over to the fax machine. They both leaned forward and read the fax as Eddie held it open against the curl. They looked at each other. Bill was frowning.

They left the fax in the machine and returned to their desks.

A few minutes later Moriarty emerged from his glass office and crossed the floor directly to the fax machine. He appeared to be in a hurry. He looked into the machine, saw the fax, grabbed it, looked around, and carried it back to his office.

Cill noticed Eddie and Bill watching all this and exchanging glances.

He wondered what the fax was about. He'd have to ask Bill over a pint sometime.

Just then Cathy Wight distracted him. She brought over a

print of the photo she'd taken of Cill and Anna Thompson at the Grosvenor House dinner.

"Should wear a DJ more often CW," she said and dropped the photograph on his desk.

Cill examined the photograph. It was black and white – Cathy did her own developing – and showed two smartly dressed people standing at a bar. The camera had taken the picture from sideways on, so the two people were seen in profile. The young women was wearing an evening gown. Cill remembered the colour as green and gold. Her dark hair was pulled back in a bun and she wore tiny diamond earrings. The visible earring sparkled against the camera flash The young man wore a black dinner jacket. They both had half pints of lager in one hand, had the glasses touched to their lips, and were about to simultaneously take a drink. They were looking directly at each other over the rim of their glass.

It was a good photo. Cathy was an excellent photographer. This wasn't any old snap. Clearly Cathy had waited for the right moment. It seemed to encapsulate something. Here were two people obviously interested in each other in the midst of a formal social setting; each one wondering if this was a start, a start leading to a small universe of endless possibilities.

Cill decided he would call Anna Thompson straightaway. He had something to show her.

23. DATE

Anna Thompson was impressed by Cathy's photo as much as Cill was.

They met up after work in the Three Tuns pub on Chancery Lane. It was full of lawyers, but Anna didn't seem to mind that. She was amused by Cill's story of how this pub neighbourhood featured one of the most valuable - and one of his most favourite – places in London. The strange French-style four-stall *pissoir* set against the outside wall of Lincoln's Inn, hidden in the alleyway alongside the pub.

"Typical," Anna Thompson said. "It must date from the days when only men worked in this city. Supposedly."

"Or at least the only ones needing to pee."

"Not only were they the only ones working, they were also the only ones drinking after work."

They both laughed.

They were sitting opposite each other in one of the series of cubicles with high-backed padded benches like an old-fashioned railway carriage along one wall of the pub. There was a table between them. It was secluded and private. Most of the lawyers, men and women, were standing at the bar.

Anna Thompson was wearing a white blouse under a black suit jacket and skirt. The skirt was short, tight and stretchy. It left exposed a long expanse of thigh from the hem to her knees.

Pompey's Pillar would be impressed, Cill thought.

He wondered if she was allowed into court in a skirt like that. Probably not, he thought. Maybe there she changed into something less arresting, trousers perhaps? Then of course she'd be wearing a barrister's robe over the top anyway? He realised obscurely he would really like to see what she looked like in her court outfit. The wig especially.

Cathy's photo was laid on the table between them.

"It's really good," Anna said. "Can I get a copy?"

"I brought that one for you. I can get another one from Cathy."

Cill took out Anna's card.

It read on two lines:

AAT

Anna Aphra Thompson

"Interesting you lead the card with your initials rather than your name?" He pointed to the letters AAT at the centre of the card.

"Yes," she said. Then she smiled her mischievous smile. "I'm always hoping people will try to pronounce it as a word. If they do it's bound to come out sounding like a Liverpudlian saying "art","" she smiled again and her brown eyes lit up.

"Aat," Cill said, repeating it a few time. "You're right. It does."

He pointed to the card again. "And why put your full name on it?"

"It's the way my great uncle always did it. I wanted to do the same."

"Tom Telford Thompson?"

"Yes." Then serious for a moment she continued: "My great uncle was a great journalist. A pioneer in the industry."

That was true, Cill thought. It was sometimes easy to forget that when your first instinct was to react against all the hero-worship.

Anna told him the story of her name and her family's peculiar naming tradition for first names.

"My first name comes from a Byzantine princess. The historian Anna Comnena. And the second is after the Restoration playwright Aphra Behn. Anna Comnena was the world's first female historian," she said. "And Aphra Behn was the first English woman to live independently through writing for a living." She sounded pleased and content to be so named.

"Pretty impressive on both counts."

"And I wanted to show them both on my business card. Of course I only usually use the first name. The second is very unusual though, isn't it?"

"Not as unusual as some," Cill said and went on to outline

151

the very odd nomenclature of his editor.

It turned out that Anna had met SA Moriarty quite a few times.

"Yes he and the MD, Growler, come to board meetings."

"How come?" Weaver asked. That was news to him. It was somehow strange too, he wasn't sure how, but it felt odd. Wasn't News World Publishers a family company?

"They've got family shares. They're shareholders in the family company."

That felt even odder to Weaver. No reason why they shouldn't have shares, of course. For some reason he'd thought everyone who actually worked at *Front Page* and News World Publishers was purely a hired hand, just like him. But it seemed not. A couple of the *gran queso* hired hands had their snouts in the family trough as well.

"Nothing to do with me," she sounded apologetic. "Yes it's all my aunt's doing. But let's move on from all that. Tell me about *Front Page*. That's much more interesting."

The way she said "aunt" told Cill there was no love lost between them.

She looked at him square on. "Your name's unusual too? What is it? Sill as in windowsill?"

"No Cill as in windowcill."

She looked confused for a moment, then spluttered a cross between a laugh and a giggle into her glass.

Cill told her about his little sister and how his name was Cyril. A name he couldn't stand. He much preferred Cill.

They began to relax with each other. As they talked about their respective jobs and what they did, each examined the other in more detail. And they both began to realise they liked a lot of what they saw. Before the evening was over they both knew they were going to see each other again.

24. PROPAGANDA

In the office Jerry Carter pasted up the front page of that day's *Sun* on the wall behind his desk.

<<GOTCHA>>

The headline said.

Many of the journalists and reporters were grouped round it.

A major capital ship of the Argentinean navy, the *Belgrano*, had been torpedoed and sunk by a British submarine with substantial loss of life. For some reason the unknown submarine in question was always described as a nuclear submarine.

Did that make it more ominous and dangerous? Weaver wondered. He guessed it did. The phrase suggested a lethal capability far beyond the mere torpedo that had been used to sink this ageing second-hand cruiser. The old codger of a field marshal no doubt relished the notion of a "nuclear" submarine. Something else Britain had which Argentina didn't.

There was considerable surprise round Jerry's desk when Liz announced that she thought the headline was pretty clever.

"You think so?" Eddie said, surprised at her turnaround. "I think it's too much."

"Why?" Bill asked.

"I thought STICK IT UP YOUR JUNTA was fine. It was just rude. It was also funny and clever. But this is subtly different. I think, to use a very odd term for me, that it's in bad taste. It's seeing war as a game. Almost as a game of conkers. You make a score and you chalk up the numbers. But this is much more than just about taking a warship off the board. It's also about the hundreds of dead sailors. This is disrespectful to them. I don't think disrespect has any place in war. Not any more."

"But isn't it just something newly old, just the latest in that fine old journalistic tradition of THAT'S ONE IN THE EYE FOR HERR HITLER?" Judy said.

"It is definitely," Eddie said. "Very much OUR BOYS. But nowadays we all think that shit by the Pathe newsreel reader whatsisname – "

"Bob Danvers-Walker," Rex said.

" – is silly and inappropriate. This is in that tradition. A nasty and unnecessary tradition. And this is worse. It's stupid and disrespectful. We don't need to do that anymore."

It was quite a speech by the normally taciturn chief sub-editor.

"All's fair in love and war surely, Eddie?" Cill said.

"Maybe that used to be the case. But I'd like to think we're more civilised now," Eddie said.

"But I think what *The Sun* is doing is just being realistic," Rex said.

"Yes," Cill agreed.

Eddie looked disdainful at this.

"It's true Eddie," Cill pressed. "If we go down your civilised route you just end up with a mismatch in viewpoints between the likes of us back home and the troops in action. While I'm sure he was "Herr Hitler" for Bob Danvers-Walker and the home audience, for the boys actually doing the fighting he was "fucking Adolf" and the Germans were "fucking squareheads". I bet they weren't calling him "Herr Hitler"."

"Not to mention a deficiency in the testicular department," Rex said.

For once Eddie had no response. He looked thoughtful.

"Those doing the fighting have to dehumanise the enemy. For the troops in action in the South Atlantic, they're going to have to kill them at some point. And part of being able to do that is by *dehumanising* them." Cill said, stressing the word. "It's part of the whole package of being a soldier. And it's the part that we back home don't talk about. Those of us back home can afford the luxury of not dehumanising the enemy. We have the luxury of being civilised; those on the front line don't."

"And *The Sun* is – possibly – just being the first to cut out that mismatch," Rex said. "It's taking the stance, or pretending to take the stance, of the soldier on the ground. And representing that in its headline."

"So it's like Bob Danvers-Walker really saying on the Pathe newsreel "Fuck off Adolf. Our boys are kicking your arse"?" Judy said and smiled at the idea.

Liz, having been silent throughout since opening the debate now chipped in.

"But war really is a game of conquers, anyway, isn't it Eddie. It's all about who conquers whom."

They all laughed, not least Eddie. Cill looked over at Tintin with new respect. Anyone good with words was good with him.

"I suppose what really rankles with this," Eddie sighed and pointed to the headline. "Oh I think you're right about the mismatch – necessary or unnecessary. But for me the trouble with this is it's not just telling us what's happened, it's telling us how to think about it. And that's not journalism, that's propaganda."

"We're being steered by this kind of thing into having our prejudices supported?" Judy said.

"Yes. And I for one don't like being told how to think. Nor to have my news outlets imagine they know how I think." Eddie moved away from the wall.

As the rest of them returned to their desks, most of them thought what Eddie had said was right. And Cill and Rex were right too. But they also thought it was a telling interception by Tintin.

As for Liz herself, she was pleased of course with the laugh she got and the appreciative glances at her wit. But what came out of it most was that it was a milestone for her. Perhaps for the first time in her professional career she felt like a journalist. That was because the more she thought about *The Sun* headline the more she fully understood now that as a journalist it didn't really matter what you wrote about. It mattered much more how you wrote it.

Another journalistic issue came up later in the day.

Cill Weaver came off the phone and went straight over to Jerry's desk,

"I just got a tip," he said, his eyes bright with newsworthy anticipation.

"Oh yes?" Jerry put down his red pen and looked up.

"I just got a call. Apparently the French have told us all they know about the characteristics of the Exocet missile. We've even been having full-scale combat and flight tests against it – us and the French air force together. Somewhere in Canada apparently, secret and well out of the public gaze."

Jerry sat back. He picked up his biro and sucked on the end of it.

"It's good Cill. Very good. But my instinct is we can't use it."

"I'm told us getting it is an exclusive. An old-fashioned scoop."

"I know. I know. I'm not saying it's not newsworthy. It is. It's great. Just that we can't use it."

Cill knew exactly why Jerry had doubts. If they published it they would be telling the enemy secrets about the capabilities of the British armed forces in wartime. In some suspicious minds – those in government for example – that could be construed as treason.

"I know where you're coming from. But I thought I'd see what you thought."

"Look. Tell you what," Jerry said. "I'll have a chat with the *gran queso*," he pointed with his fingers like a gun in the direction of Moriarty's glass office.

Cill returned to his desk while Jerry collected Eddie and they went over to Moriarty's glass den and disappeared through the door with Cuddles in tow.

A little while later Jerry and Eddie came out. Jerry passed the edge of his hand across his neck in a cutting motion towards Cill.

Cill nodded and got on with writing the next story.

But then Jerry diverted his line of direction and came over to Cill's desk.

"Essay and Cuddles agree," Jerry said. "But I've had another thought."

Cill looked up enquiringly.

"Rather than just guess about the rights and wrong and the legalities of this, I'm going to have a chat with Gonner Rear about it," Jerry said.

Jerry moved off in the direction of the interview room so he could have a more private phone conversation there.

It turned out that Gonner Rear agreed.

He agreed with Jerry that this was not the kind of thing that would be covered by a D-Notice precisely because the government and the Ministry of Defence assumed the Exocet assessments were secret and none of the press would find out about the Canadian trials, and had not issued any D-Notice to include this issue. So in theory there was nothing preventing *Front Page* from printing the story. Except of course that it could – and in Gonner Rear's opinion would – be construed as treason by a very irate Ministry of Defence.

And he also pointed out to Jerry that, aside from the legalities, it wouldn't help their circulation much in practical terms if *Front Page* got a reputation for helping the enemy.

So Cill's exclusive tip-off about the Franco-British Exocet exercises was never used during the conflict. But it wasn't forgotten. It was put on the back burner in everyone's minds ready for extraction and use in retrospectives when the Falklands war was over.

Later in the upstairs bar at the Tipperary, sitting on stools by a low round table in the first floor bay window, Weaver got an opportunity to ask Bill about the fax that had come in to the office two days before that had caused some strange behaviour by him and Eddie.

Bill looked out of the window, examining the pavement. He seemed in doubt as to what to say.

"I think it was a fax that was misdirected to our office number," Bill said. "It shouldn't have come to us at all."

"What was it?"

"It was an instruction from a firm of solicitors, I think solicitors representing the Thompson family. It was addressed to SA Moriarty and it said it was confirming the agreement between the Thompson family and Moriarty to give Moriarty "another million shares" in the family company. That's what it said: "another million"."

Cill whistled. "Bugger me. Another million. Is that worth a lot? Is that as valuable as it sounds?"

"No. Not at all. The shares could be worthless. In a family firm you can't really sell them. There's no market. There may be restrictions too on how you can dispose of them anyway. Sometimes you can't even pass them on to your heirs. They have to go back to the other shareholders in the family. They just give you voting rights in the company," Bill paused. "Most of the time."

"What do you mean?"

"There is one circumstance where those family shares could be very valuable. Very valuable indeed."

"What's that?"

Bill held up a hand. "I need to do a bit of research first. Need to ask around."

It seemed to Cill that Bill was actually concerned, worried even.

Bill stood up and made his way to the bar to get them another drink.

As he placed the pints down on the table he spoke again.

"I think if what's going on here really is going on, then we all need to know about it."

25. BEX

Bex Dudley-Thompson couldn't believe it when her husband told her how much of her money he'd lost on horses. Owning them and betting on them.

She knew she'd married an utter ne'er-do-well, fly-by-night, and total financial flibbertigibbet very soon after the wedding.

Straight after the war-delayed honeymoon on lake Garda they'd gone to live in Sidney Dudley's country house in Gloucestershire.

Brought up as she was in London Bex was excited at the prospect of country living. She'd be able to ride, grow roses, follow foxhounds, perhaps entertain on a lavish scale, join and head local charities, become a leading figure in the community.

It turned out she wasn't able to do any of those things.

Major Sidney Dudley had no money at all.

That was the first shocking thing.

He couldn't even afford a gardener to cut the lawns at the ramshackle tumbledown Gloucestershire country house known as Poitiers. Or at least she was under the impression the house was called Poitiers when she first saw it written down on Sidney's elegant business card when he first asked her out before the war. It turned out she was wrong on that too.

They'd got married in 1940 during the war. They lived in a house in Russell Square that her father Tom rented for them for the duration of the war. Soon Sidney was posted abroad, first India, then to North Africa, Sicily and Italy, Normandy and finally Germany. Bex divided her war time either alone in the Russell Square house, or back at her family home in Hampstead.

Straight after the end of the war they went on the delayed honeymoon to Italy and lake Garda. When they came back they moved out of London to live in Sidney Dudley's country house.

Then came the second shocking thing. The house was originally named Poitiers after the famous battle of the Hundred Years War won by the Black Prince in France. A battle won by the firepower of the English longbow against the massed ranks of French horse-backed chivalry.

It was thus a great shock to her to hear all the locals refer to the house as "Poyters". And Poyters it now officially was.

The Dudley family at an early stage in the evolution of their mid-19th century country seat had long given up trying to educate the locals in the proper pronunciation of the name of their – at the time - imposing mansion. So they too over time adopted the same pronunciation themselves.

So Poyters it was.

For Bex, living in Poitiers was one thing. It sounded grand and historic and sonorous and exotic and foreign. But living in Poyters was something completely different.

In time she got used to the name. She didn't like it. But she got used to it.

The third shocking was the house was a wreck. Living in it was worse than a wreck. You could abandon a wreck.

She knew Belfast sinks were fashionable now among her old set in London. But she doubted if any of them would ever have seen an original one? One that was still in place after its first fitting in a different century, lurking in the dark kitchen, the windows half-obscured by ivy, with a dirty slimy wooden drainer board alongside it?

Sometimes in summer she was sure she saw, and worse heard, things moving in the ivy through the bit of kitchen window above the Belfast sink the ivy hadn't yet covered. She refused to go near the sink until the noise had stopped.

In the scullery with the deeply-worn red quarry tile floor stood a twintub top-loading washing-machine. No modern front-loader here. But she refused to use the mangle that stood in the corner.

They didn't even have a fridge until Bex insisted. She bought it herself when they became more widely available in the mid-1950s. Before that, things were supposed to be kept cool in a little side room with shelves and a sloping ceiling called a butler's pantry.

She began to hate words like "scullery", "larder" and "butler's pantry". She longed instead to be the proud owner of a "utility room". But she wasn't.

The lighting and electrics dated from the 1950s, when the original wiring had been replaced. They even had the hideously old-fashioned dark-brown bakelite Wylex plugs and sockets, the ones with a central round pin and two offset flat pins either side.

The front door bell wasn't even electric. It was a Heath Robinson mechanical monstrosity. You pulled a knob on a wire instead. The well-worn brass knob sat in a smart but badly oxidised brass housing at mid-height on the right hand side of the door. Visitors pulled sharply on the knob. A wire attached to the knob passed all the way through the front wall, then through most of the other downstairs inside walls of the house to the back kitchen. There, high up on the side wall of the kitchen, the wire emerged from the wall. It was attached to a bell.

When someone pulled sharply on the knob outside the front door, the wire moved all the way through the walls sufficiently to tilt and shake the bell. Then you knew someone was at the front door.

Unsuspecting newcomers didn't even realise the brass knob was some kind of antediluvian doorbell, and instead ignored it and tapped on the door. In a rambling tumbledown tottering mansion like Poyters, no one heard them when they did. Many times people had come to the door and gone away again, thinking no one was at home, both literally and figuratively .

So Bex had insisted on having a big heavy door knocker attached to the door. If people didn't know how to use the doorbell, they should at least get the hang of using a knocker.

Anyway, one time shortly after Bex and Sidney had installed themselves in Bex's private hellhouse, a visitor pulled too sharply on the doorbell. Somewhere in the dusty-but-damp walls the yards-long wire snapped. The doorbell stopped ringing for good. Even Bex realised they couldn't hack all the ancient horsehair plaster off all the interior brick walls of the house to find where the wire had snapped and repair it.

Well, she thought to herself at least we've still got the

knocker.

Bex knew the major came from a long line of soldiers. Couldn't one of them, she thought, have raped and pillaged himself a fortune somewhere in some foreign field? If they had it hadn't come down to Sidney. Or if it had, Sidney himself had spent it all.

There was no central heating. Certainly there were radiators and pipes. And there was an old boiler in the scullery. Bex was never sure whether this contraption ran on gas or oil, prayers, spells, threats, bribes, incantations, astrology, necromancy, voodoo, witchcraft or magic. Either way it never worked. If you pressed the right button and tried to start it, there was a noise like a brass band tuning up in hell, following by a whooshing sound, a flame would appear with a light 'punk' sound. Then after precisely three seconds the flame would go out with a dead 'plonk' sound. Once in rage and tears and frustration Bex had repeated this sequence of operations twenty times. The boiler would still not sustain a flame.

There were fireplaces of course. It was another great shock to Bex when she found out that she was expected to lay and light the necessary fires herself in the vast fireplaces every day, if she wanted one, or go cold. She was also obliged to rake out the ashes herself and put them in the galvanised dustbin outside the scullery side door.

Husband Sidney was never there to assist. He was away at the stables, the gallops and the races.

The only room in the entire house she could keep reasonably warm was the kitchen. In there lived an ancient stinky coke-fuelled Aga, lurking like a steel-plated stegosaurus on the far wall under the old chimney breast. It had replaced the open fire at some point in the 1950s.

It looked like the last time the Dudley family had any money was the 1950s, Bex perceived.

The warmth of the kitchen drew Bex to it. Housebound, she would spend most of her day on a chair at the broad kitchen table. As long as there was nothing moving in the ivy, of course.

The one job she didn't have to do each day was fill the Aga with coke every morning. Sidney did that. Before he went off to the stables, gallops and races.

There were no servants, of course.

It was her father's death that saved Bex and the major from ruin. As his only daughter and heir, he left a substantial sum and various valuable properties to her in his will.

Tom had given Sidney Dudley a present of shares in the family firm on his wedding to his daughter. He'd also left a substantial amount to him in his will, as well as money. But the shares were far outweighed by the amount owned and controlled by Bex.

Sidney rapidly ran through the money Tom Telford Thompson had left him. And though it took a fair while, now finally the major had run through most of his wife's money as well. In the twelve years since she had been the main beneficiary in her father's will, Sidney had blown over four million pounds of her money. There wasn't much left at all.

To be fair, her total inheritance from her father was fourteen million pounds. And much of the money, the majority, ten million, had gone on a much-needed upgrade, restoration, refurbishment, revamping and rebuilding of Poyters. Both Bex and the major were astonished at the size of the bottomless pit that doing up a wreck of a country house entailed. Despite the costs, they persevered with the improvements. It was, after all, her money.

It took time too, there was so much to do, so much to undo, so much to put right. But after three years she was the proud occupier of a modern country mansion, complete with new electric wiring throughout, doorbell, stainless steel sink ("Damn and blast the Belfast sink," she'd thought with the thrill of victory) and fitted kitchen, custom-built from American live-oak hardwood, a new modern boiler and central heating system, dishwasher, washing machine, and best of all perhaps a proper utility room stocked full with the latest machinery.

That was just the start. The whole place had been gutted,

improved and done over and brought up to the required domestic standards of the last two decades of the twentieth century.

Poyters had been totally overhauled and almost completely rebuilt to her specification and entirely to her satisfaction; complete with full-time gardener and live-in housekeeper-cook.

Then, when at last she could imagine she could settle into her "older middle age", as she put it, in a comfortable modern state-of-the-art country house estate, she discovered that Sidney had wasted nearly all the rest of her money on the horses. Sidney had got through nearly four million pounds at the stables, the gallops and the races.

Sidney loved horses. He loved their size and muscle. He loved their sleek smooth-haired lines. He loved their snorting, breathy and breathtaking, willingness to run. He loved their ground-eating galloping and ceaseless mad-dashing. He loved the reckless thunder of their hooves on the long turf of the home straight. He loved them so much he wanted to place a bet on every single one running in every single race meeting in the country. If he could.

Not just on betting either. Sidney owned horses too. He had a stable at Newmarket. He had two in Ireland. He had another in France. He dabbled with yet another in the USA. But just as with placing a bet, so with buying horses, Sidney had no nose for a winner. Characteristically Sidney never listened to advice. He paid for it, but he never listened to it. He knew best. Another of his defining characteristics was to never be swayed by evidence. He believed absolutely in his gut instinct. But owning horses that don't win is perhaps a quicker way of losing money than placing bets on them. Certainly if you own losers on the scale that Sidney Dudley did. The average cost of owning a race horse was around £20,000 a year. And Sidney owned a lot of horses. One count put the number at forty-nine horses in four countries. His gut instinct was funded by his wife.

The stables, the gallops and the races; and Sidney's gut instinct: that was where the rest of Bex's money went.

With her much reduced circumstances Bex might be

thought to have grown to dislike, blame, and even hate her husband. Perhaps even seek a divorce. But she didn't. Instead she began to harbour an intense jealousy and grudge and dislike of her cousin-once-removed, Dryden. It seemed he was the fortunate one. He was the undeserving one who still had all his own money, while she, the deserving one, had lost it all through no fault of her own. Dryden was too fortunate and not deserving of his good fortune at all.

She became envious of his control of the family firm, News World Publishers. While she had been given the cash and property by her dad's estate, and some shares, Tom's nephew Dryden had been given the largest portion of the shares in the firm by her father. A portion large enough to control the company.

Bex thought she should be the one with the "lioness's share of the shares" as she often said, picturing herself as a lioness born of a lion. She was after all Tom's daughter. Dryden was just Tom Telford Thompson's nephew. She was ten years older than Dryden too. Didn't that count for something in seniority? And who had heard of the gift of family shares missing a generation anyway? That just wasn't done.

Certainly a large portion of the original shares in the firm were already owned by Tom's brother William. But no one quite knew for a long time what William owned. Or even where he was.

That was because William had announced publicly in 1940 that he wanted nothing to do with his brother's company. In fact he wanted nothing to do with his brother at all.

The falling-out wasn't anything to do with the fact the two brothers were so completely different in their outlook. So much so that Tom was interested only in arts and literature; while William was fascinated by science and technology. It wasn't that, it was something more. But only they knew what it was.

Whatever the cause of the breach between them, the practical differences between the two brothers was still stark. While his brother forged the brilliant trajectory of a career in newspapers and publishing, William just took things apart. While Tom was ennobled to life peerage as Lord Ironbridge for services to journalism by a grateful nation in the shape of a slightly awed establishment, William was busy putting things back together.

A talented electrical engineer, William had invented an altimeter. Small, compact, accurate and lightweight, William Thompson's altimeter had been used in nearly all of the RAF's planes during the Second World War. His design had also been manufactured under licence in the USA and used in American planes throughout the conflict as part of the Lend-Lease deal between the two countries.

While the brothers were still close, before the war, Tom had expanded his news publishing empire into the further realms of the English-speaking world. He'd launched daily papers in Australia and Canada. Both became highly successful.

Then he looked at the American market. It was bigger and more difficult. It was also closed to outsiders. Much of the publishing industry in the USA at the time was a closed and exclusive cartel. The members closed ranks against the brash upstart from England.

Tom tried an oblique approach. He entered the American market on the coat-tails of his brother's engineering success. He bought a small but proficient electrical engineering company in Hartford, Connecticut. Then with William's agreement the firm became the American arm of William's precision instruments manufacturing company, Thompson Telemetry. One of the main products now manufactured there was William Thompson's altimeter.

Tom Telford Thompson went over to the USA for three years between early 1939 and America's entry into the war in late 1941, to run the company.

America's service industries might manage to close themselves to outside newcomers, but technical precision instruments were a different matter. The American branch of Thompson Telemetry was highly successful, built up on the strength of William's world-beating altimeter.

Then when his brother's precision instrument manufacturing company was well-established in the USA, not only on the domestic scene, but with substantial export earnings too, Tom turned again to his first love, publishing.

But instead of launching papers he launched a series of trade and technical magazines on the unsuspecting American market.

By 1942 there wasn't a trade, profession or industry in America which wasn't represented by a Tom Telford Thompson weekly magazine and several monthlies – all as market leaders.

By the end of the war the Thompson brothers were among the wealthiest men in Britain.

In fact, as the war economy required and valued technical invention and manufacturing talent much more than journalism, by 1945 William Thompson had a fortune as big if not bigger than his brother's.

But something happened between them, probably observers reckoned, sometime in 1940, while Tom was still in the USA running his brother's company there. Certainly by the end of that year the two brothers were entirely estranged and were no longer on speaking terms.

What had caused the rift was known only to them.

After the war William carried on with his successful business manufacturing precision instruments. Then in the early 1950s he suddenly retired. He retired early. He sold his business interests, including his own company Thompson Telemetry, and went to live in France. He more-or-less disappeared off the family map.

Disappeared off the family map so much that he didn't even emerge to attend Tom's funeral in 1970.

Disappeared off the family map so much that many people forgot he was still alive.

Disappeared off the family map, that is, until Bex's trusty solicitor tracked him down.

Bex remembered that William at some point had owned a large amount of shares in her father Tom's family firm. What had happened to them she wondered?

If there were enough of them, and if William was willing enough, they might be enough to give Bex control of the family firm.

She sent her solicitor to France to hunt him out and track him down.

It turned out William was willing enough. He didn't give Bex his shares. But he did give her proxy voting powers and power of attorney over them. A legal document proudly brought back from France by Bex's solicitor gave her the right to use the amount of William's shares as her own. In essence the document confirmed that William agreed that his number of shares would effectively be added to Bex's total for voting purposes at board meetings. She thought: at last that would give her control of the company.

It almost did.

When she and her solicitor went through all the numbers they were still a few millions short. Bex's total of shares, plus her power of attorney over William's shares, was still outweighed by the total possessed by her arch-enemy Dryden, his tart of a daughter Anna and his snotty son Sam.

Bex Dudley-Thompson wasn't someone who could be defeated or cast down for long. She wasn't Thomas Telford Thompson's daughter for nothing. She thought long and hard on the problem.

Bex then tried another tack. She took the long view.

Every year now she held a lavish garden party at Poyters to celebrate the anniversary of the completion of the now-grand country mansion's refurbishment. This time she took the unusual step of inviting the long-serving managing director of News World Publishers, Sandy Growler, and the long-serving editor of *Front Page* magazine, SA Moriarty, to the garden party. They and their wives were invited to stay on for the weekend. During that time Bex had long discussions with the two men in the now grand first-floor library and sounded them out on their reaction to her plans.

They were both very willing to fall in line with what she had in mind. That was because if Bex's plans came to pass, they would be two very wealthy men indeed.

Bex's scheme gathered pace. Her plot unfolded coil by coil.

At the subsequent board meeting she urged the merits and desserts of the two long-serving publishing men to the board. She recommended that both should be given shares in the family firm as a reward for their long, loyal and sterling service to the company.

Though an unprecedented step, since none outside the family had ever owned shares before, the board agreed. Dryden thought it was a good idea. It seemed the time was right to broaden the firm's foundations, to bring in new blood, and to make some kind of reward to the two men for their long, fruitful and faithful service.

So it was done. Sandy Growler and SA Moriarty were gifted substantial amounts of shares and became shareholders in the family firm.

But it had all been agreed between the two of them and Bex on a single understanding and a single proviso. A single secret proviso that had been hammered out between Bex, Sandy and Essay during that fateful weekend of the garden party at Poyters.

The proviso was that if they became shareholders the two newcomers to the board would always vote the same way as Bex.

Because Bex and her solicitor had calculated that with the new shares issued to the new members, if added to Bex's own and William's under Bex's proxy powers, then Bex could and would have control of the company.

And Bex wanted control of the company because she had worked out a way to make a huge amount of money.

She was going to take the family firm public.

She was going to launch the firm on the London Stock Exchange.

26. TIP

The Falklands war continued. The Harrier jet proved itself not to be outclassed by Argentina's French-made warplanes, the Mirage and the Super-Etendard. The Harrier showed itself to have outstanding manoeuvrability. If caught with an Argentine jet behind it, the Harrier could almost literally stop in the air, drop vertically, or instantly change direction. The chasing jet had no such ability and its pilot had no choice to speed past and overshoot the Harrier that was suddenly no longer in its sights.

The roles were then reversed: the hunter became the hunted.

The Harrier in pursuit of an Argentine jet could then unleash the deadly Sidewinder missile. For the Argentine jet there was no escape from the Sidewinder.

The Exocet unfortunately had also proved its worth. Two days after the sinking of the *Belgrano*, and the <<GOTCHA>> headline, Britain lost the first ship sunk by enemy action since the Second World War.

HMS *Sheffield* was hit, set aflame, and sunk by a single Exocet. The ship was stationed away and to the northwest of the Task Force in what was known as a picket line.

After the sinking of *Sheffield* there was great concern at Northwood, the British forces command centre just west of London, over whether Argentina would be able to source more Exocets. The war seemed to hang on the international market for Exocets.

It was a busy time in the offices of *Front Page*. Many of them said later it was the best time they'd ever had as journalists.

As one of the service wives said to Tintin as she did a series of interviews with and features on those left back home. "I never thought I'd see the day in my lifetime when Royal Navy ships left for war from the same harbour that Francis Drake went out to fight the Spanish Armada."

It made you think, Liz reflected, how warlike a country Britain was; and how many wars it had fought and been involved with in so many places so often for so many centuries. And how close to the surface, how lurking under the gloss of peaceful apparent normality, war could be for a country with that sort of history.

Would war always be with us? She asked herself. She sighed. She'd thought she knew the answer to that question. Now she wasn't so sure.

The phone on Cill Weaver's desk rang. For some weeks he'd been getting calls about the war. They came from all sorts of people; from his regular contacts, and from contacts of contacts. Sometimes they gave him information he could use in a story, and sometimes they didn't. Sometimes it seemed they just rang up for a chat.

But there was one caller in particular. He rang very occasionally. But when he did it was news gold dust. He didn't know the voice, it seemed disguised in a metallic and husky whispery sort of way. The person never gave their name, but it was the same voice every time.

The person had first contacted him with the story about the joint proving exercise in Canada between the British and French air forces to enable the British to understand and counteract the characteristics of the Exocet.

Now the metallic voice spoke softly in Weaver's ear. It told of the great ongoing fear at high level of the Exocet. It told how in response to the sinking of *Sheffield* the British and French secret services were cosying up to each other. There was an ongoing "op" the voice said, between the two secret services to prevent Argentina sourcing more missiles on the international market.

Weaver knew he couldn't use any of this stuff. He guessed his informant knew it couldn't be used during active reporting of the war. Was he then just giving Cill a head start on any better-informed analyses and retrospectives that would inevitably be written and published after the war was over? It seemed so.

His phone rang one more time before the end of the war with a call from this same strange informant with the military knowledge and the same quiet husky metallic voice.

This time the voice asked a question before supplying the

answer.

Had Mr Weaver thought, the voice asked, how Britain seemed to know with unfailing accuracy of the whereabouts of all the Argentine surface vessels and warships?

"How did the sub know where *Belgrano* was?" the metal voice whispered in Weaver's ear.

Weaver hadn't really noticed that, he admitted. Did we have satellites spying on the Argentine ships? he asked.

The voice told him Britain didn't have any satellites covering the South Atlantic.

That didn't particularly surprise Weaver. He wasn't up to speed on the positioning of British military satellites. But he took the metallic voice's word for it.

"Americans?" he said. They had to be giving Britain secret satellite info, surely?

"Them neither," the voice said. The voice pronounced it "neether".

If not the Americans, then who? It couldn't be down to luck. He waited on the phone, breathing quite heavily.

"Only the Soviets've got satellites covering the South Atlantic," the husky flat voice continued.

Weaver doubted the Russians would be giving any help to Britain. There was, after all, a Cold War going on above and beyond this little conflict in the South Atlantic.

"Somebody's listening in to the Soviet satellites," the voice said. "Somebody close."

"Who us?" Weaver asked, keen to know.

"Not us. Somebody's listening in to the Russians. And giving us the intel. Not us. Not the Yanks neither. A neighbour. An old friend." The line went dead.

Weaver was stunned. Strangely the information made him feel warm and hopeful. We did have friends after all. Friends keen to help in the conflict.

He thought about what he'd heard. The word neighbour played on his mind. Was it one of Britain's "neighbours" then who was listening to the Russian satellite signals? And passing the details to Britain? Which neighbour could it be? France was already helping with the "op" against the Exocet market. He doubted if France had any better satellite listening capability than Britain itself had. Germany then? Could be, he thought. For want of any further insight, he assumed for the time being that Germany was somehow helping out with information it had accessed behind the Soviet Union's back about Argentina's warship movements in the South Atlantic.

For a few days he felt he understood what his metallic advisor had been telling him. That Germany was listening in to the Russian satellite signals and passing the information to Britain, he now felt certain. Specifically it was details about Argentine ship positions and coordinates.

But then one afternoon as he looked out of the office window at a passing summer storm, he realised he might have been assuming the wrong thing about the word "neighbour" his informant had used.

He might have meant not a neighbour of Britain but a neighbour of Russia.

Cill didn't need to find an atlas to remind himself that the Soviet Union had many borders in common with other countries. It probably had more "neighbours" than any country in the world.

But for the purpose in hand you could cut out many of those "neighbours" for two reasons: one, they weren't necessarily friendly enough to Britain to supply this kind of secret information; and two, they weren't necessarily advanced enough to have sufficiently sophisticated listening and interception technology.

Thus Cill's thought process on the conundrum now made him lean towards Turkey and Scandinavia. Turkey was a fellow NATO country, true, and might be willing to help. But Weaver's instinct was looking towards Scandinavia.

He now felt certain that one of the Scandinavian countries was the one referred to as the "neighbour". A neighbour of the Soviet Union.

Suddenly he finally realised that only one of the four main

Scandinavian countries might simultaneously be considered a "neighbour" to Russia and "an old friend" to Britain.

That would be Norway.

He was convinced now that Norway had some sort of listening station close to the Soviet Union – they shared a common border way up in the Arctic, after all. Norway was intercepting signals from the Russian satellites over the South Atlantic and passing the information to Britain.

Knowing where the enemy's ships were enabled Britain to do two things: attack them or move away from them. Weaver was sure now Britain had been able to do both, aided by the Norwegians.

But as before, he could not act on any of this information. He couldn't write a story making claims based on the phone calls of his anonymous informant.

But he might have a head start over every other journalists, and even historians, when it came to writing about the war afterwards.

He started a new specific notebook. A notebook dedicated to the war and all the information supplied to him by his secret metallic husky-voiced informant. When it was all over he was going to write a book about the Falklands War.

He turned over in his mind what he'd just heard. You could disguise the giveaway sound of your natural voice – hence the constant metallic huskiness. But it was another thing altogether to disguise your dialect and your natural grammar. At first Weaver thought that might give him a better insight to the man's identity. Assuming it was a man of course, that machined metallic voice could be either sex. Assuming the voice was male, was he also a northerner? At one point he'd said "them neether." That felt northern, Cill thought. But the more he thought about it the more it sounded cod-northern, a deliberate northern-style usage, a Dick Van Dyke version of a cliché northerner.

Weaver decided in the end that the voice had just thrown the phrase in to stir the mystery pot a little more. He did it because he could: it didn't mean that was his natural dialect. Which put Weaver back to square one.

Cill wondered sometimes if the one-legged captain he'd met at the Grosvenor House dinner had anything to do with these metallic husky phone calls. He thought the way the voice had used the word "op" sounded very military. As did the way he referred to "Soviets" rather than Russians. And he was the only military man he'd given his card to in recent weeks. Come to think about it, the captain had never actually said what he did and where he worked. Could it really be him?

The messages passing secret information made Weaver feel right at the sharp end of his profession. He felt right in the centre of Edge City's news reporting.

But he never did find out who the voice was.

27. TIPP

They were upstairs at the Tipperary. The low round tables surrounded by stools in the bay window of the upstairs bar at the Tipp were occupied by journalists and reporters from *Front Page*.

Bill Roadhouse had asked Cill, Judy, Jerry and Liz to meet up after work for a drink in the Tipp. Tintin felt included in this inner circle for the first time. It was a mystery. Some of them assumed it was Bill's birthday, or he was going to announce his wedding to his girlfriend Esra.

Bill got the first round in.

"Well cheers Bill," Judy said as she took a sip of her pint. "What's this all about? Congratulations or commiserations?"

Bill took a drink of his own pint. There was an excited but strangely wary look in his eye.

"I think there's a plan to launch the firm on the Stock Exchange. To go public."

There was an immediate excited – or baffled depending on who you were – murmur round the low table.

Bill went on to explain what he'd found out.

When a family firm plans to launch on the Stock Market there's a lot of sorting out to do. A lot of organising, Bill said. It was a set process. You usually had to get a bank involved. And in fact that was the route through which Bill had had his suspicions confirmed. He'd tried many of his business contacts and friends in the City. But none of them knew anything. None could report any whispers of the kind Bill was looking for relating to *Front Page* and its parent firm News World Publishers, the Thompson family firm. Then he asked Esra for help.

She worked for the London branch of the American merchant bank Shanks Sisters. A bank famous – and unique - throughout the financial world for having been set up by two New York sisters. They'd established the bank straight after the end of the First World War. They'd been funded initially by their father, a steelmaker who made a colossal fortune as his steel came into huge demand for armaments during the USA's 1917-18 war.

But there was no question that the two sisters had what it took to compete and win in the hostile male world of start-ups and company finance in the boom time of the 1920s.

Their nous had enabled their bank to survive the Crash better than many of their rivals and they persevered and prospered into the mid-1930s and beyond. The new war and its aftermath saw them and many other US companies take the American way of business into the wider world.

By the time Esra Oz joined the bank in New York's Wall Street headquarters in 1980 the two Shanks girls, though still alive, had long since retired. But they had made Shanks Sisters into one of the most successful and respected merchant banks in the world.

In due course the high-flying Turkish-American requested a move to Shanks's expanding London branch. She explained she wanted for a time to be on the same continent as her family and ancestors. There she met a keen ambitious business journalist, Bill Roadhouse.

She had not yet decided whether she would ask Bill to accompany her back to America when the time came; or whether she would abandon her adopted homeland and stay in Europe with Bill.

Esra set about finding out what she could about Bill's search for any rumours of a big Stock Market launch by a longstanding very successful family firm with publishing interests.

Esra had not yet quite got used to the British idea of the business lunch. For her, the American business world revolved purely round results: it was what you did that mattered, not who you knew. But in England she discovered that while results were thought to be important, also deemed of equal or even more importance was how you got those results. And if you got them through team-building and contact-making, then so much the better. And one of the ways you did both of those in London was by means of the business lunch. This was a heavy alcohol-fuelled affair where one exchanged anecdotes, learnt a lot from and about your colleagues and rivals, and sometimes made good and lasting acquaintances. One thing she had learned though at these very challenging lunches was to keep off the alcohol and listen rather than talk. In this way she discovered many things, useful and less useful.

It turned out that Bill's hunch was right. At a lunch at Simpson's in the Strand with colleagues and contacts of colleagues Esra found the information Bill was searching for. It was no more than a hint, a whisper of certain goings-on. But it was enough.

A small exclusive private bank, with swish offices in the Strand, was rumoured to be advising a family firm with magazine interests in a prospective launch on the Stock Exchange. The bank was well known for handling aristocratic fortunes, old money, in a discreet and sensitive manner.

"Looks like they are getting used to handling new money now too," Esra said when she reported back to Bill.

Armed with the confirmation of his original insight, now Bill thought he needed to widen the circle of knowledge and bring some of his closest work colleagues into the loop. They all needed to know what was going on behind their backs. They needed to know what it all implied for their jobs and the future of the firm they worked for. And perhaps, if they didn't like it, they all needed to talk about whether there was any way they could do anything about it.

There was a group of shocked faces round the low table as Bill made his announcement. They all looked at each other. They all in their own way each wondered what it really meant.

"Is launching on the Stock Market a good thing or a bad thing?" Judy asked.

"Good for some. Very good," Bill said. "Especially if you've got shares in the family firm."

"But how much practical difference does it make to the operation of the firm or to *Front Page* for that matter?" Jerry said.

"Well, a lot or nothing at all Jerry. I don't think it's about that. It's not about benefitting the magazine or even the firm. This is all about making a few people very very wealthy. They don't care about the magazine. They just care about themselves."

Bill sighed. Then carried on.

"Sooner or later all companies will shit on their employees, us, in the end. Usually from a very low height. They trip you up. Spit you out. Trample you down in the mud. Leave you for dead and move on; stepping over your body on the way."

Seeing the business editor so despondent really brought the seriousness of the situation home to the journalists round the table.

"If we were public, what sort of difference would that make to us?" Judy asked with a quiet voice.

"Actually I think it would mean the end of *Front Page* as we know it." That sounded very dramatic, and Bill could see some frowns. He carried on.

"It means we'd be exposed to the real world," Bill said. "For fifty years we've been protected. Our strength is our independence. We have credibility precisely because we're not part of a publishing empire. No one could buy us. No one could take us over. No big conglomerate could tell us what to do. We've had no party line to follow, no instructions from on high about what we can say and what we can't. No vested company interests we can't afford to offend. No leaders we must write supporting some company agenda or any editorial copy having to tow the party line. No big boss down the phone telling the editor what to do or say. And no corporate ads we're obliged to take; nor corporate advertorials masquerading as journalism. And at the end of the day none of our rivals could buy us out just to close us down," he held up a hand "And that's happened before, believe me."

"We've been free?" Cill asked

"It's quite likely we'd get taken over pretty quickly," Bill carried on, warming to his theme. "There's nothing companies like better than clearing out the competition by buying them out rather than compete with them on the open market. And yes, Cill, we've been free. As a limited company all that independence goes up in smoke. Up to now the only control over us has been the Thompson family. And they had no interests in the magazine

179

or what it said. As long as we made a fat profit and they all got their big packet dividend in their pocket every year they were happy. And so were we. All that will change."

"And if we're public all that goes out of the window?" Judy literally looked out of the Tipp's leaded light upstairs window down to the street below as she spoke.

"Yes."

"How do you know about this, Bill?" Tintin asked. "What made you suspicious?"

"It started with a misdirected fax that Eddie and I saw a week back," Bill said. "That's what started it all." He related how it referred to SA Moriarty being given "another million shares".

Bill told how on their own and in the family firm these shares were totally worthless.

"But when you launch on the Stock Exchange, those shares become the shares of the publicly listed company. And it often goes like this: at launch each one of those shares could be valued at least £1 each."

Judy and Jerry both whistled simultaneously. They could see where this was going.

"And our revered boss SA Moriarty possesses at least two million of them, that we know of from that misdirected fax. So on the day the firm goes public, his shares are instantly worth a total of two million pounds!"

"Jesus Christ," Cill said. "The wanker doesn't deserve it."

"That's not as bad as it could get. On launch it could be that each share is worth £10. That's very common. That would give our esteemed boss twenty million quid. And I doubt if the eminence grise *gran queso* Growler's got fewer shares than Moriarty. And I guess the family members will have a lot more shares. Which will be worth a lot more than Moriarty and Growler's," Bill finished. "The numbers will be huge."

Judy was appalled at her undeserving, incompetent and non-journalist boss possibly pocketing as much as twenty million quid.

"Talk about scum rising to the top," she murmured.

"Scum who just happens to be in the right place at the right time," Cill said and shrugged.

"But wrong person," Tintin said. All her fierce deep-felt instinct that only those properly worthy should be rewarded was surging back. It really was unjust.

"But Bill," Jerry said. "They'll only be worth these colossal numbers if they actually sell their shares, surely?"

"Very true," Bill replied. "But there's usually very strong demand for shares in new market launches right at the start. Because the launch price is basically a guess, there's always the assumption that the shares are undervalued and are bound for a while to go up, independent of the overall state of the market. They go like hot cakes, new potatoes and hot-cross buns. Some analysts and market-watchers make a living purely out of monitoring and dipping into new launches."

"Come on Jerry," Judy said." Can you imagine that Skippy and Growler will hesitate for one second to cash in when there's an absolute fortune to be made? It'll be take the money and run. They don't give a shit about the magazine."

That seemed very likely to be the case to everyone round the table.

Finally, as they finished their drinks it was agreed that those present should widen the knowledge loop and pass the information on to all the rest of the staffers. There was no way they were going to let Sandy Growler and Skippy Moriarty continue to keep this secret. Everyone would know. After all, it affected them all.

"But why would the family bother?" Cill said to Bill as they broke up to go their separate ways home. "Why go public now and upset an applecart that's been a nice little earner for the Thompson family for fifty years? Why now? What's changed?"

"I think you need to talk to your girlfriend Cill," Bill said.

"After all, she is in the family way," Judy said.

They all laughed at the pun, Cill included.

Cill thought he now knew Anna well enough to bring all this up. She even might want to talk about it. If she could and

181

wasn't sworn to secrecy in some way.

Bill carried on: "I think there must have been a big change within the power structure of the family. Something's happened there."

28. GOTCHA

It turned out Cill didn't have to worry about broaching the subject of what was going on with her family firm to Anna. She was keen to talk to him about it. She was plainly concerned.

They went for an early dinner then went to see *Bladerunner*.

As they came out of the Cambridge Circus cinema Cill told Anna that he was really pleased he was going out with a woman who looked exactly like the "replicant" Rachael that went off with Harrison Ford at the end.

"The same height; the same dark eyes, the same legs like Pompey's Pillar!"

She smiled. She would settle any time for being thought as good looking as Rachael. Though she did think she needed to know a bit more about what Pompey's Pillar was when it was at home before she liked that description of her legs too.

Afterwards they went back to Anna's flat in Greenwich together.

They caught the stopping train from Charing Cross to Greenwich.

Anna had been silent for some time. They'd chatted about the film. But then Anna fell silent. There was something on her mind, Cill knew. Suddenly she spoke again.

"Cill I have to talk to you about something. It's urgent," she said. They were walking close together, hand in hand up Croom's Hill towards Anna's flat close to the Maritime Museum.

For a moment Cill was slightly panicky. That sounded a bit like the start of a conversation he and Sarah should have had before they broke up.

"It's about the family firm," she hesitated. "Trouble is I'm not sure I'm even allowed to talk about it," she stopped again. "Oh bugger it," she said. She'd been bottling it up for over two weeks and it was finally going to come out.

She stopped and turned to face him full on, reaching out and taking both his hands in hers.

"My side of the family has lost control of the board and

there are big changes going to happen." She sighed with relief as though a weight had just come off her shoulders.

"There I've said it," she smiled at him. "I feel like I've crossed a line in the sand."

"I think I know," Cill said gently.

She stopped, pulling his hands. She looked at him.

He looked away then turned fully towards her again.

"The Thompson family is going public with the family firm. You. They. Are launching News World Publishers on the Stock Exchange."

She looked astonished.

"How do you know that?"

He told her as they carried on walking.

"Just a misdirected fax. Amazing. Bill's nice," she said. "And bloody clever. Esra too. But it's true. It's going to happen. But we don't want to do it all. But we don't have any choice. We've been outvoted."

She told the story of the fateful board meeting.

On the same day the <<GOTCHA>> headline had appeared in *The Sun*, Bex Dudley-Thompson had given the Thompson family board meeting its own <<GOTCHA>> moment.

The board meeting was held at Dryden's house in East Sussex. They'd been held there since Dryden had become chairman of the board on the death of Tom Telford Thompson in 1970.

Dryden Thompson owned a very impressive seven-bedroom country mansion. It had been designed by Edwin Lutyens in 1921 for an aeroplane entrepreneur and manufacturer, keen to live in the country but within close striking distance of London by road and rail. Dryden had bought it in the 1960s. Like many of Lutyens's fine country houses, Dryden's house looked like it was somehow meant to be there. Almost as though it had grown there, emerged from the ground fully formed as a natural effulgence, rather than been constructed. The deep russet brickwork seemed to tie the house solidly into the landscape.

Present round the long table in the study were all the current shareholders bar one: Dryden Thompson; Anna Thompson;

Bex Dudley-Thompson; Sidney Dudley-Thompson; SA Moriarty; and Sandy Growler. Missing was Sam Thompson, but his shares would be added to Dryden's in a vote either by a proxy arrangement or through an ongoing power of attorney.

Bex chose her moment with maximum psychological devastation.

She'd left it until the Any Other Business items came up right at the end of the board meeting.

Board chairman Dryden Thompson looked round the table. Did anyone have any further items?

Opposite him, at the far end of the table Bex raised her hand.

"Yes Bex."

"I want to table a motion. I think it's time to take the firm public. We should launch it on the Stock Exchange."

If a nuclear explosion could be confined in a single room the effect would be similar.

In the aftermath, like after a nuclear explosion, there was total silence.

Bex was staring with a grim determination at Dryden. He could see she was deadly serious.

The debate started.

The two newcomers to the board, SA Moriarty and Sandy Growler added little to the debate. They both said they would be happy to follow the majority.

Bex knew they were being a little disingenuous. Only with their votes would she be in the majority. But she knew she could bank on them. That was the deal.

Dryden thought the whole thing was absurd. The family firm had been operating for fifty years. No one in all that time had ever imagined going public was the right way forward for one of the country's leading news outlets and current affairs opinion-formers. Just as Bill Roadhouse had told the shocked audience in the Tipperary, Dryden knew that going public would spell the end of the independence of *Front Page* for good. He'd always kept his distance from the title – he'd learnt that from his mentor and uncle Tom Telford Thompson.

"Own it: don't moan it," Tom TT had said to Dryden when he gave him the bulk of the shares. "Make money out of it, but leave the title alone. Keep your distance. Let it be. No input. Keep well away."

Dryden had followed that advice to the letter. But he did value the high and wide respect that owning the title gave him.

Going public wasn't going to happen on his watch as chairman and majority shareholder.

Anna was present. She always said very little at these meetings. In a way she felt slightly out of her depth, and was content to follow the lead of her father. She knew that Dryden had proxy voting and power of attorney over her brother Sam's shares, and they would always be added to Dryden's count when it came to voting. She too always voted the same way as her father. That was what gave them a constant majority.

In the end Bex forced a vote. Two votes in fact.

The first vote was on whether News World Publishers should initiate the process of becoming a public limited company listed on the London Stock Exchange.

And it was then that Dryden realised for the first time the strength and depth of Bex's plan.

Dryden, plus Sam by proxy, and Anna voted against the motion to go public.

Bex voted in favour of the motion.

Sidney Dudley, "Silent Sid" as Dryden always thought of him, voted with Bex, as he always did.

Both the newcomers voted with Bex.

That wasn't necessarily a problem for Dryden, though it was a surprise and he did feel and smell the first inklings of a rat. But while there might be some kind of rat involved, possible collusion of some kind between Bex and the two newcomers, he wasn't unduly worried. He and his side of the family still had more shares than all of the others in the room put together.

That was when Bex produced the hammer blow.

Her <<GOTCHA>> moment.

Just as Dryden was about to pronounce the failure and outvoting of her motion, she delved down the side of her chair and brought out a document from her slim elegant Italian-made white leather briefcase. Smoothly she laid it on the table face down and slid it to her right to be passed on to Dryden.

When it reached him he turned it over.

Dryden Thompson experienced his second metaphoric nuclear explosion of the day.

It was a legal document, witnessed and dated by a solicitor, signed by William Thompson giving both proxy voting rights and power of attorney over his shares at board meetings of the family firm to Bex Dudley-Thompson.

Effectively Dryden's own father was voting against him.

Dryden, Anna and Sam were now outvoted.

The motion was passed.

News World Publishers would begin the process of seeking a listing as a public limited company on the London Stock Exchange at the first opportunity.

Dryden, Anna and the absent Sam lost the second vote too.

That was on a motion proposed by Bex that the board had lost confidence in Dryden Thompson as chairman. He would be replaced by another nominee.

The motion was carried.

Bex Dudley-Thompson was voted in as chairperson of the board of News World Publishers.

Anna was crying when she finished telling Cill all about the dramatic events of the board meeting at her father's house.

He put his arms round her and comforted her.

"My granddad. My granddad did it. My granddad has destroyed *Front Page*," she sobbed, heartbroken and embarrassed.

29. TAKE & STAY

Whether SA Moriarty would admit he was one to take the money and run, was a different issue. No way, in fact. Even if the magazine was to be published by a public limited company, he still saw himself as editor.

Why not?

Even though he would be unbelievably wealthy, that was no reason to give up editing *Front Page*.

If things went well, he would take the money, but he wouldn't run.

He would take the money and stay.

He would carry on as if nothing had happened. And he'd keep angling for that OBE. And in due course a knighthood. And who knew, a life peerage as well.

Why not? It had happened to editors before.

He thought back on the drama of ninety minutes ago.

Old Bex had really put the boot in to Dryden. He never saw it coming.

Moriarty and Growler were rendezvousing in a pub car park, the Bell at Outwood, not far from Gatwick Airport, and not far from Dryden's country house.

Dryden's place was a fantastic spot, Essay had to admit. But did Dryden really realise when he bought the rambling russet Lutyens–designed mansion place in the mid-1960s, did it up, and installed himself and his daughter and son in it, just how busy Gatwick would become, and just how noisy?

Not just noisy planes either. They were full of the kind of noisy people Dryden would run a mile from if he met them, Essay was sure: cheapskate families and their cheapskate charter flights and their cheapskate holidays?

Moriarty and Growler arranged to meet in the Bell after the board meetings they were now fully-fledged members of. As newcomers they felt they needed to compare notes on what they'd witnessed and how it had gone. Especially to what extent it affected them. While Dryden was chairman of the board the meetings had always been held at his house. That's one thing that will change immediately, Essay considered. The next meeting's going to be at Poyters.

The first thing Essay Moriarty wondered about when he was first invited down to Dryden's place in Sussex for board meetings was where was Mrs Thompson?

Mrs Dryden Thompson?

Moriarty thought of her in those exclusively male-oriented possessive terms. He got a kind of thrill out of thinking of the absent woman as being purely identifiable by means of her husband's name. It was so old-fashioned and out of keeping with the time as to be totally glorious, he thought to himself. I must resurrect that form of address in *Front Page*, and have it added to the House Style.

But then he held an imaginary conversation with Eddie Osmoe, with Eddie refusing pointblank to make the necessary change to the Style.

He'd have to do something about Eddie. He really would. It was about time. His constant dissent could no longer be tolerated.

Sandy Growler's S-Type Jaguar slid into the parking spot adjacent to Moriarty's BMW. Growler gave an old-fashioned foot-tap on the accelerator as he simultaneously switched off the engine.

Clown, Moriarty thought. He's going to bang the side of my car with his door when he gets out. Why didn't he park further away? In the next-but-one space, say? There's plenty of room.

There was no love lost between editor and managing director.

The only thing currently uniting them was the prospect of making serious amounts of money through no efforts of their own.

The hierarchy of News World Publishers was similar to many medium-sized companies.

Essay Moriarty ran the editorial side of *Front Page* magazine. On equal footing and standing to him was Don Phurse, the advertising manager who was responsible for the advertising content of the magazine.

Next above Moriarty and Phurse was Rod Crowcroft, who was publisher. That meant effectively that Crowcroft was boss of *Front Page* magazine. Sure, SA Moriarty was the public face of the magazine, and as editor was thought of widely as being the boss of *Front Page*. But in most publishing companies there is always a hidden anonymous boss, the money man, above the public boss, and that's the publisher. And at *Front Page* the publisher was Rod Crowcroft.

Crowcroft was an accountant. He saw his job of publisher as maximising the profit made by *Front Page*. As long as there was a profit he left Moriarty and Phurse completely alone to run and operate their respective sides of the cash-cow that was *Front Page* as they wished.

But though Crowcroft was publisher, he wasn't the boss of the whole publishing company. There was someone else above him.

Above Crowcroft was Sandy Growler, who was managing director of News World Publishers.

At the top and pinnacle of the management tree at News World Publishers was Sandy Growler. Sandy Growler was the Thompson family's man. He had been appointed to the firm by the family and answered for the firm to the family.

News World Publishers' MD Sandy Growler was an amoral adventurer, a chancer completely lacking in any kind of scruple. As Dryden Thompson often said of Sandy: "Like many such amoral opportunists who feel the normal civilised notions of right and wrong don't apply to them, he is a product of Harrow School." An old boy of Harrow and an alumnus of a cavalry regiment, he was a friend and racing habitué of Sidney Dudley.

"Silent Sid and Sandy – a right pair of talentless undeserving ne'er-do-wells," Dryden once confided over dinner to daughter Anna and wife Stella. "That ironically through no efforts of their own seem to have done very well."

How on earth then could a man of such dubious character

be appointed by the Thompson family to run their family firm?

It was Bex of course who recommended Sandy Growler for the job of running News World Publishers.

Dryden's first instinct was to veto the appointment. But he spent the night thinking on it. And in the morning had come to a different conclusion. Better he thought a completely predictable amoral adventurer running the firm than anyone with talent or his own agenda or ideas or vision.

With TTT's nostrum of "own it, don't moan it" at the forefront of his mind, Dryden undertook a long interview with Sandy Growler. As a result of that interview Dryden had no hesitation in agreeing with Bex that Sandy should be appointed managing director of News World Publishers.

That was because Sandy had no ideas. He had no agenda of his own. He had no vision of where *Front Page* should aim or how it should operate other than what it was already doing. And above all he had no intention of ever doing anything different with the firm, and especially with *Front Page* magazine, other than follow the board's recommendations. For Sandy Growler maintaining the status quo of his own position was all that mattered. He would be the family's cipher. And Dryden was happy with that. As was Growler.

Sandy emerged from his S-Type without banging the side of Moriarty's BMW. Moriarty congratulated him acidly under his breath, then clapped him on the shoulder in a gesture of bonhomie, solidarity and fellowship.

Then Moriarty, the Glasgow street urchin on the make and Growler the Harrow and cavalry chancer, sauntered into the pub together and celebrated their good fortune with a pleasant late lunch by the log fire, lubricated by a fine bottle of Montrachet.

30. FALL OUT

"Tell me about your granddad," Cill said.

They were in her flat, sitting on stools at the bar in the kitchen. The flat took up the entire top floor of a four-storey house. It overlooked, and had a view of, Greenwich Park through the bordering trees.

Somewhere a few yards away, Cill knew, was the Greenwich Meridian. The ultimate line in the sand.

Apart from an occasional breathy huff, Anna had stopped crying. She made coffee for them and they sat side by side.

Anna told Cill more details about the fateful board meeting.

She told him also something of her grandfather.

"My father and grandfather don't communicate much, if at all."

The falling-out wasn't as bad as that between her grandfather and her great-uncle. But it probably derived from the same source.

"Who does the family think was at fault?" Cill carried on when Anna looked like she didn't get what he was talking about. "I mean your granddad manages to fall out with two generations: his brother and his own son. He looks like the common denominator?"

"We never thought of it like that. We just accepted the fact that it all began years ago, before I was born, at the start of the Second World War."

"Everything seems to go back to that. But what happened with your dad? That's after the war?"

"According to my father my granddad wasn't happy at all with dad when he went to work for TT's company. He thought he should have nothing to do with it. He thought it was bad enough when my dad didn't want to be a scientist nor join his firm. Instead he wanted to be a journalist. Then his son joining brother Tom's firm felt like the final betrayal."

Over the years Dryden Thompson became much closer to

his uncle than he was to his father. Dryden became not just TT's business heir, but his family heir as well.

"I saw much more of my great uncle as a child than I did of my grandfather," Anna said, holding her coffee cup with two hands and looking into the swirling surface.

"After he moved to France I only saw him a few times. One Christmas. An anniversary or two. I think he was a mental recluse long before he became a physical recluse in France. I always liked him. There was something kindly but sad about him."

They talked for a while about the consequences of going public for the family firm.

They agreed there seemed to be two issues. There was the potential to create a lot of wealth for the shareholders. And there would probably be implications for the independence of *Front Page*.

Anna said she now realised why her aunt had persuaded the board to accept the two new members from the firm. It was all her aunt's long-term plan to get control of the company.

"She probably thought that would be enough to give her control."

"But then discovered she still needed your granddad's proxy as well?"

"Yes."

"But why was she so keen? You're a pretty wealthy family as it is?"

"She's not. As far as we know anyway."

Anna told Cill about the massive refurbishment of Poyters. There were also strong rumours within the family that her husband Sidney was a wastrel of the first order.

"My dad always calls him Silent Sid. He never says a word. Dad thinks Sidney has blown huge amounts of my aunt's money. He's horse mad."

"So the first thing she'll do when we launch on the Stock Market is sell her shares?"

"Her and him both. Yes. But I won't sell mine. And my dad won't either."

"But you're no longer in the majority are you?" Cill couldn't imagine Sandy Growler or SA Moriarty would hang on to their shares just so control of the company would stay in the family.

Anna was still very much upset. When they went to bed they didn't make love immediately. Cill held her and stroked her gently. Her breathing slowed right down and gradually, in her own time, she became aroused. She moaned slightly and opened her legs, wanting to be touched. Later, she cried again.

During the night Anna woke up. She saw Cill standing naked at the window looking out over Greenwich Park and the Maritime Museum. There was a faint red line in the sky to the east.

"Do you think William knew? Did it occur to him do you think, what Bex would do with his vote, his shares, once she had control of them?" He spoke over his shoulder as he heard her stirring.

"I doubt it very much."

"What would happen, do you think, if he found out?"

Anna was silent, thinking about it.

"It's too late now," she said.

"Is it?" Cill said. "What happened if someone told him?"

Anna looked as if she was about to make a retort about how you couldn't put the clock back. What was done was done. You had to accept that things happened you might not like. It was the way of the world. You had to accept that and move on. But subtly her face changed. A new light appeared in her eye.

"I think we have to find my granddad," Anna said. "You and me."

31. GUNÉ

On the same day that British troops broke out of their bridgehead in San Carlos Water, and the ground war phase of the Falklands conflict began, and a new word entered the mainstream of the English language, Judy Bodkin assembled a team of raiders, *exploratores* and special forces to visit El Vino.

After landing in San Carlos Water the British forces' next objective, attacking Port Stanley, was complicated by the fact that all the Chinooks – the heavy-lifting helicopters – had been aboard the supply ship *Atlantic Conveyor* when it was hit by an Exocet and sunk a few days before.

That meant British soldiers now had to walk from their landing grounds at San Carlos to invest Port Stanley, the Falklands Islands capital town, carrying all their equipment.

It was fifty miles. There were no roads. And they were carrying an average of eighty pounds a man.

In the army this sort of mulish hellish walking under maximum load over rough terrain was called "yomping".

British forces yomped to Port Stanley and the end of the Falklands War began.

"How about us all yomping to El Vino this lunchtime? I've never been." Judy was standing by the news desks.

"You realise you can't stand at the bar. And you won't get served directly?" Jerry said. "You'll have to sit at a table and get the men you're with to order for you at the bar."

"Yes. I get it. That's the point isn't it? No women. I just wanted to experience how bad it is. How about you Tintin?"

Liz wasn't sure she wanted to go anywhere near a place that was famous for not serving women. But then again, and this was a relatively new feeling for Liz, how could you have an opinion on something unless you tried it for yourself? Liz felt she needed to put her toe in the water on this one.

"I'd like to see what it's like," she said. "I guess," she added doubtfully.

"Anna was talking about this the other day," Cill said. "She said there's a case going through the courts now, a test case of some kind under the Sex Discrimination Act. I could ask her to meet us there. If she deigns to go."

"Well, I guess if the courts are going to ban it, I guess we should all experience it in all its awfulness now," Jerry agreed. "While we can."

"We better go then while it's still unchanged. Then we'll be able to tell our grand-daughters there was once a place in the centre of one of the most advanced and most civilised cities on the planet where they couldn't get served. They won't believe it." Judy said.

"Better not ask Cuddles to join us," Jerry said. "He probably thinks we're not going to such a grand old Fleet Street institution with the right attitude."

El Vino wine bar was a Fleet Street institution, that was true, Jerry thought, or that is to say, had been true. But if so, it was an institution out of place in a Fleet Street that was changing fast.

It wasn't just the new technologies that were coming in, new ways of setting type, that were changing Fleet Street; it was the change in people too that made El Vino now look like a watering hole on a road to nowhere.

The traditional ways of becoming a journalist on Fleet Street too had changed. In the old days you left school at 15 and 16 and went to work on a local paper. And you were most probably male. And you learnt on the job. It was a kind of apprenticeship. You learnt by watching and listening to the old hacks. You learnt how to get your foot in the door and never take no for an answer. You learnt how to get people to relax on the phone and say things they never intended to say. You learnt the best way of slipping a source a fiver over a pint in a local pub. You learnt how to pressurise your first corroborating source for a story by exaggerating a little what exactly your second corroborating source had said. And above all you learnt that being a journalist was nothing to do with writing. It was much more to do with getting the story. And it was entirely to do with getting the story first.

And when you'd learnt your trade thoroughly in Darlington or Warrington or Torbay or Brighton you looked at the job ads in *The Guardian* on Mondays, or the *UK Press Gazette* when it came out on Thursdays, and applied for a job in Fleet Street. The place where all the national daily and Sunday papers had their printing works and offices.

Fleet Street's people and printing, Jerry thought, types and type: both were changing. There was a revolution under way, and it was gathering pace.

On *Front Page* now, Jerry knew, of the journalist staff only Eddie Osmoe and Cuddles weren't graduates. And Moriarty, of course. Yet only ten years before the ratio would have been completely reversed. Perhaps even five years before.

Printing had been going on in Fleet Street for nearly five hundred years. It was the street where printing had been taking place since 1500 when William Caxton's co-worker and colleague the fabulously-named Dutchman Wynkyn de Worde first arrived there. He moved Caxton's press there in 1500 after the master's death.

Printing had first come to England in 1476. Invited by the exiled king Edward IV to come to England if he should win his throne back, Caxton had accepted the offer of royal patronage and set up the first printing press in England at Westminster.

At a low point in the revolving-door-of-a-war between York and Lancaster, Edward and younger brother Richard of Gloucester had fled England to find sanctuary with their sister Margaret in Burgundy. Margaret's husband Duke of Burgundy Charles the Bold (or the Rash, depending on the translation and depending on how you saw his disastrous attempt to conquer Switzerland), lord of the Low Countries, was the wealthiest monarch in Europe.

Richard Neville, earl of Warwick, the Kingmaker, chief backer and promoter of the Yorkist cause, the man who had first planted Edward on the throne, had changed sides. He'd hauled the hapless hopeless hype-less Henry VI out of the Tower after ten years and thrust him back on the throne. Outmanoeuvred,

Edward and Richard fled to the safety of their sister's court in the Burgundian possession of the Low Countries.

There in the merchant town of Bruges they met William Caxton, head of the community of English merchants in Bruges. He demonstrated his printing press to the ex-king and his younger brother.

Impressed, Edward told Caxton there would be an offer to come and set up a press in England, should he win back his crown from the Kingmaker.

He did and there was.

And so in 1476 Caxton set off for London and installed himself in Westminster with the first printing press in England.

After Caxton died Wynkyn de Worde moved the press to Fleet Street. The street had been the home and hub of printing in England ever since.

Wynkyn de Worde is often thought of as Caxton's assistant, as well as printing heir; but he may have been much more than an assistant, perhaps a partner of Caxton's capable of providing the necessary professional expertise as Caxton tried to see off the new challenge and competition presented by the second printing press established in England, that of the mysterious John of Lithuania, in 1480.

Strange and interesting, Jerry thought, that two out of the first three printers in England didn't have English as their first language.

For five hundred years very little changed in the printing industry. The big hot-metal machines became bigger and more complex and more efficient and were increasingly operated by fewer and fewer men. But Gutenberg and Caxton and De Worde and Lithuanian John would still have recognised the methodology involved in printing a broadsheet in 1980 as they would have done a book of knightly manners or courtly love in 1480.

But slowly the technology began to change. New optical methods of typesetting came in. Before the digital age, before computers, printing was searching like a blind planarian worm for a computerised printing model. Computerised printing would come; but not yet.

And as new ways of printing and setting type emerged in the 1970s and after, so did new ways of becoming a journalist.

Until very recently most of the reporters and journalists working on the national papers and magazines headquartered in Fleet Street had started out as 16-year-old school leavers.

But then along with the incipient new technology, the breeze of change affected the personnel too. The latest generations of reporters and journalists were almost invariably university graduates.

And that inevitably meant there were now many more women among them than there had been traditionally.

By the early 1980s to be a journalist meant to be a graduate. And as often as not with accelerating percentages it meant to be a woman as well.

In the light of these changes, this evolution of journalism from trade to profession, from male to female, the lunch at El Vino became something of a raid into enemy territory.

There were six of them in the party. Jerry, Rex, Cill, Judy, Liz and Cathy. Plus a seventh, Anna Thompson, who would join them if she could, if her court schedule allowed. It was a Wednesday, the day after press day, so more people felt they could take a lengthy lunch than was possible on the other days of the week.

For Cathy who had brought one of her cameras along there was no such thing as a social occasion. Everything she did had the potential to be snapped.

El Vino was towards the west end of Fleet Street, in the direction of the law courts and the Strand. It tended to be filled with as many lawyers as journalists on any given day.

The *Front Page* team strolled down the street and entered El Vino. It was surprisingly quiet and they took a table towards the side of the main room. A well-known columnist from *The Sun* was at his customary place on a barstool at the bar. He was chatting to the group surrounding him. Jerry recognised a couple of reporters from the news desk of the *Evening Standard*. Another group at the far end of the bar identified themselves as barristers by their black jackets, striped trousers and white ties. Everyone in the two main groups at the bar was male.

They examined the drinks menu. They decided on a bottle of white from Burgundy. It had to be Burgundian wine, Jerry thought, to show solidarity with Caxton. Jerry and Rex took the order and went to the bar to get it. One good thing about El Vino that nobody questioned was you could get a very good quality wine there at a very reasonable price. They came back with a bottle of white wine and six glasses.

"Cheers," Judy said, holding up her glass. "Here's to the end of a male-dominated world."

They all drank to that.

Except as soon as they'd taken the toast Rex said: "I have to confess I did add a mental "depends on the context" to that."

They all laughed.

"And I'm not sure it's the kind of toast they'd be having in San Carlos Water right now," Rex added.

"Women soldiers will happen," Liz said. That was something else she'd learned from talking to those left behind by the soldiers, sailors and airmen sent to war. Not everyone female was against war.

To her slight mystification Liz was discovering that she'd become a lot more flexible in her thinking than she ever thought she was.

Which was worse? she thought, war or the fact that women weren't allowed to take part in it?

She'd realised only recently, talking to women during this current conflict, that the worse of the two concepts was that women weren't allowed to fight.

War might be bad; but worse was stopping women doing it if they wanted to.

This new realisation benefitted her work too. For the first time in her career she was describing the world as it was rather than as she wanted it to be. She had become a reporter.

Cill thought she was right. Women on the front line would come. There was nothing really to stop it if you thought about it. But it would probably be a while yet before it happened. Changing the way things were done always took time. Generations sometimes. Take this place for example, he thought, looking round the bar. But one thing was certain: nothing stayed the same forever. In the short run, of course, things actually became entrenched, took on a siege mentality, more set in their ways, as the forces of stasis and conservatism dug in and prepared for battle. But change always won in the end.

Yet also in a strange way change didn't really change anything, he thought. Because afterwards you often looked back and wondered what all the fuss had been about.

Anna found their table.

"I won't ask you what you're drinking," she said with a smile. "Because it won't get me anywhere. But can one of you men go and get me a glass so I can join you?" She placed a five pound note on the table. "Better get another bottle too."

Cill did as he was bid.

When he returned to the table with Anna's wine glass and a second bottle, she was telling the group about the ongoing case to get El Vino to mend its ways towards women.

"The case comes up before the Court of Appeal later this year – in the autumn. The two women, a reporter and a lawyer, who tried to get served at the bar here and were kicked out, who then took El Vino to court for discrimination, lost in the first instance. But Gonner Rear reckons they'll win on appeal. He reckons if they shift their tactics from one based on the Sex Discrimination Act to one based on restraint of trade. He thinks that'll work. I do too."

"How do you mean "restraint of trade"?" Cathy asked.

"Well if this place really is, as it claims to be, the centre of gossip in Fleet Street, then women are missing out on that if they're not allowed to stand at the bar," Anna said. "If only men are allowed to stand at the bar and there's a lot of work-related gossip going on there, it means women are excluded from benefitting from that gossip in their profession, trade or job"

"And that counts as restraint of trade?"

"Exactly. It's enough. Gonner Rear thinks that has a better chance of success than any appeal based on the Sex Discrimination Act. The act's quite complicated and not as straightforward as it should be."

"Is Gonner Rear involved in the case?" Jerry asked.

"No, but everyone's interested," Anna said. "Everyone's taking a view."

"You usually find with these things that the people doing it always claim it's for "women's protection"," Rex said. "Like they're doing you a favour." He gestured to include the four women in his comment. "Like somehow you're benefitting from being excluded. Bizarre."

"It's awful," Liz said. "But I'm glad we came."

"Shows you how far we've come. But also how far we still have to go?" Judy said.

"Yes."

Just then there was a disturbance at the bar. Some shouting and jostling.

They all looked across to see what was going on.

At first glance it looked like a group of four women had entered the wine bar, were stood at the bar and were demanding to be served. Quite right too, Liz thought. She wished she'd had the nerve to do the same thing.

On closer inspection they could see that wasn't quite right.

The four newcomers at the bar were men dressed as women.

As soon as he took it in, Cill nearly pissed himself laughing. And the four women at the table raised their glasses in a mock toast towards the bar and cheered.

Three of the four men dressed in women's clothes were quite young; the fourth was a bit older. They were all wearing dresses, wigs, stockings and high-heeled shoes. One even had evening gloves up to the elbow. Another had a large string of pearls round his neck which he kept swinging with one hand in a swirling arc in front of him like a propeller.

They looked surprisingly good, Jerry thought: much better than a pantomime dame convention. Apart from the older man, that is. He wasn't wearing a wig but had a large bonnet on his head tied with ribbons under his chin. Just like Bo-Peep, Rex thought, except he had a beard too.

The men weren't pretending to be women. They were just wearing women's clothes. They were requesting a bottle of wine at the bar.

The bartender was refusing to serve them.

It seemed an impasse had developed. The cross-dressers demanded a bottle of wine. The bartender refused to serve them.

The scene was broken up when the manager emerged from a back room and after a few words asked the quartet of cross-dressers to leave the wine bar.

Cathy Wight was first to react. She leapt up from her stool, grabbed her camera and took several shots of the four men in women's clothes lined up at the bar.

After a huddle of conversation between them, the four cross-dressers trooped out of the door with a great clattering of their high heels on the floor, accompanied by hoots and claps from the observing drinkers.

Cathy followed them outside. She couldn't see Moriarty wanting any of her shots in the *Diary* column, but maybe they could go somewhere. And anyway, she was sure she could sell the photos to some other outlet.

The four men were out on the Fleet Street pavement laughing at their failed attempt to get served at the bar.

Identifying herself and waving her camera, they identified themselves to Cathy. They turned out to be two·reporters from the *Daily Express*, another reporter, the older one, Bo-Peep, from the *Daily Telegraph* and the fourth was a lawyer. They readily agreed to be photographed in their female clothes by Cathy for possible inclusion in *Front Page*.

As they lined up outside the black and gold front of El Vino, Cathy asked them on what grounds had their bid to be served failed?

"We were certain, absolutely convinced they had to serve you. How could they not?" Cathy said. "You're men, they have to serve you."

"We forgot we were men!" the older one said. The others laughed in agreement.

Cathy didn't get it.

"We weren't wearing ties!" he explained.

It was a good point. Women wouldn't be served at all. But if you were male you were also obliged to wear a jacket and tie to be served in El Vino.

Cathy was right. Moriarty refused to have any of her photos of the cross-dressers appear in *Front Page*'s *Diary* column.

So she sold the main one to the *Daily Express*. It appeared in its *William Hickey* diary pages under a pseudonym Cathy used when she sold photos to rival publications.

32. ADDRESS

Anna and Cill knew they had to make a plan. It was a few days after they'd both agreed wildly in the middle of the night that they should head off to France and find Anna's grandfather.

In the cold light of a June Sunday morning Cill wasn't so sure that it was such a good idea to go charging off to France to find Anna's grandfather. After all, as Anna's first instinct had suggested, what difference would it make?

They were sitting at Anna's kitchen bar drinking tea. They'd had forty-eight hours to think over the idea. Cill wanted to make sure Anna really did think it was a good idea. Anna was still keener than Cill.

"But if we don't go. If we don't just go and talk to him, we'll never know if it might have made a difference, do we?" she said.

That was true, he thought. Though he was playing devil's advocate by pouring water on Anna's plan, inside he agreed with her. His own instinct said the worst thing to do in any situation was do nothing. He was just trying to make sure Anna really did want to find her grandfather, and wasn't just trying to make Cill feel better about the prospects of his job and the independence of the magazine he worked for.

But it was her grandfather. Her family, not his. And something he had learnt since meeting Anna was she came from a very troubled family. If they did go to France to look for her grandfather, it had to be her decision and hers alone.

"If we do go, do you really think it's a good idea just to turn up out of the blue?" Cill persisted. "He has kept his distance from you for all these years after all. Presumably he's had his reasons. And I doubt if they've changed?"

"I think it's best if we don't give him any notice. I want to see what his first instinct is, rather than his rational decision. If he sends us away. Fine. So be it." Anna said. "We can still have a holiday."

"Is he there alone?" Cill asked. "I mean what happened to your grandmother? Are they there together?"

Anna explained that her grandmother was dead. She'd died soon after the split between Tom and William.

"Agnes? She didn't actually go to France with William. She stayed at the flat in London. The family rumour was she'd had an affair with Tom at some point. I don't know if that's true, but she spent some time in America. Anyway they got divorced soon after the split."

Anna had seen quite a bit of her grandmother when she was a child. But then Agnes had died quite young of thyroid cancer.

"You come from quite a tragic family."

"It seems so, doesn't it. Well I think it's time for all the tragedy to stop. I think it's about time we became a normal family!"

She was also beginning to think this family feud, this deep mystery that no one talked about, had gone on long enough. She was old enough now, and independent enough, to make her own judgement about the family rift. And whether it was still justified. Or was just made ridiculous and unworthy through the passage of time. She wanted to find out.

She'd already decided she was going to go, with or without Cill.

She's already decided she's going to go, with or without me, Cill thought.

That clinched it for him.

He put his teacup down on the kitchen island top.

"Okay," he said. "Let's do it."

Having decided to go and look for William, they began to make a workable plan.

They realised they needed to go as soon as possible. Cill said he could take a week or even a fortnight off straightaway. Anna said she too could get away with only a week's notice.

"But I need to be back for the next board meeting. So we can only go for eight days." She hated the thought now of going to the board meeting. Traipsing out to Poyters wouldn't be the same as the easy train down to her dad's house. And the thought of seeing Bex at the head of the table, triumphantly running the meeting, gave her a kind of shudder. But she knew her dad wanted and expected her to be there. So she would. He would probably drive them both there.

"That should be plenty."

With a wrench she refocused. Cill was planning the holiday. Well, she thought, it wasn't so much a holiday as an expedition.

They'd drive there, taking Cill's Renault 4, he was saying.

But where was "there"?

That was one question.

Another was should they inform Dryden of their intentions?

Anna thought not.

They debated how open, or not, they should be about their search for William.

It may be a wild goose chase, she said. Nothing may come of it. Her granddad may refuse to see them. Even if he did, he might refuse to talk about his agreement to give Bex his proxy. If they failed, or if they succeeded, better no one should know about it for the time being.

Cill agreed. Again, it was her family after all, not his.

Likewise, they had both agreed there was no point in asking aunt Bex for her uncle William's address. That would only raise her suspicions. The less Bex knew the better.

So on the face of it they were going to go on a holiday to France together.

"Supposedly that's the quickest way to break up a romance," Cill said. "Go on holiday together."

Anna laughed. As did Cill. But he crossed his fingers as well.

They decided it should have the appearance of a walking holiday. That would give them flexibility to be unspecific with friends and colleagues about their destination, other than to vaguely say "the French Alps," or "the "Alpes de Provence," or "the Pyrenees," or even "various places," when asked.

"Actually that might be something nice to do together anyway," Anna said. "If William refuses to see us or kicks us out of the door as soon as we arrive, we could use some fresh air and a bit of hiking about, don't you think?"

Cill agreed. They would take their boots and plan a real walking holiday as cover.

That left the matter of her grandfather's address.

Where did he actually live?

Anna had a plan for that too.

She was due to go down to her father's place for Sunday lunch. This was a regular date they both tried to keep up as often as possible. It was about the only time nowadays father and daughter had a chance to see each other.

Cill had learnt early on in their relationship that Anna's mother had died. Her father was the only parent she had.

"How old were you when she died?"

"It wasn't long, a few years, after Sam was born. He was four. I was ten."

It must have been hard, Cill thought, for all of them.

"What happened," he asked, not sure she would answer. The Thompson family seemed to attract tragedy like a magnet. They were surrounded by a sad and tragic force-field.

"Oh, a car crash. Someone drove Stella, my mum, off the road. The car hit a tree. Just kids having fun, overtaking each other on a blind bend. They weren't even drunk. She was trying to avoid the head-on collision."

"She was the only one in the car?"

"Yes. Coming back from visiting a friend."

"And your dad never remarried?"

She smiled and shook her head. Anna thought her mum would be always the only woman for her dad.

Coming down to East Sussex to have Sunday lunch with her dad had become a regular item in her diary. She knew her dad looked forward to it. She was glad to keep doing it when she could. She also knew that quite soon she would ask Cill to come down there one Sunday too. She knew already she wanted her dad to meet him.

This time while she was at her father's place Anna intended to take the opportunity to slip into the study and look though her dad's Filofax in a search for William's address in France. She knew he usually worked at the head of the long table in the study, and left his Filofax there.

"He keeps everything in his Filofax," Anna said. "I introduced him to them a couple of years ago. And now it goes everywhere with him. And I know he puts almost every bit of information in it that's vital to him. God knows what he'd do if he lost it."

Anna had occasionally seen her dad refer to the address pages in it at board meetings. If her grandfather's address was anywhere it would be in her dad's Filofax.

Anna and Cill arranged to see each other back at Anna's place that night. If she didn't come back with William's address, they'd have to think again.

They walked to Greenwich station together and caught a Blackfriars train. There they spilt, Anna on the tube west to Victoria to catch a train south, Cill on the tube north to his own flat.

They arranged to meet at Victoria station that evening when Anna arrived back in London on the Gatwick Express before travelling on to Greenwich.

Cill spent the day cleaning and tidying his flat. He tried to do it on a fixed schedule now that Anna would often be staying. It was more often than he used to do it, he admitted.

After that he read the papers. This was an essential part of his weekend. He bought all the leading Sundays – he could claim for them on his monthly expenses – and went through them minutely. He also bought all the Saturday papers as well. They were increasingly looking like the Sundays, and rivalling them with multiple "weekend" sections.

It was essential as a news reporter, he knew, to see how the other major news outlets covered the same stories he and *Front Page* did. And also to check they hadn't got exclusive stories that *Front Page* had missed. You could learn a lot by both seeing what they'd done, how they'd done it, and what they'd got and what they'd missed.

It wasn't just the news stories he scanned and compared. He

went right through the papers, paying particular attention to the comment and opinion pages. He was particularly interested in the leaders – the place where the paper expressed its own opinion on matters in the news. This was both for professional and personal reasons. Professional, to see what the other papers thought about the issues of the day and to compare that to how *Front Page* saw them. And personal, so he could get a broad appreciation of the stance a particular paper took on these things. That would be essential to know should he ever be applying for a job at one or more of them over his career. It was essentially know your enemy until they became your friend.

In the same way he always listened to the *Today* programme every weekday morning on BBC Radio 4 before he went to work. He didn't particularly like radio news. He felt much more at home with *News At Ten* on the telly. Nor was he impressed by how ignorant and scathing the *Today* presenters were about science and technology items. They almost seemed to take the view that civilised people never need know anything about science. And that made Cill want to kick their collective arse. Once he nearly threw the radio out of the kitchen window into the rain when one of the presenters gave an embarrassed laugh when introducing a news item about astronomy – as if to say how can cultured civilised people be expected to know anything about this silly science-and-tech stuff? But there was no question that *Today* was possibly the most important current affairs programme on radio. It was the one show on which any minister in the news would appear, or agree to be interviewed. If you were in news journalism yourself you had to listen to *Today*.

He and the other members of the news desk would scan the weekday papers in the office. One of Carmen's jobs every work day morning was to go down to the post room and pick up the papers. It also gave her a chance to have a quick chat every day with Jan Yoonick, the young tall and blond Dutchman who ran the post room. She looked forward to that.

Then as afternoon turned to evening, Weaver ducked down into the tube system again and was waiting at the platform gate at Victoria station at the appointed time.

He saw her in the crowd stepping off the train and waved. She smiled and waved back as she walked along the platform towards him.

They greeted and kissed each other and moved on across the concourse and down the steps to the tube.

"How did it go?" he asked.

"The lamb was excellent," she replied mischievously. "My dad's a good cook."

He looked at her.

"Don't worry. I've got it," she said. "Wait till we get home."

They moved on across London and talked of other things.

Afterwards, at Anna's flat, after they'd made love in the shower, they were drinking a glass of red wine together, sitting on high stools at the kitchen island.

Anna took out a folded piece of paper from her bag. She opened it and placed it on the kitchen worktop.

Cill looked at it.

"Great name for a house," he said with a broad smile.

On the paper Anna had written the words:

Manoir de la Pisse, Ceillac 05600, Hautes Alpes, France.

33. MAP

On the Saturday morning five days after Monday 14 June when the military governor of the Malvinas, general Mario Menendez, surrendered his troops in Port Stanley to British forces, Cill Weaver and Anna Thompson set off for France. They travelled in Cill's Renault 4, with both of them insured to drive it.

On the actual day of the Argentinean surrender, the day after Anna came back from East Sussex with her grandfather's address, Cill went to Stanford's map shop again. This time he was looking for maps of France; specifically the right IGN 1:25,000 scale sheet or sheets for Ceillac. He found them; sheet numbers 3637OT and 3537ET. He also bought the relevant 150,000 scale yellow Michelin map no 334. As well as the red Michelin road map of the whole of France.

The Manoir de la Pisse wasn't specifically marked on the IGN sheet. But there was a Cascade de la Pisse at the end of the Mélezet valley, where the road ran out not far beyond the high Alpine village of Ceillac. And not far from the waterfall the 25,000 scale map showed a small square dot with the abbreviated word "*mr*" next to it.

Cill thought "*mr*" might stand for "manoir".

That must be the place, Cill thought.

"Doesn't look an easy place to get to," Cill said to Anna.

"There are roads though?"

"Yes all the way. But it looks like your granddad has chosen a place to live that's as isolated as isolated can be in western Europe in the late 20th century."

That same Monday night they were looking at the maps together, spread out on the kitchen island.

Anna could see what Cill meant about isolated.

Ceillac wasn't even marked on the Michelin road map of the whole of France. Cill showed her where it was on the large scale map. It was south and then a little east of the great Alpine fortress town of Briançon.

With his interest in things military, Cill knew about Briançon and its citadel built by the legendary military engineer Sebastien Vauban who fortified the whole of France's eastern frontiers for Louis XIV in the late seventeenth century. Vauban's fortifications meant you could beat Louis's armies outside France, as the allies under Marlborough and Eugene frequently did, but you couldn't follow that up by invading France.

"I'd like to see Briançon anyway," he said. "It's a fortified town guarding the approaches to France from Italy through the high Alps. The citadel is one of Vauban's masterpieces."

"Okay," Anna said, neutral.

Cill grinned at her.

"Okay, forget the military stuff."

"Another time?" Anna said.

"Looks like from Calais we head southeast across eastern France," he said, tracing a finger across the map. "Calais. Arras. St Quentin. Great First World War sites along there--"

Anna punched his arm.

"--Rheims. Troyes. Then south to Dijon and Lyon. And then after Lyon we turn east towards the mountains. Grenoble. Then Briançon. And after that we'll need the larger scale map. But it looks like we head out of Briançon on the Gap road. And finally we turn off the main road here."

Anna leaned forward. Cill's finger was pointing to the little town of Guillestre.

"Or we could take a more direct route from Briançon on a minor road via here." His finger pointed to Chateau Queyras. There was a high pass there on that road too. The Col d'Izoard. It rang a bell for Cill.

"I think the Tour de France goes over this pass. Every once in a while."

"Which is best? The main road or the road the Tour takes?"

"Depends on the road I guess. But either way it's going to be pretty spectacular. There are some serious mountains here."

"So let's take a view on that when we're there?"

He agreed. Though if his hunch or memory was right, any

road the Tour took had to be in good condition. So the Col d'Izoard might be the best option.

Something they talked about was what exactly a "manoir" was in France. They assumed it was something like a "chateau". Was there a difference? They didn't know, but doubted it. They decided both words could be applied to large country mansions, something in size perhaps between her father's Lutyens country house and a family seat like Poyters.

Whatever kind of place William lived in, Anna knew he was in possession of considerable wealth. At one time her grandfather had a lot of money. And presumably still had.

Another thing they talked about was the various outcomes of their unannounced arrival at William's place.

They had agreed they would give him no warning. But there was something else, another scenario that troubled Cill.

"When did you last see him?" Cill wondered if Anna would actually recognise her grandfather.

"Fifteen years ago. He came to my mother's funeral. He liked my mum more than my dad I think."

William had turned up at the church. He hadn't come to the crematorium, but had sat at the back of the church in his customary black suit. He had also refused to attend the wake afterwards.

The last time Anna saw him he was standing bareheaded in the rain by the plot in the churchyard where Stella's ashes were interred.

Anna knew what Cill was asking. "I'd still recognise him. I'll still know him."

34. PISSE

Five days later they caught an early ferry at Dover. They left England on the Saturday morning and would return back over the Channel the following Sunday, eight days later.

It was warm and sunny. The A26 motorway, the Autoroute des Anglais, tore through the rolling countryside, laying claim to the landscape. Leaving Arras behind, they ran through the big bread-basket of France. The vast unhedged lolloping fields of wheat stretched away to the sky on either side.

Then it was Champagne country.

"Do you like Champagne?" Anna said. She was driving.

"Not really," Cill replied gazing at the fields. "Don't see the point. You can celebrate with any old bottle of fizzy wine." He'd never been particularly convinced by the two types of champagne glasses either, he reflected: the old-fashioned broad-topped one and the newer flute type. The first one only had echoes for him of the Babycham advert from years before; and the second one seemed deliberately designed to stop you getting a good swig in. For Cill swig beat sip every time.

"I think I rather agree with you," Anna said. "But it's always nice to have a few bottles in. So no detour to have a tasting and stick some boxes in the back?"

"Maybe on the way home?" Thinking, we might need a few bottles of Champagne to drown our disappointment.

"Gonner Rear said it quite well," Anna smiled at the thought. "He said Champagne was a very successful way of getting rid of some very nasty white wine."

"Yes, very pithy," Cill said. "Gonner Rear takes the pith well."

As wheat field turned to vine the landscape changed from undulating fields to wooded hills, with trees left and curtailed and shaped on the hilltops like Henry V's haircut, and then lower down beneath the trees came regimented ranks of vines marching all round the shoulders of the hills like rows of terracotta warriors.

They got almost as far as Macon that first day.

They spelled each other at the wheel, taking two hours each. But by 4pm after eight hours on the road they'd both had enough and began to cast their eyes around for a place to stay the night.

They found a place off the motorway in a village north of Macon; a clean and perfectly acceptable two-star family hotel in the Logis de France network, with the yellow and green hearth logo on a metal plate swinging in the breeze over the door. The plumbing worked and neither the floorboards nor the double bed were intrusively or disconcertingly creaky.

The hotel seemed full. They were the only English. The rest were mostly Belgian and Dutch.

"Clearly we're in the Low Countries' corridor to the sun here. They're either staying in this region to taste the wine, or they're passing though to the south," Cill said at dinner, looking round the room.

"Or both. What is it here, Burgundy?"

"Yes. I think so overall. Maybe specifically Beaujolais. I'm not sure."

"There's a Macon white, isn't there?"

"Yes. And then you get into Cotes du Rhone country after Lyon."

"Let's go local," Anna said.

So they enjoyed a bottle of Macon white with their dinner.

Next morning back on the motorway they pushed on to Lyon. Cill was happy to go through the middle of Lyon, but Anna insisted they take the *rocade*, the by-pass on the east side.

"We're going east anyway. So there's no point in going through the city centre."

"I just fancied seeing the Rhone in the city centre – it's huge apparently. But you're right. *Rocade* it is."

They followed the motorway to the east of Lyon. Then took the turn-off towards Chambery. Then the turn-off from that road towards Grenoble.

All the while the terrain stayed flat and uninteresting. There was a distant loom of mountains in the east, first on their left as they headed south then ahead as they turned east at Lyon. But it wasn't until they branched off the Chambery road towards Grenoble that they experienced the first climb. The road headed away from the Rhone and Saone valleys and began to slant upwards. Ten minutes later they were still climbing. The superbly engineered toll-road took the ups and downs out of the climb and created a constant gradient by means of cuttings and viaducts.

The 850 cc of the Renault 4's engine engaged the gradient in a constant battle. But with only two people in the car and a couple of suitcases they could bat along at a constant 65 mph, even up the seven-mile and more climb. Anna had her foot and the accelerator flat on the floor and was enjoying the car's enduring struggle with the long slope. She felt it was a battle she was in charge of; and one she and the car were going to win.

The road levelled out and they both realised they were now in the mountains.

On their left the big white peaks of the Massif de Vanoise defined the horizon. Turning left and craning his neck, Cill could make out the huge lump of Mont Blanc with its surrounding white fangs of lesser peaks at the utmost edge of vision to the northeast. Ahead the city of Grenoble was walled in by the tops of the abrupt cliffs of the Vercors plateau and the consecutive standout heights of the Chartreuse range. And then beyond and behind the city to the south stood the limiting white heights of the Massif des Ecrins rising to 4,000 metres.

There were cement quarries everywhere you looked, Cill noted. Later, as they moved further into the mountains there would be hydro-electric power stations too. But around Grenoble it was limestone quarries for cement works that pocked the cliffs and mountain slopes.

The scenery became even more spectacular as they travelled along the Briançon road out of Grenoble. They stopped for lunch on top of the easy 2000-metre Col du Lautaret, no more than a lump in the road. It was a picnic in a old loop of road with an ancient stone bridge, by-passed by re-engineered new work. They were in a deep valley cloven by the rivers Romanche and Guisane between the 3,500 metre serrations of the Pic de l'Etendard, Pic Bayle and Mont Thabor to their left and the 4,000 metre dazzling-white incisors of Mont Pelvoux, La Meije and Barre des Ecrins to their right.

The heights on both sides of the road stepped back in a cascade of shades of green, darker lower down with waves of Alpine conifers, giving way to lighter shades of green and distant grey as grass took over and emerged from the treeline into high meadows. Green and grey then disappeared into white as the heights continued to climb and succumbed, then gave way completely, to seasonal and permanent polar conditions. And everywhere you looked through the green, the grey and the white there were vast cliffs, ragged rocks and abrupt precipices with dark shadows, and the occasional glint of turquoise and blue as the edge of a glacier caught the sun.

They approached Briançon. They could see it stood on a great plug of rock overlooking the Durance river. From their direction, above a sprawl of outlying suburbs by the station, lines of tall three-storey houses with multi-coloured corrugated metal roofs stood above the walls of the old city. Above the corrugated roofs was a second military wall, housing Vauban's high but squat stone citadel, dominating the town and the valley approaches.

There were salients, re-entrants, embrasures, enfilades, bastions, glacis, ouvrages, casemates, ravelins, redoubts and revetments, forts and blockhouses everywhere you looked in the citadel and outside the town on the heights around. All this state of the fortification art, Cill knew, was designed to make the citadel impregnable to attack and create a killing ground for those attempting to invade France by means of the Durance valley.

Vauban and Louis XIV were obviously deadly serious that no one should be able to invade France by this route.

They agreed they wouldn't stop, though it was a wrench for Cill, since he'd never seen so much military engineering gathered together in one place. They'd have a better opportunity to see it all on the way home.

Cill wondered about the metal roofs. Maybe it was to ensure there was no build-up of snow on the roofs in winter. Heat from the interior would constantly escape thought the thin metal sheets, ensuring that any falling snow would melt. Snow building up then avalanching off the roofs would be deadly to anyone caught below in the streets. But it'd be a bugger for your heating bills, though, he thought.

Now they came to the choice of road. The question was carry on along the main road down the Durance valley or turn off to Chateau Queyras and the Col d'Izoard?

They decided to keep going on the main road, heading now for Gap.

Just over thirty kilometres further on they came to another Vauban citadel, Mont Dauphin, guarding the approaches to Briançon along the Durance river from the south.

Here they turned east towards Guillestre and Ceillac. It was getting on for four in the afternoon.

They passed through Guillestre and began the final climb to the high Ceillac valley.

The road rose through trees. A series of hairpins took them round a bluff, still climbing. More trees. More bends. There was no other traffic. They were the only car on the road in both directions.

Even though they'd been in spectacular mountains all day long it wasn't until a series of long thin sticks appeared by the side of the road, standing tall out of the ground surface fifty metres apart, that they realised just what being in the mountains meant. The sticks were three metres high and painted yellow and black, alternating half metre a time for each colour.

Cill wondered aloud what they were for.

Anna was in the passenger seat. She was staring hard at the sticks.

"They're for showing where the line of the road is when it's covered in snow!" she said. There was both certainty and a kind of wonder in her voice. "And to show how deep the snow is too."

"For snow ploughs?"

219

"Yes. And for when the valley is completely snowed in."

It was a bright sunny June day. But they both now knew they had passed into a realm where that wasn't always the case. They had entered a world where weather ruled. A world where humans who lived there would be unwise ever to forget that fact.

Eventually the steep road eased up. They crested the rise and came out through sparser trees onto the floor of a broad green valley. Anna looked at the map. The valley floor was around 1800 metres above sea level.

"We're up around 6000 feet," Anna said, doing the conversion, the large scale map on her lap. "You get ski slopes lower than that."

"What a spot," Cill said. "A lost valley."

"Yes. A lost world. When do we see our first dinosaur?"

Cill pulled over into a gravel lay-by beside the road and stopped the car. They looked around.

The valley was surrounded by mountains in all directions. The Melezet valley had only one way in and one exit. The only way in or out was the road they had just taken. Ahead and to their left flat on the valley floor was the small village of Ceillac, made of stone houses, tin roofs, and wooden barns and outbuildings. Higher up to their left, north, above and behind the village were separate detached houses built into the hillsides. They were more modern and bigger than the houses in the village. At a guess, Cill thought there were more houses outside the village on the hillsides than there were in the village. A larger building stood out, overlooking the village. It was a hotel.

We can stay there tonight if William won't see us, he thought.

Far to the east, but dominating the skyline and rising above the nearer peaks and the lesser heights around it was the impressive isolated steep rock pyramid top of Monte Viso.

Their road curved round to the right away from the village and followed a small torrent, the Melezet, gradually climbing higher into the southern distance. While still unusually broad and flat, the valley narrowed inexorably as it climbed.

"Let's follow the road," Anna said, looking at the map.

They left the village of Ceillac behind and headed south. The road was still asphalted, following the line of the Melezet stream down the right hand side of the valley. The valley side closed around them on the right, and the steep mountain flanks approached the stream and the road. But less so on the left where it was still open, broad, green and flat. All the way along the road, on both sides now, were the three-metre yellow and black sticks, fifty metres apart.

In two more miles the road ended in a wide gravelled parking area. Cill stopped the car again.

On the right a connected series of waterfalls ran down the mountainside.

Anna looked up from the map and pointed. "That's the Cascade de la Pisse," she said. "Worth a taste, don't you think?"

"What? Drink the water?"

"Yes. I'd like to take the Pisse," Anna said with a giggle. "I think we should fill up our water bottle here in celebration. And take it home."

No sooner said than she reached into the back seat, grabbed their litre size blue metal Sigg water bottle, left the car and did a kind of rotating waltzing dance with the bottle, holding it outstretched with two hands, like a naiad performing some kind of ancient water ritual. She pranced and danced over to the pool at the base of the last plunge of waterfall. She went round the pool to the far side and stood by the edge of the fall, on a boulder, reaching into the falling water with the bottle, its unscrewed cap dangling on a string.

She came back to the car. She unscrewed the cap and took a sip.

"Well," she said. "I've taken the Pisse."

"I'd like to take the Pisse too," Cill said.

She handed him the bottle. He took a short sip and screwed the cap back on.

Anna was looking at the map again.

On the left of the parking area was a low stone wall topped

with black-painted iron palings shaped like spears. It appeared out of the trees behind and disappeared out of sight into the trees ahead. Creating a gap in the wall were two high square stone pillars with wrought iron gates. Each pillar was topped by a stone coping above which there was a round stone ball. The gates were open and a stony gravel track passed between the pillars and disappeared over a low rise into a clump of conifers.

Cill heard Anna take a deep breath.

"I think this is it," she said very quietly.

For some reason this reminded Cill of what Brigham Young was supposed to have said when he led the Mormon ox-wagons west and first spotted the huge Salt Lake from the top of Gobblers Knob or somesuch place in the mountains and spied Ensign Peak, the mountain of his vision. "This is the place," Young said gazing intently down at the lake in the plain below. Cill wondered if he'd known the gleaming lake far below was actually salt he wouldn't have been so confident that "this is the place". After all, if they'd gone on another couple of hundred miles they'd have reached California – surely a better place to settle than the middle of the Utah desert next to a vast dead salt lake.

Anna folded the map and put it away. She clasped her hands and rested them on her jeans in her lap. She looked at the waterfall. She gazed up at the mountain heights, stepping back in echelon in all directions except behind.

"It is a great name for a house," she said and laughed.

Cill started the car again. As they drove between the pillars they could both see there was a plaque on the left hand one.

It read *Manoir de la Pisse*.

35. WILLIAM

The stone and gravel drive passed into the trees. They went up and over a brow and headed slightly downhill. After a hundred yards they came out of the trees. The vista opened up and the manor house was right ahead of them.

It's Marlinspike Hall, Cill thought, only smaller. But not much smaller.

A central square tower section of four storeys was sandwiched between, and slightly proud of, two three-storey wings. Both wings and tower were topped by the steep roofs characteristic of France, rising to ridge lines on the wings, and to a tall pyramid shape on the central tower. The top, second, storey on both wings and the central square tower, and the third storey in the tower, were in the form of dormer windows in the roof. The tower then had two dormer windows in its pyramid shaped roof, one above the other.

The drive curled away to the left of the mansion as they looked. The ground fell away from the front of the house on two large terraces. The upper one immediately in front of the house was a broad gravelled parking area. Both terraces were bordered by a low stone wall. The drive ran in to the parking area from the left of the house. At the far end of this terrace on their right beyond the house hidden under trees the gravelled drive ran on to a group of outbuildings, garages and barns, made of brick and wood. The lower terrace carried a lawn. Stone steps at the midpoint connected both terraces. At the lower edge of the terraced lawn, down a second short flight of steps, the ground reverted to nature with an uneven mixture of grass, low shrubs, bracken and protruding rocks before the trees through which they had just passed took over.

Behind the mansion there was another terraced lawn bordering on to a natural thick conifer forest beyond, which was flat for a stretch before rising up slowly, then abruptly, and eventually merging with the grassy meadows and lower rocky cliffs of the mountainsides where the trees became sparser before dying out completely.

The walls of the manor were mainly rendered, except for the stonework on the corners, lintels, and round the doorways and windows, which had all been left uncovered as natural stone. The render was painted a bright creamy-ochre colour, which made the whole house seem to shine warmly in the late afternoon sunlight.

A flight of six steps went up to the front door, which was in the base of the square central tower.

It did indeed look a little like Marlinspike Hall; the country mansion of Tintin's seafaring friend Captain Haddock.

The sound of a two-stroke engine alerted them to a tractor-mower moving along in straight lines on the terraced front lawn, where a woman was cutting the grass. Two sheepdogs were running alongside the mower.

They drove on up to the house and parked next to the two cars already there, a grey Citroen DS21 and a black Citroen DS19.

Anna looked at her watch. It was five-fifteen.

"Just in time for a nice cup of tea," she said and opened the car door.

Cill touched her arm before she stepped out of the car.

"Are you okay?" he said. "We can turn around and go. Now."

But she knew she would always regret it if they did. She would always wonder what if?

She smiled and shook her head and got out of the car. Cill went up the steps and joined her by the front door.

Though the building looked at least a hundred years old, Cill reckoned, there was an electric doorbell. He also noticed that the glass in the heavy glass-panelled door was triple-glazed. Some serious money's been spent here, he thought. The only way you could live comfortably in a place like this at 6000 feet up in the mountains was if it had been seriously, effectively, efficiently and comprehensively modernised. Again, serious money, he thought. The kind of money that Captain Haddock had come into after discovering the buried treasure of the pirate Red Rackham. Or from selling a very successful manufacturing operation and living on the proceeds and your royalties.

Anna pressed the doorbell. In the bulky dark interior distance of the house they heard it ringing.

After a while they could see someone approaching the inside of the door through the glass. He opened the door.

He was a tall thin white-haired gentleman dressed in black suit trousers, a black suit waistcoat, and a white shirt with the sleeves rolled up to the elbow. He wore a red silk cravat round his neck. He had black socks and high quality black lace-up leather-soled shoes on his feet. He wore circular heavy black-rimmed glasses.

In good shape for eighty-five-plus, Cill thought immediately.

Beside him Anna drew in her breath.

"Granddad!" she said.

The white-haired man seemed totally stunned. Taken aback. Lost for words.

He frowned slightly as if unsure of place or time. He gave a minute shake of his head. He stared at her intently. He glanced once at Cill, then shifted his look back to Anna.

"Anna?" he said. He repeated it: "Anna?"

Then he smiled.

"Anna."

"Yes it's me granddad. I came to see you."

William Thompson opened his arms. Anna moved forward and they embraced.

"Wonderful. Wonderful," he said. "It must be fifteen years."

Cill realised he had been holding his breath. He let it out in a long silent sigh.

William was holding Anna at arms length.

"Fifteen years. Dear me. You were ten."

His voice to Cill sounded a little old-fashioned. Someone perhaps whose accent and dialect had not evolved over the decades through exposure to radio chatter and particularly to television. Even the queen now sounded nothing like she did back in the 1950s. Indication of self-imposed isolation? Cill wondered. But there was something else too. He couldn't quite place it. Was there a touch of Birmingham or Black Country there? Yes definitely. He tried to chase the echo in his mind. Then he got it: Neville Chamberlain.

Cill had been to the Imperial War Museum in London, at Kennington south of the river, many times. One time there they had a recorded loop from the wireless with the voice of Neville Chamberlain telling the people of Britain over the BBC on the third of September 1939 that Britain was at war with Germany. It was the echo of that voice that he heard now in William Thompson's clipped and dated tones: just an old and fading echo there of the dialect that might be called "Midlands manufacturing".

I have to tell you now, he thought, *that no such undertaking has been received. And that consequently this country is at war...*

Maybe for Anna and William the current moment was as dramatic in its own way as the third of September 1939 had been for the whole country.

Cill forced himself back to the here and now.

Anna was talking fast and furiously, thinking on her feet.

"...in the neighbourhood...walking holiday...Alps..." she was saying; "...drop in...hope you don't mind..."

"Of course not. Lovely. So pleased," William said. But he looked askance at his granddaughter, as though he suspected there might be more to it.

He pulled the door fully back.

"Come in. Come in."

"Granddad, this is my friend Cill."

William seemed to take the strange name in his stride.

He extended his arm. Cill took the handshake.

William smiled: "Sill as in windowsill?"

Cill laughed aloud at the verbal echo between grandfather and granddaughter.

"Not quite. It's my younger sister's corruption of Cyril."

"You'll stay the night? A few days? What are your plans?"

William turned his attention back to Anna.

"We'd love to. We don't have any plans really. We were walking in the area. It's fantastic! Cill wanted to examine all the military architecture," she said, extemporising.

"There's a lot of that in these parts," William said with a smile.

"And I remembered you lived somewhere around here."

Again, Cill thought William's eyes gleamed with something behind his glasses – as though he accepted the story for the time being but wondered if there wasn't more to it. But maybe he imagined it, Cill thought. Those black circular glasses reminded him of something, of someone too. Again, as with the verbal echo of Neville Chamberlain, Cill followed the fleeting image round his mind.

He got it. Arthur Askey. The glasses were just like those worn by Arthur Askey. They looked great on him, better than they looked on Arthur Askey. So long as he didn't suddenly break into the *Busy Busy Bee* song.

"Good. Good," William said. "Well, come in, make yourself at home. How about a cup of tea?"

He ushered them deeper into the mansion.

First hurdle over successfully, Cill thought. At least he hasn't sent us packing, refusing to see his granddaughter.

They followed William through the house. They passed from the front reception area to a large back reception hall with an imposing double staircase rising in the middle, which split into two at a half-landing with each side journeying on upwards opposite each other to feed into its own wing. Beyond and under the staircase a broad passageway took them to a huge stone-flagged kitchen at the back of the house. The kitchen had a series of windows overlooking the back terrace, but was also brilliantly lit with striplights and spotlamps. It was packed with all the latest cooking appliances and gadgetry.

A woman aged in her mid-fifties was sitting at a big solid table in the centre of the room, reading what looked like a cookbook.

"*Marcelle, du thé s'il vous plaît,*" William's French was fluent, Cill noted, but still had that element of Midlands manufacturing in it. A strangely attractive combination, he thought, French and Midlands manufacturing.

They followed William through a door at the side of the kitchen where another broad corridor led and opened into a long wide day-room. The lounge overlooked the lawn and forest at the back of the mansion through a series of high windows. There were also two french windows, Cill noticed. He thought fleetingly: what do they call a french window in France?

Cill could see that all the windows were actually modern triple-glazed units sitting in the reveal formed by the original windows beyond. Even the french windows were actually double doors, with modern triple-glazed doors fixed into the space in front of the original french ones beyond.

Clever he thought. You keep the looks from the outside of the original mansion architecture, but you made sure the inside was warm and comfortable with the triple-glazed units to the latest modern standards.

"Sit down, take a seat." William gestured to a settee and armchairs grouped round a large hearth. "Or we could go out on the terrace?"

Outside through one of the french windows Cill could see there was a group of heavy white iron tables and chairs on the stone patio that jutted into and above the grass terrace like a promenade on a beach.

"How about outside while it's still sunny?" Anna said.

William nodded and opened one of the two door and french window assemblies. Anna and Cill followed him out on to the terrace.

The air was chilly out of the sun. But the first table and six chairs round it were still squarely in strong sunlight.

They sat down. Cill looked over to the mountain wall beyond the mansion. It was staggeringly spectacular. The forest rose in waves across the valley towards the mountainsides. Then it crept up the sides of the mountain, broken in places by crags and cliffs. His eyes moved upwards. The thick belt of trees became thinner as the ground became steeper and the climate colder. Less carbon dioxide too, he wondered. And then the forest finished in a series of irregular fingers feeling for purchase far up the mountain. At that point grass and meadow took over, interspersed now with bigger crags and more frequent cliffs. Then the grass too struggled to gain a footing in the battle against gravity, slope and temperature. It became patchy, and suddenly as he looked even higher, there was no grass at all: just rock. The rock came in two species, scree and fixed. A belt of scree defined the area between the grass and the fixed rocks and cliff. Upwards again the rock and cliff merged into snow. And above that there was only white. The white of the snow merged imperceptibly with the wispy white of the sky.

From where he looked it was the wall of the world.

Cill was diverted from his dreamlike scanning of the surrounding mountains by the arrival of tea.

"The thing about mountains," William said. "Is you always want to know what's on the other side. And for humans what's the single most important thing above all else about a mountain wall?"

Cill smiled and shook his head.

"It's where is the way over?"

Perceptive, Cill thought.

Marcelle, who Cill guessed was some sort of housekeeper, brought out a tray of tea and madeleines to the terrace. There was even a jug of cold milk too.

"*Merci Marcelle,*" William said. "Marcelle is actually a shepherd," he added. "Or used to be. Her daughter Nicole still is one. You probably saw her on the tractor cutting the grass."

William explained there was less work as a shepherd these days. Especially for those living up in the high pastures such as the Melezet valley.

"Modern shepherds live down in civilisation and come up here on quad bikes. The days of the traditional shepherd and their lifestyle on the high pastures are gone. No one wants to live up in the cold with the sheep and goats any more, eh Marcelle?"

"They are soft and idle," Marcelle said in strongly accented English. "*Mollassonnes!*" she said with an amiable grin and made a kind of exaggerated and dismissive motorbike noise with her lips, representing Cill guessed, a quad bike.

Cill wasn't sure by any means, but the way she said it convinced him that "*mollassonnes*" was a French equivalent to what Eddie Osmoe would have called "mardy babs".

"There's less work for the high shepherds nowadays. So I provide what employment I can," William explained. "I, and this place, wouldn't be able to survive here without the locals."

He asked Anna for news of the family. But was his heart really in it, Cill wondered. Was he just being polite?

Anna talked of her father and her brother. She passed on information about health and so forth on the other side of the family. After a while William stopped her.

"Anna. It's lovely to see you. I've missed you I realise. It's been too long," he took a breath. "But there's more to this visit than just being in the locality or accidentally passing by, isn't there?"

But before Anna could answer he held up his hand.

"But let that be for now. After tea I'll show you to your room. You must be tired. Then let's all have a good talk over dinner. Agreed?"

"Yes, granddad." Anna said. "Agreed."

Their room overlooked the back terrace. It was on the first floor. They had a view of the forest on the rising slopes right up to the tops of the mountains. You could open the triple-glazed interior window unit, and then open the outside casement beyond that. Anna tried it, but shut it rapidly. The sun had gone behind the mountains and it was getting cold.

"He's sharp, isn't he?" Cill said.

"Quite abrupt too," Anna replied. "I thought we'd have a lot more chatting and smalltalk before we got to the nitty-gritty."

"I guess he's used to his own pace – his own pace of politeness."

"Yes. And at least we're here. He hasn't sent us away."

"I think he's missed you too."

Cill also thought that William was only just beginning to realise just how much he'd lost by cutting himself off from his family. You sent a course of action in motion. Then it gained a life and a momentum of its own. It could become very difficult then to alter or steer it, and stopping it would be out of the question.

They were both lying on the broad king-size double bed.

William had told them to rest, shower, and sleep if they wanted. He suggested they join him for a drink at 7pm in the day–room they'd already seen.

After being shown to their room, Cill had gone back outside to retrieve their suitcases from the car. He took the opportunity to look round.

He walked across the gravelled terrace at the front of the house and followed the drive into the complex of outbuildings. In the first one he found the person he now knew to be Nicole stowing away the tractor-mower. Her two sheepdogs came out of the lean-to shed to investigate, wagging their tails. He kneeled down to their level and made a fuss of the dogs and said hello to them in English. They looked at him as though there was something wrong with the way he spoke.

He smiled and said hello to Nicole. He tried his best French.

"*Vous êtes une bergère?*" <<you are a shepherd>> or at least that's what he hoped he'd said.

"*Oui c'est vrai. Aussi je suis la jardinière pour monsieur William.*" Nicole smiled. She pronounced the name in three syllables, "will-i-am". She was incredibly lean, taut and muscular. Her face, neck and bare arms had an endemic tan integrated into the skin. The outdoor life, he assumed. Despite the wear and tear of the outdoor life as a shepherd and a gardener - *jardinière* - on her skin she looked about thirty or less – which was younger than she probably was, he thought.

"*Il est bon pour lui. Très bon d'avoir des invités,*" she said with a smile. But Cill didn't understand what she'd said. But the way she'd said it made it sound good.

He smiled and waved and wandered back to the front door.

Just after seven o'clock they left their room and made their way back to the ground floor lounge. Cill wore a blue light cotton jacket over his jeans and polo shirt. Anna had changed into a long skirt and a loose flowery shirt. She carried a shawl across her shoulders. On their feet he wore his customary Timberlands: she wore tennis shoes.

William met them in the lounge and before drinks offered to give them a quick tour. They both agreed rapidly to the offer. William showed them round the whole house and outbuildings. First he led them outside.

The biggest of the outbuildings was a large stone-built barn. This was where William had his workshop. He had a second workshop inside the mansion on the second floor of the east wing. He had removed the interior walls and converted the whole of the wing's third floor to a workshop.

"But obviously there's going to be a lot of heavy stuff I couldn't lump up two flights of stairs."

So he'd run the house's electricity across to the barn and installed a second workshop there.

Back in the house he first took them below ground. A basement ran about two-thirds the total length of the mansion. It was part wine cellar and part storage.

They followed William up the main staircase. The first floor in both wings was for bedrooms. The second floor above that on the west wing was a library and study.

The second floor in the tower was a second, smaller study.

And third floor, right up in the pyramid roof, accessed by a helical staircase from the second floor, was a miniature observatory. It contained a large telescope and a padded office chair on castors. To Cill it looked like a 20x power telescope or even bigger. There was a opening roof window in each of the four faces of the pyramid.

"Obviously the mountains cut out the line of sight in all four directions," William said. "Compensated by the absolute absence of light pollution."

Though it was a big place, William seemed to be using most of it.

From his little observatory William led them back down to the ground floor.

Cill took a beer when offered his choice of drink. Anna chose a glass of red wine. The three of them stood in one of the wide windows of the lounge looking across at the forest and the rising mountainside.

"Well master Cyril, Cill, what's your line of work?"

When Cill told him he worked for *Front Page*, William tilted his head on one side like a dog wondering which end of a bone to start on first.

"Do you. Do you indeed. Interesting times in the South Atlantic if you're on the news desk?"

Cill said he was and it was.

William said they'd be eating in the kitchen.

"I do have a dining room, obviously. But I like the kitchen. And there's only three of us. Marcelle's made some kind of boeuf bourguignon. She's gone home now so we'll have to help ourselves."

Anna asked about Marcelle. What the arrangement was.

"She comes every day. Cooks and kind of hangs around--"

he smiled "--In case I need anything. She even helps Nicole out in the garden. I think she prefers to be outside anyway."

William explained he had a cleaner too who came in once a week to clean and do the washing.

"Nicole comes every day too?" Anna asked.

"Most days. She's a shepherd, as I said. But once the flocks are up on the slopes they don't need much looking after. It's just moving them around that's a lot of work for her and the dogs. And there's always lots to do here. You should see her swinging an axe to cut logs. Marcelle's a dab hand with a felling axe too. I've got enough logs to withstand a siege."

William took a sip of his drink, a *kir bourgogne*, which he'd explained was a classic French "apero" - aperitif – made of red wine and crème de cassis.

"And of course," he said. "They work for me all year round. Whereas up here there's no shepherding once the flocks have been taken down off the mountain for the winter."

"Do you still get that thing here," Cill said, searching for the word. "Transhumance?"

"Yes they do," William said. "The seasonal shifting of the flocks and herds to high and low pastures. They've no choice really."

William finished his drink and placed the glass down on the windowcill.

"Shall we go and eat?' he said.

They sat at the end of the big heavy table in the kitchen. William sat at the end with Cill and Anna either side of him. They helped themselves to the stew while William opened a bottle of red wine.

Then they had cheese and bread.

William asked Anna about her career. He didn't know she had become a lawyer.

William took a sip of his red wine. He cut a small slice off the tomme de savoie cheese and nibbled at it on his knife before placing it on a piece of bread.

"I think you want to talk to me?" he said, smiling.

In fact, Cill thought, it looks more to me like you want to talk to Anna.

Anna looked hard at him across the table.

"I'll be perfectly honest granddad," she said. "There's two things I want to talk about. If you're willing. I perfectly understand if you don't want to talk about the second one. That's a family matter. But the first one is a business thing. And it affects not just me but Cill as well."

"And what are these two things," he said. He was smiling at her. Cill realised it had done his heart good to see his granddaughter again. And he seemed to be very pleased she seemed so direct and animated, and independent as well.

"The first is: why did you give aunt Bex power of attorney and a proxy vote over your shares in great-uncle TT's publishing company?"

"And the second?"

"The second is: what happened between you and my greatuncle all those years ago. And why have you had no contact with your family in all these years?"

William still smiled gently at her. He nodded a few times.

"You're right," he said. "Enough is enough. But if you don't mind I'd like to talk about your second question first."

Cill looked at Anna.

"Would you like me to leave the room?" he said. "It's a family matter and not necessarily for my ears."

Anna looked enquiringly at her grandfather.

"No. No," he said. "Please stay. That may make it easier to talk in a way."

He took a deep breath and began to talk, staring at his granddaughter constantly.

"I should have spoken about this a long time ago. It's gone on too long. My anger with one generation has hurt other generations, and I never intended that. I'm glad you came."

He took a long breath and touched Anna on her arm. Then he refolded a shirt sleeve which had become loose.

"I broke irrevocably with my brother," he said, "During the

Battle of Britain. On *Adler Tag* to be exact."

37. BREACH

William looked at them both on either side of him. He could see the young man understood what he meant, though there was an element of great surprise there too. His beautiful granddaughter clearly did not understand the relevance of the German phrase. But clearly he could also see that she was certain he would explain. He could see now she was certain that he would no longer leave her in the dark.

More than ever now he felt the full force of time, almost the entire crux of his life concentrated inside one singularity. The years of hurt and blame and isolation began to drain away inside his mind. More than ever he realised now the time had come at last to tell his story. He carried on.

"That was the 13th of August 1940. We call it Eagle Day. I think Goering himself called it *Adler Tag*. The Germans sent over 600 planes in waves. It was their biggest attempt to destroy the RAF. At the end of the day the RAF was still intact. There were many many German planes shot down. Many historians think the Germans lost the Battle of Britain that day.

"Three days later I was visited by two young men in suits. I thought it strange they should be in civilian dress and not in uniform. It turned out they were from MI5, the secret service.

"They showed their identity passes and asked if they could talk to me. I couldn't think of any reason why I needed to talk to the security service. But they were very polite and equally I couldn't think of any reason why I shouldn't talk to them. So I agreed.

"They came in and we sat round my kitchen table – a bit like this." He gestured to the table where the three of them sat. "And they explained why they had come.

"It turned out that among the German planes shot down on *Adler Tag* there were quite a few Messerschmitt 109s, the leading German fighter plane of the day. And quite a few of those planes were brand new. Less than a year old, according to their serial numbers, they told me."

William paused and looked away through a kitchen window into the dark. He was also looking into the dark history of his memory, Cill thought.

"Each one of those new fighters had an altimeter made by my company."

William looked at Anna intently.

Cill held his breath: what he'd just heard was very serious.

"And they wanted to know why."

"What did you say?" Anna said quietly.

"I had no idea. There was nothing I could say. I certainly hadn't sold any to Germany in the previous twelve months. I had no idea how my altimeters ended up in recently-made German planes when we were at war with Germany, and had been for nearly a year."

"Were they old instruments?" Cill interjected.

"Not at all," William replied. "They were brand new."

"So what happened?" Anna almost whispered.

"They left after asking me to find out. They said they would be back."

"Did you find out?"

"Yes I did."

It turned out that Tom Telford Thompson, in charge of William's instrument manufacturing company in the USA, had been selling altimeters to German armaments manufacturers.

"And when I asked him – instructed him – to stop, he refused."

The USA was not yet at war with Germany and Tom could see no reason why he shouldn't carry on making vast amounts of money selling products to countries the USA was not at war with.

"The really bad thing, the thing that made me sick to my stomach, was that he couldn't understand why I wanted him to stop. I didn't know my own brother.

"It turned out I couldn't stop him either. He was obsessed with accumulating enough money so he could bully and muscle his way into the American publishing industry. Thompson Telemetry was just a means to an end for him. But for me it was everything.

"I'd made the mistake of giving him too much control of the American side of the company. That was a lot easier than going over there all the time myself. And I trusted him to do a good job. Which he did. Running back and to across the Atlantic would have been no way to run a successful company. And then when I needed to it turned out I couldn't stop Tom. I'd have to instruct lawyers – possibly even go over to the USA myself, not easy in wartime – and go through the courts. And it would all take time. I did start the process of having Tom sacked and removed from the company, but it took a long while, and by then the USA was at war with Germany too, and the Americans themselves stopped the exports anyway.

"Tom had moved into publishing in America by then. He left my company when it suited him."

William filled his glass. Cill got the impression that Anna's visit had acted as a catalyst for him. Perhaps the presence of his granddaughter had switched something on – or off - in his mind. Whatever it was it looked like for the first time William was at last able to see a context for the great things that had happened to him and his brother forty-two years before.

"When I spoke to Tom on the transatlantic phone, and he refused to stop selling the instruments to Germany, I vowed I would never speak to him again."

He fell silent, breathing heavily. Anna reached forward across the table and placed her hand on his.

"You were right," she said.

"But I wasn't right to take it out on Dryden when he joined Tom's publishing empire. I should have accepted that."

"Did MI5 come back?" Anna asked. "Did they visit you again?"

"Yes they did."

The government blamed William.

"They couldn't prove anything really. Couldn't prove I had any culpability. But they wouldn't believe I couldn't stop it. They thought I'd turned a blind eye."

"But you hadn't done anything wrong!" Anna was indignant.

"It didn't matter. They made it clear that when the conflict was over there would be no government or public contracts coming my way. When we won the war, I would be finished."

He looked through the window again, into many types of darkness.

"The only way for the company to survive – all those jobs – was for me to go, to sell out, to leave, my own company, my life's work, and never come back."

He reached over and touched Anna's arm in turn.

"You were right to come. It has gone on too long. But perhaps I had arrived at the stage where I couldn't make the first move. One reason why, perhaps to answer in some degree your first question, I gave Bex what she wanted. She reached out to me, and a kind of dam began to break."

Anna had tears running down her cheeks. She dug a tissue out of a pocket.

Cill was shocked into breathlessness. You never heard about this kind of thing in the history books. This kind of nasty human detail was overlooked or never talked about, or never quite reached the surface, or was successfully brushed under the carpet. And afterwards everyone could pretend it had never happened. It was the English way.

He wondered what he would have done if he'd found himself in the same position. He didn't know. He realised that for all his interest in war, he had no idea what it was like to be in one. Especially one as vast as the Second World War.

Anna was sobbing audibly. "Oh granddad," she said. "I'm so sorry. I just thought you couldn't stand us." She sobbed again."

She got up and went to find one of the downstairs cloakrooms off the main front hall.

She thought of all the Christmases they'd had as family when she was a child. Tom always there. The jovial celebrated editor always brought the best presents. And they'd never given a thought to this lonely man walled up in his own self-imposed exile.

She felt the kind of hurt that history often has for the present.

And she knew that all you felt when you felt that hurt was a need to undo what had been done.

If you could.

While Anna was out of the room, the two men remained silent. Cill felt William Thompson had not yet finished talking about the family breach and he didn't want to break the atmosphere or divert him.

Anna came back into the kitchen and and fetched the bottle of wine off the worktop by the sink. She refilled her grandfather's glass.

"I'm so glad you told me," she said. "Did my father never know?"

"No. No I never told him. I fell out with him without him ever knowing the reason. That was wrong. I felt he betrayed me by going to work for Tom. I couldn't see straight. Not for a long time."

He smiled and took a sip of wine. "I'm not sure I'm seeing particularly straight even yet. But things seem a lot clearer now."

Anna was thinking about her family. It made such a difference now they knew what had kept William away all those years. With knowledge came the ability to accommodate it, work round it, allow for it, perhaps even get over it – on all sides. Water under the bridge was all very well, but it helped enormously when you knew the name of the river too.

She wondered: if she asked him, would her granddad join them for Christmas this year? She hoped he would. He might. All she could do was ask him.

"So Bex sent someone to see me," William was saying. "Even though she didn't come herself, I felt she was making overtures. And I responded to that. I signed the documents her representative brought. To be honest I didn't give it much thought. After the break with Tom I never bothered with his company. I did before, when he first set it up. I enjoyed it in those days. He seemed to have a mission to change the way news is presented in England. He had a vision of a completely independent newspaper or news magazine. Independent at every possible level, editorially and commercially.

"I remember one of his great bugbears was how all the editors in the land had got together and agreed not to publish anything about Edward's affair with Mrs Simpson. He was really incensed by that. He called them a cartel and said it was news by permission."

Amazingly, William gave a short laugh.

"Tom said the newspapers of the day might as well all get a royal warrant and wave it from their mastheads: *News by appointment to His Majesty Old King Cole or to The Court of King Caractacus.* Or whoever. Take your monarchial pick.

"He was disgusted. He set up his own company so that kind of thing would never happen again. I thought that was good."

Cill made a mental note to ask Alison Wong when he got back what *Front Page*'s coverage of the 1936 Abdication Crisis and the preceding Simpson Affair had been like. As bad as every other news outlet? Or better? It would be an interesting exercise to check.

"So, Anna dear if you're asking me why I signed the documents that gave Bex a proxy vote on my shares, my answer is I couldn't see why not."

William looked out of the dark window again.

"I guess I was pleased after all these years to help a member of the family, when they asked. Even though it wasn't direct contact with the family again: it was indirect and I thought it was a start. In fact it seemed to me that it was my fault; that Bex was actually frightened to seek me out face-to-face and had sent an agent, a go-between, in case I maintained my distance." He pulled a face. "Are you telling me now I shouldn't have agreed to see him. Or do as Bex requested?"

Anna said "No of course not. I understand. But I can give you a brief idea of why we think it's not good. And I can tell you a lot more about what I think Bex's motives are." Her granddad was way out of touch after all. "But Cill can give you a much better analysis than I can of why it's bad for *Front Page*."

"You said just now you thought it was an exciting time when Tom set up the magazine?" Cill said. "And how he thought it was absolutely important to try to establish a news outlet that was totally independent on every level?"

"Yes," William said.

"Well, I think *Front Page* has always been that, right from the day Tom Telford set it up. But Bex having your proxy will effectively destroy that independence."

Cill went in to the background. The rumour becoming a certainty that the magazine was going public. And why being a public limited company would probably spell the end of its independence. He realised he sounded just like Bill Roadhouse giving the same speech in the Tipperary. He didn't mind: Bill had spoken well.

"I'm not saying Tom Telford was right in any way to do what he did to you. He clearly wasn't. But I think he was right to try and launch – and keep going – a truly independent news outlet. Britain thinks it has a lot of those. But it doesn't really. They all, without exception, have their own agendas, their own constraints and commercial and financial slants and realities, the BBC included. *Front Page* doesn't."

When he finished Anna took over. She told the story of the fateful board meeting. The skilful way Bex had staged the coup. The shock and a kind of despair on her dad's face. It was almost as though he felt he'd let Tom Telford down, she remembered. She also passed on all the family rumours about Bex's motives: the humungous doing-up of Poyters at vast expense and the wastrel Silent Sid's antics with race horses, owned and backed.

When she finished William was silent.

The three of them had talked themselves out.

It was late.

William stood up and left the room. In a few minutes he came back carrying a down-filled jacket.

"You've given me a lot to think about," he said. "I'm going for a stroll. It helps me think. Helps me put things in place in my mind."

He opened a drawer and took out a large torch.

"Don't wait up for me," he said as he opened the kitchen door and disappeared into the night.

Cill and Anna looked at each other across the kitchen table. "What d'you think?" Cill asked.

"I think he's been waiting for a night like this for a long time."

"It's a breakthrough, isn't it. Such a sad story though."

"Yes. But I hope he might come to England, now, to visit us."

"I wonder why he didn't start to make overtures to your family as soon as Tom Telford died?"

"I think at that stage his ire and melancholy, and the sense of betrayal, had latched on to my dad Dryden as well."

"I guess feeling you've been betrayed is not a good feeling at the best of times," Cill said. "And to feel betrayed in wartime is probably even worse. You feel – I imagine – you have a responsibility not just to yourself but to the country."

"Especially if you manufacture products which might benefit the enemy if they get their hands on them. An even greater sense of public responsibility."

"And so an even greater sense of betrayal."

Anna looked at Cill with an exaggerated lustful leer: "Let's go to bed," she said. "I feel a weight has been lifted off me somehow."

They went upstairs to bed.

They saw William at breakfast next morning.

The first thing Anna did was ask her grandfather whether he would like to visit her and her father over Christmas? And stay the holiday with them?

"I'd like it very much. But doesn't it depend on your father?"

Anna knew it did. But she intended to do something about that as soon as she and Cill arrived back in England. When her father learnt William's story she was sure he would be more than pleased to see his father again – knowing that his father was very keen now to see him.

"I'll talk to him," Anna said.

"Regarding the other thing," William said. "I fear it may be too late now to reverse the decision. Bex has set the train of events in motion. These thing pick up a momentum of their own. They may now be unstoppable. Not reversible until too late. I will however talk to my lawyer in Gap. He'll advise me what I can do, if anything. Anna dear – and Cill – please understand that I wish now I hadn't done it. But I hope you can understand why I did."

Anna did. She was also beginning to realise just how smart her aunt had been. She'd struck just at the right moment. Just when after forty-two years William was finally feeling that the breach with the family and his self-imposed exile had gone on too long, but didn't know yet what to do about it, Bex's emissary had arrived. Her timing was perfect.

"You realise granddad that it's not you she cares about? It's just your shares."

"Do you really think so?"

"I'm afraid I do, yes." And the more she thought about it the more certain she was. "Dad is convinced she really really needs the money."

"Can't she downsize?" Cill interjected. "Sell that huge pile? Must be worth a fortune now it's been done up." Then he held up his hand in apology. It was none of his business. But couldn't resist carrying on: "Would just suit a City barrow-boy-cum-trader made good."

Anna smiled. Bex would be horrified, aghast and mortified that anyone should think her pride and joy would fall into the hands of a "barrow-boy". She'd do better to get rid of Silent Sid, instead or as well, Anna thought but didn't say. And his horses. That would solve all her problems in one go.

But Anna had to admit that Poyters would now be anyone's pride and joy after its massive rebuilding programme.

"Dad and I will be there for the next board meeting."

"When is that?" William asked.

"A week on Saturday. The Saturday after we get back home. Dad is definitely not looking forward to it."

William Thompson frowned and looked thoughtful. But then brightened up.

"Now," William said. "Will you stay for a few days? Explore the mountains here." He smiled across the table at Cill. "There are some fabulous military sites in these parts – as I'm sure you've seen already. This is frontier country after all. Why not do some day-trips and take a more leisurely look?"

Anna looked at and Cill looked back.

They both said yes they'd love to, simultaneously, and then burst out laughing.

William joined in. He didn't remember the last time he laughed.

It was an excellent few days. They both realised they needed a break, needed some fresh air. They put their boots on and scaled the surrounding high trails. William told them a long–distance footpath known as GR5 entered the valley from the north and exited it over the col above the Cascade de la Pisse to the south.

"You can't get lost," William told them. "The trail is marked by flashes of red and white paint on trees and rocks. That shows the way."

So they went exploring back up the trail in the north to the col at that end of the valley, and followed it up the mountainside above the waterfall to the col at the southern end. Both walks were long and steep and made them realise how truly the valley was a lost world, more-or-less inaccessible.

They ate a picnic on top of the Col Girardin at the southern end of the valley beside the spring that fed the waterfall. High above the waterfall, Cill looked down and imagined that the world could truly pass you by in this valley, even though it was in "frontier country" as William said. The issues and ebbs and flows of the world, and the vicissitudes of the frontier, and the comings and goings of war would all have little meaning in this high remote valley. You could lose the world here. And the world could lose you.

Maybe that was why William had chosen it.

Anna joined him on the cliff edge. She interlocked an arm with his and leaned against him.

"I needed this," she said.

He smiled and nodded.

"Sounds silly. But I always think mountains give you perspective."

"I think you just said whatever's the opposite of an oxymoron." She tugged on his arm.

"The bleeding obvious?"

"Yes. But I like it. It's true too."

"Can we come again," he said. "And stay longer?"

"Oh yes," she said.

Over dinner one evening Anna asked what it was like in winter in the valley. Did they get cut off?

"Oh yes, Quite often. For a couple of days at a time. Perhaps even a week," William said. But sooner or later the snow plough made it up the road from Guillestre, he said.

"Those are interesting times when it happens. The whole valley becomes united by the isolation. There's a kind of safety and survival committee – sounds dramatic I know – but it's less kind of life-or-death in French. But one of their jobs is to check every house and farm in the valley when we're cut off. Make sure people have enough food and fuel."

William told how he often took in families in the manor house during the snowed-in times.

"People can miscalculate, or the weather can suddenly descend in the mountains, and catch you out, so quite often I've had families here when they run out of food or fuel in their own places. The children love it."

It sounded to Anna that her granddad liked it too.

They took two day trips out to look at the fortifications. One day they spent in and around Briançon. The other they visited Mont Dauphin and Chateau Queyras, both small towns fortified by military engineer Sebastien Vauban.

Each day they had breakfast and dinner with William Thompson. Anna enjoyed these times tremendously. She felt she was getting to know her grandfather for the first time.

She was fascinated by his workshop, by the history of his company, by his interest in mechanical and electrical inventions.

She was also beginning to realise that she didn't care what her father thought. She didn't care if her father refused to make peace with William. She had made peace herself. She knew she would come and see him again. Whether Dryden liked it or not.

The Saturday came when they must leave. They would spend a night somewhere on the road and cross the Channel sometime around midday on Sunday. They would both be back to work on the Monday.

They stood on the steps leading to the front door.

William shook hands with Cill.

"I'm sorry I couldn't do more about the company. We are all trapped in our own circumstances and it takes a lot to break out. Some never do."

Anna knew it was done the way it was done because Bex had the greater need. Everyone really was now just reacting to things that Bex had initiated. Yet if Bex hadn't done what she did, Anna would never have come, and would never have become reconciled with her grandfather. Whatever happened, in a way she owed Bex that.

Cill walked down the steps, leaving the two Thompsons at the top step.

Grandfather and granddaughter looked at each other. They embraced.

"I'm so glad I found you granddad," Anna said then ran down the steps to join Cill in the car at the base.

William waved them off. He kept waving all the way to where the car disappeared into the trees.

He turned and entered the house. He closed the front door and leaned back against it. He breathed a heavy sigh. But his heart felt lighter than it had for a very long time.

As Anna drove out between the stone entrance pillars of the Manoir de la Pisse, Cill in the passenger seat said: "Well we came here to do two things. And we've done one of them."

"Which one have we done?"

"You've finally understood the root cause of the division in your family. And I reckon you've gone a long way to healing it."

"Yes," Anna agreed. "But too bad about the other thing."

Yes it was too bad, Cill agreed to himself. He'd been hoping somehow that William would spring into action and annul the agreement he'd made with Bex. He should have known the wheels of the law and the machinery of business didn't work like that. Once set on a course, it was like a supertanker trying to stop or reverse course. It could be done but it took a hell of a lot of time and effort.

Well, at least they'd tried.

39. PUBLIC

When Cill returned to work on the Monday, it was to discover that SA Moriarty had made an announcement to the staff during the previous week while he'd been away.

Sandy Growler had intended to speak to the assembled employees in the large basement. It was standing-room only, but the floor was big enough for the whole company to be grouped together there.

But Essay insisted that he should be the one to inform the editorial staff.

"It's my team, my team," he said.

But Sandy insisted as managing director it was his responsibility to inform the whole of the staff.

Essay insisted it was his job to inform the magazine.

The deal they came up with was described by Bill Roadhouse as "preposterous".

Essay would tell the magazine staff. Then Sandy would inform all the staff, including the magazine. So *Front Page*'s employees would be told twice.

Both Essay and Sandy would be telling the employees the same thing: the company was going public.

The knowledge that News World Publishers would be launched on the stock market was now in the public domain.

"He was even more like Piffy on a rock-bun than ever," Eddie Osmoe said.

They were in the Printer's Devil after work on Monday evening.

"Yes, really pleased with himself," Judy Bodkin agreed. "He couldn't stand still."

At both briefings, Sandy's and Essay's, Bill Roadhouse had asked the key question: how would *Front Page* benefit?

"They didn't really have an answer, did they Bill?" Judy said.

"That's because either they don't know or they don't care," Cill Weaver said. For his part he was glad he'd missed both employee briefings.

"I think it's both," Bill said. "If they cared, they still don't know."

The conventional answer, Bill said, was that it would give the company more investment capital.

"What that means is we'll have capital, or can raise it, to take over other magazines."

"Do we want to do that?" Judy asked.

"I guess it's conceivable that we might," Bill exhaled in exasperation. "But that's missing the point, it really is. The real point is the reverse of that: we can be taken over by other publishers, someone who has more capital than us. Someone who makes the shareholders a good offer, one they can't turn down. It doesn't have to be a publishing company either. It could be anyone. A corporate raider. A multinational. A foreign firm. A company wanting to get into publishing. A company wanting to control all the stages of the paper-and-print process. Anything. All they have to do is have sufficient funds to make the shareholders an offer per share they can't refuse. And there's going to be nothing we can do about it. The fact they're not admitting that means they don't care."

"So it really is for them a matter of taking the money and run?" Judy spat the words.

"Yes. It's obvious. They've got pound signs in their pupils."

"So what do we do?" Cill said.

He'd spent the time over his first pint of the evening explaining the attempt to get William Thompson to step in and stop the process. He admitted that they had failed.

"The best thing we can do," Bill Roadhouse said. "They only thing in fact. Is live with it and lump it. Or look for another job."

"Yes, believe it or not," Eddie said. "I think we'll look back at this time as a golden age."

They all laughed, but when they thought about it they realised there was a lot of truth in what Eddie said.

While events concerning the future of the magazine and its parent company inched towards the next stage in the launch process, for the magazine it was business as usual.

Much of the time that week at work was spent on Falklands retrospectives.

Everyone knew it was far too early to be wholly accurate. It would take years for the full Falklands story to come out. Cill Weaver intended to write one of the earliest books about it.

But they could write about what was known, and how the campaign had gone, on the face of it. In particular they could analyse the political events leading up to the outbreak of hostilities. They could, and did, take a view on the competence of the government and its relations with Argentina before the crisis. Was there any blame? Was there anyone to blame? Could the crisis have been handled better? Should the political masters have been wiser – or was that just being wise after the event?

There was a lot of discussion about these topics at *Front Page* as they attempted to find a consensus among themselves.

They all agreed that once Argentina had invaded South Georgia and the Falklands, the British response had been first-rate, expert and totally professional.

"We have, after all, being doing this kind of thing for a long time," Cill Weaver pointed out in one news meeting.

"You mean, sending expeditionary forces overseas to take on third-rate opposition?" Eddie said. Eddie was in the school of thought that said it should never have come to a shooting match. The situation should have been sorted out well before that stage.

"If you like, Eddie," Cill agreed. "But nevertheless it is something we are very good at."

They agreed that throughout the fighting part of the crisis, Britain always seemed one step ahead of Argentina. And in the end they tended to agree with Cill's point that "We knew how to do this kind thing. They didn't."

Where they also agreed the magazine should take a position was on whether the government had been at fault leading up to the crisis.

In a number of leaders, Bill and Cill and Jerry pointed an accusing finger at the government for sending confused and confusing signals to the Argentine junta over Britain's interests in the

South Atlantic, and over its commitment to the Falklands.

In one leader Bill said the government had been lax, possibly even incompetent, in not realising that Argentina was serious when it made a claim, years before, to possession of "Las Malvinas". That should have sent huge warning bells through the ranks of the British government. That Britain made no response to the claim – and even seemed to be retiring its single Antarctic research vessel without replacement and cutting military expenditure - could only send one message to the junta: that Britain wasn't interested in the Falklands and would even turn a blind eye should Argentina attempt a takeover.

That was wrong and incompetent. And worthy of blame, the leader said.

Regarding the blow-by-blow details of the fighting, *Front Page*'s team was aware that it was far too early for the full facts to emerge. They knew that what seemed straightforward was unlikely to be the full story. As Cill Weaver knew from the anonymous tips he received, there was as much action going on covertly behind the scenes as there was on the ground in the Falklands.

For that reason the magazine tended to stay away from commenting on or analysing the actual fighting.

"We can leave that to the historians," Jerry Carter said. And everyone with one silent demurral agreed.

The demurrer was Cill Weaver. He had already decided he would write a book on the conflict. For the time being he would keep that information to himself. Together with the fact that he was desperately racking his brains to discover some way in which he could get in contact with his anonymous tipster.

Assuming for the moment that the one-legged captain he met at the Grosvenor House dinner might be the best candidate for his informant, the more he thought on it the more he realised there was one route that he could pursue to get back in touch with him. He could ask Anna's father Dryden how the guest list to the dinner had been compiled. Somebody must have thought the captain worth inviting, and thus know who he was.

Another thought struck him: who was responsible for the

seating plan? Had the captain engineered it somehow so he would sit beside Cill?

He felt he was on the right lines. He also knew that what had taken him so long to perceive what he now saw quite clearly was the illusion of central position. We all think we are the centre of the universe, Cill recognised that. So it comes as a suprise when you realise someone else has manipulated you and put you in a situation of their choosing, not yours.

Cill was feeling more and more confident that he was looking in the right direction. He hoped that Anna would invite him to meet her dad very soon.

Someone whose writing profile was much enhanced by the Falklands War, but in a non-military and non-political way, was Liz Tintwistle. Her series on "Those Left Behind" was up for a number of press awards.

Much to her surprise this success and recognition did not seem to be resented by her colleagues. They really did seem genuinely pleased for her. It might be expected that the editor and deputy editor would want to congratulate her, the magazine after all would benefit in the marketplace from having an award-winning writer on the editorial team. But she didn't expect the apparently heartfelt congratulations from her writing peers, Cill Weaver, Judy Bodkin and Bill Roadhouse. She also remained grateful to Jerry Carter and Judy Bodkin for commissioning her to do the project in the first place.

And when Eddie Osmoe took her aside one morning and told her she was probably now the best writer on the magazine, she became all breathless and nearly burst into tears.

For the first time in her career as a journalist she felt that's what she was, a journalist. She also felt she belonged in the profession and belonged at *Front Page*. She now enjoyed coming to work.

40. SHARE

For Anna the Saturday at the end of the week after she returned to England was the day she had been dreading.

It was going to be the first board meeting of the owners and shareholders of News World Publishers to be held at the home of the new chairperson.

The meeting would be chaired by Bex Dudley-Thompson and would take place at eleven-forty-five a.m. in her new grand first-floor library at Poyters.

One good thing that came out of her return was it was clear her father was as deeply touched by William's story as she was. And as equally sorry for the past estrangement. He was as keen as she was to make amends, to make up for lost time, to meet up, and definitely to invite William to the next family Christmas.

"Will you call him?" she asked.

Dryden wasn't sure. Face to face was better than phone to phone.

"I think I might do what you did. Just turn up."

Anna thought that was a great idea. She wanted her dad to do it as soon as possible.

"Why not go straightaway?"

"I will. I will," Dryden said, with a smile at his daughter's intensity and keenness. He had already decided he would go straight after the looming board meeting. Which he too was dreading.

It'll be nice to get away, after that, he thought.

"I'll give you the maps we used," Anna said. "It's a fantastic place. But you'll need the maps." She still couldn't get over the remarkable isolation of the Manoir de la Pisse and stunning scenery of Ceillac and the Melezet valley.

On the Friday evening, she and Cill met for dinner after work. Then Anna caught the train down to Sussex to stay the night at her father's place. Dryden thought it would take two and a half hours next morning to get to Poyters, even in his Porsche 911.

They didn't talk much on the journey. They had an early breakfast and set off for Gloucestershire. Anna knew it was going to be an ordeal for her dad. For herself, though not neutral by any means, she knew she was a relative junior, a makeweight when it came to share ownership and voting power. But after this meeting she was seriously considering giving her dad permanent proxy power over her vote so she wouldn't have to attend any more board meetings. Of course, going public would mean the days of these family board meetings were nearly over anyway. Who knew? This might even be the last one?

They made good time and turned off the road under the gated archway over the entrance to Poyters's drive at eleven-thirty.

Poyters had two main drives, Dryden knew. This one, the prime one, and another one, the back drive. He often wondered if the local fire brigade knew about the back drive, because there was no way a fire engine would fit under Poyters' entrance arch. The back drive had no arch, just brick pillars and gates.

The main drive was designed as the show-route to the house. You crossed a small stream by means of an imposing stone bridge far bigger than the size of the watercourse necessitated, then crested a meadow-banked hill, and Poyters was immediately set out all before you in all its renovated glory.

As they approached the broad sweeping drive, lawns and cedars in front of Poyters a man stepped out of the rhododendrons right in front of their car and held his hand up in an instruction for them to stop.

Good thing I was going slowly and was admiring the view, Dryden thought. He recognised the man as the gardener.

He approached the driver's window and Dryden pressed the button to open the window.

"Madam says parking is over there," the gardener said.

He pronounced it "muddum" which Anna thought particularly apt.

Dryden followed his pointing finger and saw the designated parking area was on the cobbles in front of the stable block to the left of, and well away from, the house. Very well, he thought. Bex doesn't want cars spoiling the looks and lines of the façade.

There were two cars already parked on the cobbles, a Jaguar S Type and a BMW. Dryden parked his Porsche alongside them.

Dryden collected his briefcase from the back seat. It contained his trusty Filofax.

The door was opened by the Dudley-Thompsons' live-in housekeeper. Anna never knew her name because Bex had never bothered to introduce her.

"Clearly Bex is too grand now to open her front door herself," Dryden said as they followed the housekeeper along the corridor and up the staircase, which had been designed deliberately with low risers and easy goings, to the first floor. He didn't care whether the housekeeper heard him or not.

They crossed the broad landing and the housekeeper opened the library door and held the door open, letting them pass inside ahead of her.

As they entered the room the housekeeper's thin high-pitched voice announced them.

"Mr Dryden Thompson and Miss Anna Thompson!"

God, what century are we living in? Anna thought. This country seat lifestyle had clearly gone to Bex's head.

Bex was sitting at the head of a heavy oak table. Sidney was sitting in the place at her right hand.

SA Moriarty and Sandy Growler were already seated. One at Bex's left hand, the other one place beyond that.

"Dryden, so good to see you," she boomed.

The books must be absorbing the sound in here, Anna thought, otherwise at that volume there'd be an echo.

"Take a seat." She gestured towards the seat beyond Sandy Growler.

Dryden ignored that position and took a chair at the other end of the table opposite Bex. Anna took the chair on his right. The long table now had two groups of people centred on each end of the table with a wide gap of empty seats between them.

Both Growler and Moriarty stood up to say hello and shake Dryden's hand. They both said hello to Anna, but neither of them offered to shake her hand. She thought that was particularly rude. She wasn't sure whether they did it because she was very much the junior here; or because she was a woman. Either way she was incensed. She did not reply to either Sandy or SA. She put her bag down and came to the head of the table to give her aunt a peck on both cheeks. Then as she returned to her seat she approached both Sandy and SA in turn to say how do you do and shake their hand, so making them stand up again to do so.

Silent Sid lived up to his nickname. Sidney just smiled and waved without getting up from his chair. He'd do much more than that if we were horses, Anna thought. Getting his priorities right, obviously.

All board members being present, Bex called the meeting to order and began to go through the agenda.

The main item was Bex's report on a meeting with the bank in the Strand which was advising News World Publishers on the move to go public, and steering them through the process. There was actually nothing much to report, she said. She had been informed that certain documentation was in the course of being printed and would be ready for the board's perusal in time for the next board meeting in a month's time.

Another item involved public announcements. Should they continue to endeavour to keep the launch secret or should an announcement be made? Bex herself favoured maintaining secrecy. Dryden said he had no view on that himself. Nor did Anna.

At this point both Growler and Moriarty informed the board that they had both made announcements to the staff of News World Publishers.

So in effect the secret was no longer secret.

Bex scowled and gave a kind of harrumph sound and an audible sigh. Dryden wondered what her problem was. Maybe she just didn't like publicity. Maybe her natural instinct was for covert operations.

In the light of the new information the board held a vote on whether a public announcement should be made. It was passed. Dryden and Anna abstained.

This is going to be one of the quickest board meetings on record, Anna thought. With Dryden clearly sulking and Bex driving the whole thing at speed, we should be out of here in less than ten more minutes. We'll zip through Any-Other-Business and be gone. I won't be sorry, she thought, if this does turn out to be the last family board meeting.

Just then they could hear a commotion on the landing outside the library door. A shrill woman's voice could be clearly heard calling for someone to please stop. The other voice was a man's voice, but it was much quieter and indistinct.

The library door flew open and a tall thin elderly man in a black three-piece suit stepped into the room.

It was William Thompson.

"I believe I have a place at board meetings." he said calmly. It wasn't a question.

Behind him the housekeeper was apologising to Bex that she had let him in, but couldn't stop him marching up the stairs to the library. Bex waved her away. Her mouth was still hanging open at the sight of William Thompson in her library, at her board meeting.

Aside from Bex, the most surprised person in the room was Dryden Thompson. He had not seen his father for fifteen years. Not since the day of Stella's funeral.

Sandy and Essay looked at each other and shrugged. Strange family the Thompsons, the look said.

The least surprised person was Anna. She was delighted to see her granddad again so soon.

William had a presence, there was no question of that. Already he seemed to own the room. He went round the table in turn saying hello and introducing himself. He embraced his niece Bex and kissed her on both cheeks.

"So nice to see you again," he murmured.

Bex could only gurgle an incoherent splutter in response. He shook Sandy and Essay's hands. He embraced his granddaughter and kissed her lightly on both cheeks. Silent Sid waved. He didn't smile this time. William ignored him.

Finally he came round the table and stood in front of his son.

They just looked at each other.

"I'm so sorry," William said.

"It's good to see you," Dryden said, with an effort.

"We have a lot to talk about. I came to see you."

Then William turned to the table to include them all and said "But first things first. This is a board meeting. Please carry on."

He sat down in the empty chair at Dryden's left hand. Now the two poles at the table ends were much more even.

There was nothing Bex could do. William was a member of the board. Admittedly he hadn't shown up to a meeting almost beyond living memory. But that didn't mean he didn't have a right to attend. He did.

She regained her composure. "We were just finishing in fact," she said. "Any other business?" she was asking the table, and looked around.

"I think that's me," William said. "Why I'm here."

He had a slim briefcase with him. He laid it on the table in front of him and brought out a document in an orange stiff paper folder.

There was absolute silence in the room. Each one in their own way was wondering what exactly was William doing? What was he doing and why was he here?

William slid the document towards Bex's end of the table.

"I herewith revoke giving you my proxy vote. I hereby cancel giving you my power of attorney over my shares for the purposes of board meetings. This document supersedes and replaces any and all previous documents on this matter."

"No! No. You can't!" Bex almost shouted. "It's too late."

"I can. And it's not too late," William replied. There was steel and stone in his voice. It reminded Anna that this was a serious businessman. Compared to William everyone else in the room was an amateur.

"I now propose a motion under Any Other Business," William said. "I propose this board stops the process of launching News World Publishers on the stock market."

Apart from a shocked indraw of breath from Bex, there was a stunned silence round the table. Anna felt her heart lifting. She wished Cill was there to witness this.

The quickest to react, in a way, was Moriarty. He saw the vast money he thought he was going to make slipping out of sight like a longship into a fog bank. He slumped in his chair.

"Oh fucking hell, hell," he said. At that point he didn't care who heard him.

Bex had no choice but to table the motion. There was no debate. Bex, Silent Sid, Sandy and Essay voted against the motion. Dryden, Anna, Sam by proxy, and William all voted in favour of the motion. The motion was carried by weight of share.

News World Publishers would not be seeking a listing on the London Stock Exchange as a public limited company.

Bex staggered to her feet. She almost fell over. Sidney attempted to bolster her elbow. Angrily she shook him off.

"Get out," she shouted. "Get out of my house now. All of you. Get out. Out. Go," she screamed the last word.

They did as they were bid.

41. AFTER

Outside under the trees, Dryden and William were talking. It wasn't the talk they both knew they needed to talk; it was just expedient talk about whether William would stay at Dryden's place – he would. They would talk the necessary talk there later.

They would travel back, the three of them in Dryden's Porsche. Anna laughed at the fact that she was the one who would be expected – by reason of age and suppleness - to squeeze into the tiny back seat area. She'd done it before, and knew it could be done, if she sat sideways with her feet up across both seats in the back.

An early question she had for her dad on the journey back was what would happen to the board now?

"Bex will resign as chair," Dryden said. "She has no choice. She may not even come to the next few meetings. I suspect we'll be having all contact by means of solicitors letters for the foreseeable future."

Quickly William told his side of the dramatic events of the day.

He'd had a meeting with his lawyer. One thing had worried him: theory and practice. In theory he knew he could stop giving Bex his proxy vote at any time. He could of course undo what he had done. But could he do it soon enough in practice to make the necessary difference?

He talked to the lawyer. And it was as he had suspected – but had not mentioned to Anna and Cill – that it might not be too late in practice to change and rescind giving Bex his proxy vote and cancel Bex's power of attorney over his shares for board meeting purposes. But he had to do it quickly. He had to act before the listing process developed a life and momentum of its own.

But with a board meeting looming and the listing process gathering pace he began to realise that to do everything by solicitor's letters would be too slow. He knew from his own business experience that decisions needed to be reversed while they were still private, before any press releases had been issued or statements of intent been made publicly. Apart from anything else, a stream of letters back and forth might also forewarn Bex and allow her to come up with a counter-strategy.

He realised the best and only option was to turn up in person at the next board meeting. He'd driven to Lyon and caught a London Heathrow flight. He'd then taken a taxi immediately to Gloucestershire. He had only just made it.

"Talk about a *deus ex machina*," Dryden said. "I was absolutely astonished to see you when you forced your way into the meeting. Not just because you were the last person I ever expected to see; but also for the drama that immediately unfolded."

"Yes. Since I saw Anna I've been wondering about just dropping in on you. Like she did to me. That seemed to work. But this business had to be confronted most urgently."

Dryden was beginning to follow through in his mind more ramifications of "this business".

"I think as well as Bex going, our editor and managing director will also fundamentally have to consider their positions," Dryden said. "They are seriously compromised."

"Yes," William said. "Clearly they'll both have to go. They've lost the confidence of the board."

Dryden wondered about Bex. What she would do now. He knew launching on the stock market had been her big plan to make serious amounts of money. And he knew she still needed the money. Well, he thought, maybe the failure of her plan will jolt her into some kind of reality. Getting rid of Silent Sid would be a huge beneficial start. Or if she couldn't yet go that far, then getting rid of his horses at least. Selling off all those stables in four countries should fetch her quite a bit of cash. She'd probably also have to sell Poyters too in time. Well at least now it was sellable.

Anna was looking forward to seeing Cill that evening with all the news. She couldn't wait.

It would also be good to let her father and grandfather have the house alone for the rest of the weekend too. She knew she would see her granddad again before he returned to France.

Though there were long silences on the drive back from Gloucestershire, they were companionable. All three occupants of the car felt like a family for the first time in as long a time as any of them could remember. It was a family they were sure that could face the future now on a much more solid footing than any of them had ever have thought possible. For the three of them it was time to start again.

Anna caught the Gatwick Express back up to London. Her father and grandfather announced they would go out for a celebratory dinner together. Then retire to Dryden's study to talk and make inroads into a bottle of Scotch.

Cill was waiting for her in the Greenwich flat. She had given him a key immediately on their return from holiday. It had seemed less of a big deal at the time than she expected. And the holiday together had not broken up their relationship either.

He wished he'd been there.

When Anna told him about what had happened at the board meeting, his first thought was to wish he'd been there himself.

"But it's amazing," he said. "Amazing."

Anna thought she'd ask Cill to come and stay a few days at her father's house straightaway. She wanted her dad to meet him; and knew Cill wanted to see her grandfather again. Strange she thought, that my boyfriend should meet my granddad before he meets my dad.

Cill liked the idea as well. One thing he hadn't had a chance to do when they'd been in France at William's place was to talk about what it was like to run a factory making key instruments for fighters and bombers during the Second World War. Cill was looking forward very much to picking William's brains on that.

He was also looking forward to meeting Dryden. Mainly because he was Anna's father. That was natural. But also because he was a route into discovering who the one-legged captain was, who might or might not be his anonymous informer during the Falklands War.

Anna persuaded Cill that the big news could wait over the weekend. He didn't have to phone Bill like he first wanted to do as soon as he heard. It could all wait till Monday morning.

In the office on Monday, Cill was first in. He took an early train to Blackfriars and walked to Fleet Street from there.

He told Bill first. Then he stopped at Jerry's desk and told him and Liz. Then he told Eddie and the sub-editors. Then he went to the features desk and told Judy and Rex. Then he saw Cathy at the lift and went over to inform her. "Sod me," she said characteristically. Then he had a quick word with Alison Wong in the library, and a brief conversation with Carmen. She told Cuddles. By ten o'clock everyone knew.

Essay didn't know they knew.

Anna had also told Cill what her dad had said about the position of the editor and managing director being untenable as a result of the recent board meeting.

Cill was not particularly surprised therefore when SA Moriarty called all the staff of *Front Page* together in the middle of the editorial floor at the end of that week.

Moriarty announced that he was moving on. He had handed in his notice and would be leaving in four weeks time. Moriarty claimed he was going on to better things and had a "couple of projects on the go that are on the go just now." No one believed him. And they were all glad to see him go.

"What's that Skippy?" Eddie Osmoe said in an appalling attempt at an Australian accent. "You're leaving to do better things?" He carried on, switching to a Dick Van Doolittle mock-cockney: "Don't fink so Skippy old son. Word on the street is you've bin given the boot. The old 'eave-'o, me old china. You bin stitched up."

At the same time an internal memo was circulated among the staff saying that Sandy Growler had resigned as managing director. He had been replaced by Rod Crowcroft. And he had been replaced in turn as publisher by Don Phurse, the former advertising manager.

Cill was a little surprised by a subsequent announcement that Colin Cuddleigh-Cook would take over as editor of *Front Page*.

"It's only till he retires," Bill Roadhouse told Cill and Judy upstairs in the Tipperary. "In three months' time. And there's something else."

Bill, Jerry and Eddie had been asked to attend a meeting with Dryden Thompson, the chairman of the board of News World Publishers, Rod Crowcroft the managing director of News World Publishers and Don Phurse the publisher of *Front Page*. Bill looked at Cill as if he surely must know what it was all about, as he had a girlfriend in the family?

Cill did know. But he had been sworn to secrecy. And for once in his life he did keep quiet.

It turned out that Eddie had already been approached by Dryden and Crowcroft to be deputy editor to Colin Cuddleigh-Cook. But Eddie had refused. He preferred to remain as chief sub-editor.

At this coming meeting with the company's *gran quesos*, Dryden therefore was going to offer the deputy editorship to Bill. With the understanding that he would be made editor when Cuddles retired. And at that point Jerry Carter would become deputy editor.

And so it turned out.

42. FLEET STREET

Liz Tintwistle sat on the number 11 bus. She was earlier these days. And she worried less. She'd got used to being called Tintin. To be honest she quite liked it. Though she couldn't deny that she had changed, she thought it more that those around her had changed more.

She listened to the conversation around her. She realised she was listening less critically, less sadly. It all gave her much less of a heavy heart.

There was another thing too which made her heart lighter these days.

She had been awarded the accolade of Feature Writer of the Year in the Press Awards.

She remembered quite strongly the Press Awards dinner. It was all still fresh in her mind. The entire editorial team had taken several tables. There had been speeches, most prominently by one of the two news readers from *News At Ten*. He'd spoken quite movingly of the need for journalists and reporters to always bear in mind the human side of big stories. It was all too easy to lose track of that reality. Sometimes reporters came along that put the right story back on track. It took Liz a few moments to understand he was actually talking about her, and leading up to the presentation of her award.

And there was actual cheering when she got up and walked through all the tables to the dais to receive her framed certificate. And when she said a few words of thanks there was absolute silence in the room. And then more cheering came as she walked back to her table.

And perhaps what was most surprising to Liz, to the old Liz as she now thought of herself, was that she took it all in her stride. She wasn't fazed or embarrassed or tried to hide at all. She took it all in, met it head on, and rose to the occasion.

She was now one of the senior reporters on the news desk of *Front Page*. She was senior enough to attend news meetings. She felt included.

She had won the award while Cuddles was still editor.

One of the first things Cuddles had done as editor was have a copy made of her Press Award. Her own original was hanging on the wall of her flat. The copy took pride of place in the editor's glass office on the wall along with all the other awards *Front Page* had won over the years.

It was a strange time. Everyone knew Cuddles would be editor for only three months. He was aware of that. But as he said himself, it had been a time of trauma and transition for the magazine, so what better man to run it than a transitional editor?

It was quite amusing. And to be fair, Cuddles had grown into the job. He seemed to have relaxed a little. It seemed clear now that what had most worked against Cuddles and soured him in the minds of the staff was his belief that he was being by-passed and overtaken by lesser journalists, such as previous editor SA Moriarty. In retrospect his belief was clearly right. Most of all now he seemed to have learned how to both devolve and listen to other people and respect their viewpoints. In the end he turned out to be a safe, good, kind and gentle editor. Everyone was genuinely sad when his retirement day came.

And now Bill was editor. Things were highly professional, and better for that, and happier in many ways, Liz thought. Jerry was both deputy editor and news editor, combining both jobs which worked well enough. Thinking back she realised that the magazine under the previous regime of SA Moriarty had not been a happy place to work.

At one time it was thought likely that Cill Weaver would be appointed news editor. But he had made it plain he didn't want the job. He actually confided to Liz in the pub that he'd refused it mainly because he preferred to be a news reporter than a news editor. The jobs were different. Reporters went out and got stories; editors stayed at their desks and planned the pages. But there was also something else, he'd told Liz. He was thinking about looking for a new job. For Cill Weaver the time had come to move on.

He didn't say, but Liz thought it might be something to do

with Anna Thompson, Cill's girlfriend. It must be strange, to say the least, she thought, for someone who worked on the magazine to be going out with someone who was part of the family that owned it. Liz wished him well. She and Cill had got off on the wrong foot. She had misjudged him, she knew. She'd read recently a quote by Mark Twain: "People are nicer than you think they are." And it seemed to sum up her relationship with Cill. It was fine now. They were as close as work colleagues could get. And Liz was most definitely a member of the clique that formed around Cill and Judy and Bill.

Now the bus had penetrated to the edge of the City of London and in a phase-change made the quantum leap between the Strand and Fleet Street, between the City of Westminster and the City of London. Liz's spirits rose a little. She stood and made her way to the back of the bus and waited on the Routemaster doubledecker's open platform gripping the white pole for the next stop.

She stepped off the still moving bus, hefted the strap on her bag to a better position on her shoulder, and headed with a spring in her step for the sandwich shop at the bottom of Dunstan's Court to pick up a coffee.

She stood on the northern pavement of Fleet Street. She looked down the street, east towards St Paul's. She turned and looked west towards the Strand and the law courts. She turned back again, looking east, taking in the whole street. Just yards away was the sign for *Ye Olde Cheshire Cheese* with an arrow indicating the pub was up the alley.

I work here, she thought. Wow. This is my street. Fleet Street.

Amazing, she thought, printing's been going on here for five hundred years.

Long may it continue, she thought.

Then she made her way up the alley towards her office, humming a song.

She pushed firmly against one of the pair of glass doors, the one that said *News World Publishers* and *Front Page Magazine* on it. The door opened and she entered the lobby.

She smiled warmly at the receptionist who was holding the phone to her ear as though it was a flaming barbed-wire hosepipe with a look of utmost distaste welded to her face. Then Liz noticed the bandage round each wrist.

Oh no, she thought, Lydia hasn't gone and slashed her wrists again?

Mark Moore
Casita Galgo 2016
86,500 words

66376720R00151

Made in the USA
Charleston, SC
17 January 2017